THE PINES WERE WATCHING

LINDA NORLANDER

Copyright © 2025 Linda Norlander.

All rights reserved.

No part of this book may be reproduced in any form or by any electronic or mechanical means, including information storage and retrieval systems, without written permission from the author, except for the use of brief quotations in a book review.

Severn River Publishing
www.SevernRiverBooks.com

This is a work of fiction. Names, characters, businesses, places, events and incidents are either the products of the author's imagination or used in a fictitious manner. Any resemblance to actual persons, living or dead, or actual events is purely coincidental.

ISBN: 978-1-64875-648-1 (Paperback)

ALSO BY LINDA NORLANDER

Sheriff Red Mysteries
And the Lake Will Take Them
The Pines Were Watching
What the Fields Saw

To find out more, visit
severnriverbooks.com

For John and Jan

1

TOMMY

The lifeguard stood in the hallway of the Lykkins Lake clinic, outside one of the tiny exam rooms. She wore a terry cloth robe over her swimsuit. Her legs were lean and muscular.

"I pulled him out of the pool because he was fighting with a couple of other boys. He was wearing a T-shirt. When I grabbed it, I saw the welts on his back." She looked at Red with pain in her eyes. "Who could hurt a kid like that?"

Ten-year-old Tommy Henley sat sullenly on the exam table, his chest bare. He was a small, wiry boy with large ears exaggerated by his cropped haircut. Angry, raised welts peppered his back.

"Hi, Tommy." Sheriff Red Hammergren walked into the room. "How are you doing?"

He looked down at his dangling toes.

Red pulled up a chair to be at eye level with him. "Listen, Tommy, it's wrong for anyone to hit you. Does it hurt?"

Tommy continued to look at his feet.

Gently she touched his chin and tilted it up to her. The dark smudges under his brown eyes etched an aged weariness onto his little-boy face. Red wanted to take him in her arms and hold him tight. Instead, she gazed at him with a steady kindness. "I need to know who hit you so it doesn't happen again."

The sullenness disappeared from his eyes with the gentleness of her voice. For a moment he looked frightened, then his eyes flooded with tears.

"No one," he said softly.

"No, Tommy. Someone hit you."

He shook his head. "I fell." Again, he looked down at his feet.

"Did your mom hit you?"

A tear rolled down his cheek and onto his knobby knee. Tommy Henley refused to say anything more.

Outside, in the hall, the lifeguard whispered to Red, "I heard one of the other boys talking. He said that Tommy said a guy in a green jacket did it."

Red sighed. How often do kids like this lie to protect their parents? She knew that his mother, Arlis Henley, lived in a rundown trailer outside of town. Last she had heard, Arlis was working up at the Golden Deer Casino. She was known to have regular male clients she "partied" with on weekends. Red had never arrested her.

The morning was already heating up as she pulled in front of Arlis Henley's trailer. It sat outside the city limits in a township with no zoning. Trailers like this one were dotted throughout Pearsal County. A rusted Tonka toy truck with missing wheels lay at the foot of the rickety metal landing surrounded by dry, scraggly weeds. Arlis's old red van, with its smashed passenger window, sat parked on a dirt patch off the driveway. A battered overturned child seat rested next to the van. Otherwise, the mostly dirt yard showed no evidence that Tommy lived in the trailer.

Red stood in the doorway of the trailer, listening to Arlis swear. It was close to noon now. She hoped to get this business taken care of before the meeting she'd scheduled with three other county sheriffs in the area this afternoon. They were applying for federal funding to share a deputy position. The feds wanted them to use it for "homeland security." The sheriffs needed the position to deal with the increase in drunk drivers coming out of the Golden Deer Casino. "I think we can classify anyone driving a car while intoxicated as a terrorist, don't you think?" Red had said to her colleagues when she invited them to the meeting. The sheriff from Dickson County failed to see the humor in her remark.

The Pines Were Watching

Arlis Henley's grating voice rose from inside the trailer. "You can't come in here and take my Tommy. I didn't do nothing!"

Herman Winstead, the county child protection worker, stood inside the door of the trailer. "Sorry, Arlis, but Tommy looks like someone beat him."

"I didn't do nothing! Tommy falls a lot."

Herman turned away from the door with a shrug. Over the years, Herman had seen a lot of "falls," and Red could tell from his weary expression that the social worker was worn out. Or burnt out would be a better phrase.

"Don't do this," Arlis begged, stepping to the doorway. Tears streaked down her face. Her skin had a ruddy, grainy texture. She was as tall as Red, with a thick, boxy body. Georgia, from Red's poker club, would have called her "a backwoods Helga"—one of those sturdy women descended from a long line of mothers who bore the children, plowed the fields, and chopped the wood.

Arlis stared directly at Red, her eyes hardening.

"Do you think I'm dumb enough to beat the crap out of my kid and send him where everyone could see it?"

That's a good question, Red thought. Arlis wasn't the brightest light in Pearsal County, but she was wise to the system.

"I'd like to come in so we can talk." Red motioned toward the door.

Arlis walked back inside without replying.

Inside, the trailer was cluttered but clean. Dishes were stacked in the dish rack, and the place smelled of the flowery scent of dish soap. Red sat down at the small table across from Arlis. A housefly buzzed near the window.

"So, what happened to Tommy?"

"I don't know." Arlis grabbed a pack of cigarettes from the kitchen table. She lit one, drawing deeply, then blew the smoke in Red's direction. "Maybe it happened at a friend's house."

"What about a guy in a green jacket?"

Arlis froze for just a second, then turned nervously away. "I don't know nothing about a guy in a green jacket. Tommy lies a lot."

Sure, Red thought. *Ten-year-old boys make up stories about strange men beating them up all the time.*

"Arlis, let Herman Winstead help you out."

"Herman Winstead is a toad," Arlis hissed.

Red kept her voice even. "We're going to see that Tommy is taken care of until the hearing."

"I've got friends who'll get him back. Just you wait. I've got money, too. I'm getting myself a lawyer." Arlis shot Red a fiery look. Red ignored her. The Arlis Henleys of the world had a special instinct for survival. She'd have Tommy back within a month.

Red noted the gold bracelet Arlis wore. It didn't fit the backwoods Helga look and didn't appear to be a cheap piece of jewelry. "Nice bracelet."

Arlis touched it.

"Looks expensive."

She pushed her lower lip out. "I got a job now. I can buy things for myself."

Cartoons played on a flat-screen television in the living room. Arlis's gaze strayed to the sound of the television as Red waited for her to say more. The tight T-shirt she wore advertising Cuttery's Bar emphasized her large breasts and muscular arms.

Looking at those arms, Red didn't doubt for a moment that Arlis was physically capable of doing the damage she'd observed on little Tommy's back. A dull ache gnawed at Red's temples as she watched the woman.

"Arlis, do you understand why we had to take Tommy?"

Arlis continued to stare beyond her at the television set. Her bleached hair frizzed in the humidity of the trailer. She bore the ageless look of one who has been raised on cigarettes, beer, and abuse. As if to confirm this, Red caught a glimpse of a grocery list scrawled in a childish hand on a cheap manila tablet on the kitchen table. The list said, "Milk, cereal, beer and cigarets."

"Nice television," Red commented. Arlis winced for a moment before her face went slack.

"I'm thinking that television and the bracelet are worth a paycheck or two. Where did you get the money, Arlis?"

Arlis stabbed out the cigarette into an ashtray on the table, her brow wrinkling.

The Pines Were Watching

"Where did you get the money?" Red asked again, keeping her voice flat.

"I'm working steady, and I hit the slots one night." Arlis did not meet Red's eyes.

Red shrugged and decided not to pursue the items, since none had been reported stolen.

It was clear she would get no more from Arlis. She stood. "Herman will be in contact." She rubbed her neck as she walked out of the trailer. Her shoes crackled on the worn linoleum floor.

Climbing into her car, Red pulled the door shut and rested her head against the heat of the steering wheel while colors danced in her peripheral vision. She had a bad feeling about Arlis Henley and Tommy.

Turning quickly in the driveway, she headed west, away from Lykkins Lake, deeper into the north woods. Driving sometimes soothed her. She radioed Billie, the dispatcher, and told him she was taking a half-hour break.

"Ten four, over and out," Billie replied.

That kid has been watching too much television. Red reached over and flipped a Van Morrison CD into her player. Van Morrison had been a favorite of her late husband, Will. As "Moondance" played, she thought for a moment about the times she and Will had sat on their patio, drinking beer and listening to the words, "What a marvelous night..."

"God, I miss you, Will," she whispered out loud.

Gradually, as the music surrounded her, the tension in her shoulders eased. The backroad gravel pounded a staccato rhythm on the bottom of her car. She remembered what Georgia had said at one of their poker nights.

"You know, Red, the abuse hasn't changed much over thirty years. Fractured families, horrible poverty, toxic parents—always the same. You know what has changed, though? Now they all have guns."

Ten minutes later, Red passed the old St. Joseph's cemetery. She slowed, taking in the neglected gravestones surrounded by high grass and shaded by the watchful old pines. A red pickup approached from behind, not changing speed as it passed her. Derek Grandgeorge sat behind the wheel, slightly hunched. Red watched the truck kicking up a spray of gravel in its wake. A crumpled dark tarpaulin flapped in the bed of the truck as Grandgeorge disappeared down the road.

She remembered a conversation she'd had with Will before he died. They were talking about the things you wish for in life. Will was thin and wasting, his lungs struggling against the disease that ate them away.

"What you want in life changes. At one time, I wanted a big house like the Grandgeorge Place. I used to talk with old Carl Grandgeorge, and he'd tell me he was making a replica of a house down in Louisiana. He was obsessed with it. It cost him all his money, and he never lived in the grandeur he hoped for." Will had taken a long, shuddering breath before he added, "All I want now is a place under an evergreen to rest my bones."

After that conversation, Red had avoided driving by the Grandgeorge Place. *Funny*, she thought, *that I headed this way today*. She followed the still settling dust trail left from the pickup to a silver mailbox, which marked the beginning of the Grandgeorge driveway. She rolled to a stop at the mailbox. She wondered how much the property had deteriorated in the last few years.

The radio next to her crackled to life.

"Sheriff, I've got the secretary over at the public health nursing office on the line. She thinks one of the nurses, Joanie Crea, is missing."

2

MISSING NURSE

Red returned to the office to find that the meeting she'd arranged had been canceled. One of the participants was dealing with a domestic crisis and asked Red to reschedule it. Since she wouldn't be talking grants and funding, Red decided to check out the missing nurse report rather than assign it to one of her deputies.

The Pearsal County Public Health Department office was in an old building on Main Street that once housed a video store. Red used to haunt this place as a teenager, looking for classic movies. After the last tenant, a questionable consignment store, left, the building had been empty for a decade before the county leased it.

"Hello?" Red called out. A window air conditioner rattled but couldn't keep up with the outside heat. A rotating fan propped up on a chair blew around the tepid air. The receptionist's desk was empty.

A woman nearly as tall as Red and rail thin walked out of one of the offices. "Yes?" Her hair was kinked and untamed by the humidity in the office.

Red introduced herself. "Sheriff Red Hammergren. I understand you called worried about your nurse Joanie Crea."

The woman didn't extend her hand. "I'm Clarise Manson. I'm the director. It was my admin who called. I hope it's nothing. Maybe a staffing mix-up. I'm down a nurse, so things can be crazy."

Red indicated the office behind her. "Can we sit down and find out what the concern is?"

The director's small office consisted of a desk, a laptop computer, and a couple of bookshelves. It was clear to Red that the commissioners weren't being generous with funds for housing public health.

Clarise spoke in a husky voice. "I don't know. Joanie is always so responsible. When a patient called this morning to say Joanie had missed her appointment to fill her insulin syringes, I became worried." She grabbed an inhaler from her desk and took a puff. "Sorry, I have allergies."

Red wondered about mold in the office but said nothing. "When did you last see her?"

"Um...well, I was in a meeting all day Friday. But Lynne, my admin, said Joanie called on Friday afternoon and said she'd be going right out into the field today and wouldn't be back in the office."

"Is that usual?"

Clarise blinked. "Of course. Like everything else, we work remotely as much as possible."

Red remembered Scotty, her poker club friend, mentioning a rumor that Clarise spent much of her time in meetings outside the office. Gazing around the office, Red could hardly blame her.

"Lynne called her cell phone and checked with Angela, the other nurse. No one has seen Joanie today, and her car isn't in her driveway."

"Where was she going for her first visit?" Red immediately wondered if she'd had car problems. More remote parts of the county didn't have cell service.

Clarise blinked at her. "Uh...I can't reveal who her patients were. Data privacy, you know."

Red took a deep breath. Bureaucrats like Clarise who strictly and often incorrectly interpreted the patient confidentiality law were an ongoing irritant. Red didn't push it because she was sure Lynne would be happy to tell her.

She asked a few more questions but determined that Clarise knew very little about Joanie or the patients she visited. While they talked, Clarise kept checking her phone, a sheen of perspiration forming on her forehead.

"Am I keeping you from something?" Was she overheated or nervous, or something else?

Clarise's eyes widened. "Ah, no. Or, ah, I have a meeting in Brainerd. I really need to go."

Escape, more likely. Something was off with the director.

While they spoke, Lynne came back from lunch, breathing heavily. Lynne had been with the public health nursing office for years. Scotty, a previous director, called her a receptacle of patient knowledge who broke data privacy on a regular basis. "We got along fine as long as I didn't lecture her about patient confidentiality. Of course, nothing is confidential in this county."

Red stood and once again offered her hand to Clarise, who once again ignored it. "Thank you for the information. I hope I didn't make you late for your meeting." She walked into the reception area and waited as Lynne settled into the chair behind her desk. Lynne walked with a slight limp and groaned as she sat. "Good to see you, Sheriff."

"Your boss said you could help me."

Unlike her boss, Lynne was happy to talk and to share the names of patients on Joanie's caseload.

"We are down a nurse, and she can't seem to get around to hiring someone." Lynne glared at Clarise's now closed office door. "Poor Joanie and Angela, trying to manage all those patients and still do the well-baby visits."

Red nodded sympathetically. She was in the same spot of not having enough staff.

She pulled up a chair across from Lynne's desk. "Tell me what you know about Joanie and where she might be."

Lynne appeared eager to talk. "Reliable and always gets her paperwork done in time. For me, she is a treat. And her patients really like her."

"Anything unusual I should know about? Threats or that kind of thing?"

Lynne hesitated at first and then leaned forward in a confidential manner. "She is separated and planning to divorce her husband, Jimmy. They split up this spring."

"Jimmy Crea, the accountant?"

Lynne nodded. "She didn't share much, but I got the sense he was kind of controlling."

"Have you talked with him? Since Joanie missed her visits?"

Lynne pointed to a legal pad on her desk. "I made notes of everyone I called this morning. It turns out Jimmy has been in Duluth at some religious conference. He's one of the deacons in that church that took over the building from the Methodists. I left him a message."

Red nodded. Lynne was referring to an evangelical church that had been established a few years ago. She knew little about them other than a call from Rose Timm, the secretary who reported that funds were missing. After Red took the information to investigate, Rose called her back and told her it was an accounting mistake and everything was in order.

Lynne told her Joanie Crea was a good, efficient nurse but not particularly friendly. Staff had invited her to a few after-work functions, but Joanie had declined. "She always had an excuse, but we wondered if Jimmy kept a tight rein on her."

"Does she have other friends in town I could talk with?"

Lynne shrugged. "She's never mentioned anyone. Angela might be the closest to her."

The picture that was emerging was of a woman isolated by her husband. "Did she ever talk about her husband?"

"She hardly ever talked about anything outside of work. But I know things weren't going well with him."

Red's neck muscles tightened. "Why?"

"A couple of months ago, Jimmy moved out of their house and rented a room with Norma Elling up the street." She leaned close to Red. "It's confidential, but I found out that two days ago, she gave Clarise her notice and said she planned to move back in with her parents down in Southern Minnesota." Lynne sat back. "I mean, poof. Just like that. We wondered if Jimmy was having an affair or something. Even those crazy Christians stray."

The conversation would have continued, but Clarise emerged from her office with her purse. She registered surprise that Red was still here. "Uh...I have a meeting, and I'll be gone the rest of the day."

The Pines Were Watching

"Have you figured out what to do about Joanie's patients?" Lynne glowered at Clarise.

"See what you can do with Angela. I'm sure she can fill in for some of the visits." She swept out the door.

Red watched through the window as Clarise slipped into an older-model Lexus parked in front of the building. Before pulling away from the curb, she took pills from her purse and washed them down with bottled water.

Red turned to Lynne. "If you are down to one nurse, couldn't Clarise be seeing patients? Isn't she a nurse?"

"Worthless," Lynne muttered. "She wouldn't lower herself to care for people. Might chip her manicured nails. I don't know where they found her. Must have come cheap."

Even with the fan and the air conditioner, the office was stifling. Red needed fresh air. "If you think of anything else, let me know."

Once outside, she walked two blocks to the Town Talk Café. Scotty, the former public health nursing director, was the owner and chief cook and baker. Her food was bland and filled with healthy ingredients, but the place was always busy for both breakfast and lunch. For dinner, folks headed to the Golden Deer Casino. Scotty closed at 4:30 so she could help Lou with the family planning clinic located in an old, deconsecrated church on the edge of town.

Since it was now 2:00 p.m., the restaurant was nearly empty. The bell on the door jangled when Red walked in. Scotty sat at the back table, reading the newspaper.

"Hey." She set the paper down. "I hear you've been busy today."

Red slid into a chair opposite her. "No comment on ongoing investigations."

Scotty smiled. With her graying hair pulled back into a long braid, she had an Earth-mother look to her. "But you want to know all the town talk. Right?"

"I want a cup of your very bad coffee and something greasy and unhealthy to eat."

Scotty pointed to the coffee. "Pour your own while I find something that will clog your law enforcement arteries."

While Scotty busied herself at the grill, Red scanned the local paper. The *Pearsal Gazette*, like many local rural newspapers, struggled to stay afloat. Most of the paper was devoted to either feel-good stories about Lykkins Lake or high school sports. When Scotty returned with a hamburger and fries, Red pointed to an article. "I see we're going to have a championship football team this fall."

"Bah! All those young boys bashing their heads. Why don't they take up fencing?"

Red laughed. "Tell folks you're fencing and they'll ask how much barbed wire you need."

The hamburger was so-so and tasted more like oats than meat. Red suspected it might also have some shredded cabbage and carrots in it. Just like Scotty to sneak it in. Normally she'd harass her about it, but today, between Tommy Henley's beating and the missing nurse, she didn't have the energy.

Scotty jumped in before she could ask. "You want to know who beat up that little boy and where the nurse has gone off to."

"I'll double your tip if you tell me." Red shook salt onto her fries.

Scotty folded her arms on the table. "Sorry, I can't help you with either. No one said a word today about little Tommy, and the only thing I heard about Joanie was that she ran off with some guy."

"Really? Some guy? Left her patients in the lurch and ran off?"

Scotty shrugged. "It's the best I can do."

"Any thoughts about her husband, Jimmy?"

"I've heard he's involved in the church and does the taxes for some of the businesses here."

"Including yours?"

"Ha! Do you think I can afford a CPA? I used to have old Nelson do them. After they carted him away to the home, I got a fancy computer program. Screw it up every time. I'm guessing the IRS will be calling one of these days."

Red finished her hamburger after dousing it with ketchup. Scotty peered at her. "You're worried, aren't you? I know your sheriff's 'spidey sense.'"

For a moment, the abandoned cemetery with the watchful pines flashed through her head. Something bad was in the wind, and Red couldn't grasp onto it.

She stretched and stood without replying.

"See you tonight at poker. I have a feeling I'm going to wipe all of you out."

Red smiled at her. Scotty was the worst poker player she'd ever met. "No doubt."

3

THE POKER CLUB

Red glanced at her cards with an impassive expression. Three deuces. Stacked neatly in front of her were twenty-five dollars in chips. On the wall behind her, in the cluttered back room of Georgia's Antiques, hung a garish blue, black, and green velvet tapestry of cigar-chomping dogs playing poker. Tacked beneath the tapestry was a sheet of paper entitled, *Rules of the Florence Nightingale Memorial Poker Club:*

- *Must be a nurse to play*
- *If not a nurse, must be a county sheriff*
- *No talk about bowels or other bodily functions allowed during game*
- *No smoking and no spitting*
- *Winner will donate proceeds to the betterment of humankind*

"Call," she said, placing the cards facedown in front of her. She was weary and distracted. Rubbing the back of her neck, she announced, "Ladies, I think this will be a short night for the sheriff. I'm beat."

Georgia raised an eyebrow. "You're not beat, you're perseverating."

"I knew it!" Scotty fingered the one chip in front of her. "I said so this afternoon."

The Pines Were Watching   15

Red enjoyed her poker nights with the three nurses, but she tried to never talk county business with them. The little boy and the missing nurse were foremost in her mind. Second to that was the ever-present public safety budget. For months she'd been locked into a stalemate with the county board. She needed to give her staff raises, replace the antiquated computer system, and find funds for a new vehicle. On top of that, one of the commissioners was putting on the pressure to merge her department with the bordering Dickson County. Their sheriff was on leave, and they were ripe for a merger. Her head ached.

Mostly, though, she was thinking about Tommy Henley and the welts on his back.

Lou, sitting across from her, appeared to read her mind. Her eyes reflected sympathy as she watched Red flip up her cards. No one else had anything better than an ace high. She raked in the chips.

Georgia walked stiffly to the little refrigerator in the back of the store. She took out four Summit Pale Ales and set them on the table.

"We need to loosen this game up a bit."

The beer tasted cold and refreshing. Red relaxed and won the next two hands.

"More money for the Church," she said, observing the pile of chips in front of her. The Church was the family planning clinic set up in the old Norwegian Lutheran Church that Lou and Scotty ran with a patchwork of grants and donations. Since they opened it over two years ago, the teen pregnancy rate in the county had dropped by half.

As she dealt the hand, Scotty said, "Do you think Arlis will get Tommy back?"

Lou looked at Red with a neutral expression.

Scotty dealt the next hand and set the remaining deck in front of her, flipping up a jack of spades. "Oh, come on, you two! Don't look at me like that. I know all about the privacy rules. What is said in this room stays in this room."

Georgia muttered, "Like hell it does."

Scotty put the cards down and turned to Georgia with a dark expression. "What did you say?"

Before Georgia could snap back, Red put her hands up. "Let's not get into a brawl here. I might have to arrest Georgia for running a tippling house."

Lou chuckled, sorting through her hand.

The back room of Georgia's held the heat of the day, and even though Red had cooled Scotty and Georgia down, she knew she had to change the subject or the temperature would rise.

"I was out on County Road Six today and drove by the Grandgeorge Place. Every time I see it, I wonder what those walls would say if they could talk."

The conversation quickly turned to the Grandgeorges and away from Tommy Henley. Red relaxed. Behind her, a moth fluttered at the light from the open window. A tepid breeze seeped in.

"I hear it looks bad on the outside, but it's in pretty good shape, considering that it hasn't had upkeep in years." Scotty was now in her element as she related the story of the Grandgeorge family.

Carl, the patriarch, showed up with grand plans for his bride, Rebecca. They had two sons, Clyde and Derek.

"Derek was in my little brother Lad's grade, I think," Red commented. She looked at the hand of useless cards and pulled out three to discard.

"Sad story, though. Carl died when Derek was a teenager. His brother, Clyde, came home from college to take over. Rumor has it the first thing he did was knock up Geraldine Baker. Arlis Henley's cousin."

Damn, Red thought. *Back to Arlis Henley.*

Scotty was bright-eyed as she continued. "He married her, and before the baby was born, he took off to parts unknown. She lives in that place with Rebecca, the grande dame, Derek, and the daughter—Caddie."

Red noted that Lou drummed her fingers on the table. This usually meant that she was nervous. Caddie was probably one of their patients at the Church.

Before Scotty could get into more trouble, Red threw in her hand. "Fold." She stood up. "Time to cash in. As usual, give the ill-gotten gains to the Church."

Georgia looked at her watch. "Wow, it's past nine, the bewitching hour for us old folks."

Red stepped outside into the humid late summer evening. Downtown

The Pines Were Watching   17

Lykkins Lake was deserted. Six blocks away, a motorcycle roared down the highway. She could tell by how quickly the sound faded that the cycle was breaking the speed limit. She hoped the state patrol was out but doubted anyone would catch the cyclist.

As she walked to her car, an unease tugged at her shoulders. Will used to say, "Honestly, Red, your body knows more than you do. Listen to it."

Once inside her car, she snapped on her seat belt and tried to figure out what her body was saying. On her way home, she detoured down Pine Street, slowing in front of the house where Joanie Crea lived. It had belonged to the Skoglunds before the Creas bought it. She remembered riding down this street as a kid on her bicycle. The yard was always filled with neighborhood kids playing. Mrs. Skoglund used to bake cookies for them. A regular Norman Rockwell painting—except it all ended when Mr. Skoglund hanged himself in the garage after being diagnosed with lung cancer. The house was a rental for years until the Creas bought it.

A light peeked through the blinds of the front bedroom. The driveway was empty and the garage door closed. Joanie Crea must have made it home. Red pulled in and got out of the car. The humid air smelled of late summer tinged with lingering smoke from a distant wildfire. She took a deep breath before knocking on the front door and calling out.

"It's Red Hammergren, the sheriff. Sorry to bother you. I'm just checking to see if you are all right."

The house remained silent. Red took out her cell phone and tapped in Joanie's number. It went immediately to voicemail. She tried knocking again and heard nothing but the crickets in the lawn and the distant rumble of cars on the highway.

Walking over to the garage with her flashlight, she peered into the window. The garage was empty. For a moment, she wondered what Mrs. Skoglund thought when she found her husband hanging from the rafters. It happened while Red was away at college, but she remembered her mother telling her that Mrs. Skoglund was never the same after that.

At exactly ten o'clock, the light in the bedroom snapped off.

"Light on a timer," Red mumbled. "No one home." She pushed back a lock of her hair. "Where are you, Joanie Crea?"

4

THE BODY

Red woke up with a start. The sheets were tangled around her feet, and she was bathed in sweat. Fragments of the dream that woke her still floated in her head. The Grandgeorge Place, Will alive yet dead, a dark shadow of something old and evil.

She opened her eyes to the sleeping dog nestled next to her shoulder. Blue snored, blissfully unaware of Red's distress.

"I thought dogs were supposed to be psychic and know when we humans were upset."

The little poodle opened his eyes and half-heartedly licked her shoulder.

"That's better."

Her digital clock numbers glowed green. It was 3:24 a.m. She stared at it, unable to shake the sense of something bad. Outside, thunder rumbled. Red pushed herself to a sitting position. An ache in her jaw radiated through the right side of her head. Aches like this often meant changes in the weather, but this time, she felt it was caused by something else.

"Honestly," she said to the dog. "The older I get, the more I sound like my mother." She remembered when she was younger the array of painkillers in the medicine cabinet for her mother's "migraines."

It took several ibuprofen and a cup of hot tea before she was able to go back to sleep. Even then, her dreams were troubled.

The next morning, Red sat in her office with the latest financial spreadsheet. One thing they never talked about on the television crime shows was how much time law enforcement spent with bureaucratic paperwork. The best sheriff was not the quickest draw; the best sheriff was the one who could stay within a budget, not work her staff to death, and be a good servant to her constituents.

She was interrupted when Billie came bounding in the door. His face was flushed with excitement.

"Sheriff? A body. They found a body out at the Grandgeorge Place. They think it's Jimmy Crea's wife."

It took Red exactly twelve minutes to reach the Grandgeorge driveway. Behind her, she left a choking spray of dust and gravel. She hardly noticed the rhythmic swerve of the back of the car as she sped down the road. The radio crackled with voices. She glanced at it, lips pressed into a tight line. Her neck ached as she gripped the steering wheel.

In the distance, she could see large pillars supporting the roof of the graying mansion. The coloring of the house changed as she sped down the graveled drive. First, in the sun's glare, the house was an eye-aching white, then as she passed through the mottled shade of tall pines, it turned a shadowy gray.

Taking a deep breath, she eased up on the accelerator. If her information was correct, all the power and speed in her car wouldn't help Joanie Crea now.

The house stood three stories high with a sloping gabled roof supported by Doric columns. One of the third-story windows was boarded shut, and another had a gaping hole in it. A wing jutted to the right, ending in an unfinished three-car garage. Paint had peeled everywhere, leaving great sections of exposed weathered boards.

Tall grass surrounded the house, some reaching as high as the porch. A row of scraggly rosebushes scraped against the edge of the house in the scorching breeze. A few delicate pink buds clung to the ends of the thorny shoots like survivors of a shipwreck.

She pulled into the U-shaped turnaround in front of the house, switched off the car, and sat still for a moment. Three women waited for her on the weathered porch.

Before Red could greet them, Geraldine Grandgeorge stepped forward. She wore an oversized pink T-shirt, beige spandex Capri pants, and white canvas sneakers. She was at least seventy-five pounds overweight, but her hair was shiny and sleek as it cascaded to her shoulders. Her face still had a prettiness about it that the fat could not hide. Her cheap, modern attire seemed out of place on the sagging porch of the mansion.

"My girl found her out in the summerhouse." Geraldine pointed vaguely behind her.

"Is everyone else all right here?" Red kept her voice calm and steady.

Geraldine hugged herself. "Whoever did it is long gone, I'd say. She's been dead awhile."

Red surveyed the women. Next to Geraldine stood her seventeen-year-old daughter, Caddie. Caddie's fingernails were painted a deep purple. Her fingers were flying as she texted. When she finally looked up, her expression was a mixture of fear and sullenness. She was a thinner version of her mother except for the thick, dark eyebrows and curling hair.

Red did not know the third woman. She sat on the top step with her head between her knees. Red walked up to her.

"Are you all right?"

"Just a little faint," the woman said softly.

"She's a nurse," Geraldine said in an edgy voice. "She's the one who said Jimmy's wife was dead—as if you couldn't guess by looking at her."

Red pulled a notebook out of her back pocket and said, "Can you tell me what happened?"

The woman sitting on the steps looked up at Red. Her eyes were sea green, a perfect match for her red hair. Her face, so pale that it looked translucent, betrayed a deep fear.

She knows something that she doesn't want to tell, Red thought.

"Could I get your name?"

The woman stared at her blankly, her lips slightly parted.

"She's one of the county nurses," Geraldine interrupted impatiently. "She doesn't know anything. Just came by to look at Grandma Rebecca's leg."

"Your name?" Red gently prodded.

"Angela Driver." The words were whispered.

Geraldine glowered. "I told you. She doesn't know anything. Ask my girl. She's the one who found her."

Caddie Grandgeorge nearly jumped when Red looked at her. The words tumbled out, as if someone were threatening her with a stick.

"I was just out walking in the back. Uncle Derek has the summerhouse back there. It's cool and nice inside. I just go there sometimes." She looked tentatively at her mother, who nodded. "I found her on the bed. The smell was bad, and I didn't touch her or anything. I knew it was that nurse, Mrs. Crea, because she used to see Grandma Rebecca." Her voice dropped. "And me." She said nothing else.

Before Jason could arrive with sirens screaming, Red had most of the story from the women. Caddie had found the body around ten this morning. She'd run back to the house to tell her mother. Angela Driver had walked in about that time to change a dressing on Rebecca Grandgeorge's ulcerated leg. Angela and Geraldine had gone back to the summerhouse to confirm Caddie's story.

As the cruiser roared down the driveway, a warbling voice called from inside the house.

"Girl, could you quiet things down out there. I'm trying to take a little nap."

"Shit." Geraldine turned to the house. "Thought she'd sleep through all this."

Red looked directly at Angela Driver. "Mrs. Grandgeorge?"

Angela nodded. "She's confused a lot. She thinks her son Clyde is here. Only Derek lives here now."

"Where is Derek?"

Two spots of color grew on Angela's white cheeks. She looked away without answering.

"Any idea why Mrs. Crea would be here?" Red directed her question at Geraldine. Geraldine looked beyond Red toward the stand of pines on the west side of the house.

"Poor Jimmy." Her voice dropped off.

Red turned to Caddie. "Any thoughts?" The girl drew back when she spoke to her. She shook her head, shifting her eyes to her feet.

"Angela?"

The nurse did not even look at Red. She bowed her head and began crying, a dry, hacking sob.

Guided by a reluctant Geraldine, Red and Jason followed a path into the woods behind the Grandgeorge house.

The summerhouse stood in a small clearing, a quarter of a mile from the mansion, surrounded by ivy and bloodroot and a lush green mossy carpet. Shafts of sunlight danced through the tall pines onto the pointed roof. It looked like an old-fashioned screened-in bandstand with a new coat of gleaming white paint.

Red stopped, taking in its simplicity with a shudder. In the midst of the ruin of the Grandgeorge Place, this little building stood like a well-kept temple.

"Who do they worship here?"

"What did you say?" Jason glanced at her, clearly eager to get to the scene.

Red, sensing what was ahead of them, didn't share his enthusiasm. "Just surprised that this place is so well kept."

Geraldine sniffed. "Derek was obsessed with it. Wouldn't fix the broken window in the attic, but always kept this place up."

Jason pointed to the door. "Should we go inside?"

As Red approached the building, she noted the sickly sweetness of decay. "Wait. Let's take it slow. I want a good look around before we go inside." She blinked away the image of a temple and concentrated on the outside of the summerhouse.

"But… " Jason's voice rose in impatience.

"What's inside will keep, believe me."

Geraldine pressed her lips together in a grim expression. "I need to get back to Caddie." She hugged herself. In the deep forest sunlight, she looked like her daughter.

Red sent her back to the house before walking slowly to the screened

The Pines Were Watching 23

door. She noted how the ground cover was flattened on the south side of the door. Jason walked eagerly behind her. Pointing to the mangled fern and ivy, she said sharply, "Don't step there."

Jason stared. "Why?"

Red shook her head. "I don't think she was killed here. Whoever did it put the body down there before opening the door."

"Wow, how did you know that?"

Red wasn't sure. "An educated guess, Jason."

She stood on the threshold with the screen door wide open. Joanie Crea lay on top of a single bed tucked up against the wall below the screened windows. She was on her stomach with her face pressed at a funny angle into a pink floral pillow, a cord wrapped around her neck. She wore khaki shorts and a T-shirt, and her arm dangled over the cot as if she'd been thrown there in a hurry. Grass-stained white socks covered her feet. The heat and decomposition had caused the body to bloat, but even from a distance, Red saw that she was a small woman. Probably no taller than Caddie.

She motioned Jason to stay at the doorway as she walked carefully into the room. Even though it was obvious that Joanie was dead, she needed to confirm. As quickly as she could, she observed the body. Joanie's eyes were open and reminded her of the deer Will had shot several years ago, opaque and lifeless.

Without touching anything, she leaned close enough to whisper, "We'll find who did this."

Backing away from the body, Red switched on the flashlight and swept the room. "Notice anything unusual?" she asked, signaling to Jason.

"No shoes?"

"That's one thing. Now look carefully around the room."

He squinted as she pointed the flashlight at the floor.

"It's so neat and clean."

"Considering the state of her socks, it looks to me like the floor has been swept. We have a very meticulous killer." While they stood in the doorway, she took out her phone and called the state Bureau of Criminal Apprehension. She needed the forensic team as quickly as possible.

"Waltz here."

"Sheriff Red Hammergren from Pearsal County. I've got a body for you."

"Have you examined it?" Waltz's line crackled with poor cell service.

"Only to determine the victim is dead with a rope around her neck. I'm leaving the rest up to you and your experts."

"At your service. We'll be there in an hour."

While they waited for the forensic team, Red directed Jason back to the house to get statements from the three women. After he left, in the thick quiet of the woods, Red retreated from the doorway of the summerhouse and sickly sweet odor of the body.

A slight breeze whispered through the pines. She stood on the edge of the clearing under one of the tall trees. Its scent was a welcome relief from the smell in the summerhouse.

Murder was not common in Pearsal County. During her tenure as both a deputy and the sheriff, she'd only investigated two murders. One was a domestic murder-suicide that left three children without parents. The other, last winter, had been a teenage boy caught up in drugs.

Will had warned her when he'd hired her as a deputy that deaths would stick with her even after the cases were resolved. "It cuts a piece out of your humanity when it happens."

Thinking about the nurse who had once been a vibrant human being, she was struck with how carelessly the body had been dumped on the cot. The killer was either rushed or very angry. She inhaled the scents of the forest and closed her eyes. The quiet here would not last long.

5

THE FORENSIC TEAM

A voice startled her. "The troops have arrived."

She turned to the stocky, fiftyish man with wire-rimmed glasses and dark hair peppered with gray.

Maynard Waltz stuck out his hand. "Nice to see you again. I was a great fan of your husband and pleased to hear that you succeeded him."

His friendliness threw her off. She'd met Waltz several times at law enforcement conferences but didn't know him well. He was considered an expert when it came to interviewing suspects. He also had a reputation for working his team hard.

Clearing her throat, she indicated the summerhouse. "Uh, sorry, I needed to get away from the smell."

He nodded. "I always carry my jar of Vicks. Not perfect, but it helps. Care to join me?"

She followed him to the summerhouse, where he put on paper shoe coverings and exam gloves. "I can observe from a distance, if that's okay."

He studied her for a moment, then nodded.

Jason guided three more people to the site. Waltz's forensic team. As Waltz had put it at one of his lectures, "My teammates here are scientists. Unlike what you see on television, they don't carry guns, and they don't chase the bad guys. They collect evidence."

Waltz was slow and careful, handling the body with a delicate touch. When he was done, he motioned to two of the team members. "Let's get her to the coroner, who will be able to tell us more."

He approached Red, who was on the phone to the office with an update. "Sheriff, walk with me. I need to air out."

They walked together back toward the house as the van that would transport Joanie to the coroner's office in St. Paul drove carefully down the grassy pathway. Once out of the clearing, Waltz took a deep breath. "I hate these scenes. Bad people doing bad things."

"I promised her I would find who did it." Red blushed at the burst of emotion. "What can you tell me?"

"Probably been dead less than forty-eight hours, although with the heat and humidity, it can be hard to pinpoint it. Strangled with a piece of rope. We'll get it analyzed, but I doubt it will tell us much. It looked like standard rope you can get at any hardware store. She also had a gash on her forehead, like she'd fallen or been thrown against something."

"Signs of sexual assault?"

He gazed up in the sky. "I don't know. We'll let the medical examiner figure that out. I didn't see anything overt."

"The place looked like it had been recently swept. Was she strangled there?"

Waltz furrowed his brow. "My gut says no. My team will have more once we get back to the lab."

Red nodded. "I noticed the grass stains on her socks—like she'd been dragged."

A crow landed on the branch of a tree and cawed at them. Waltz looked up at it. "What do you know about her?"

She relayed the little she knew about Joanie. Respected nurse, quiet, kept to herself. Amid a divorce from her husband. Reported missing yesterday.

Waltz raised his eyebrows. "The husband. What do you know about him?"

"He's a pillar of his church. An accountant and involved in a number of community activities. Local guy—grew up around here. I've never had a report on him or any indication of trouble."

The Pines Were Watching 27

"When can you get him in for an interview?"

"He's at a church conference in Duluth. They're trying to locate him now."

They were interrupted by one of his team members. "Waltz? Need your thoughts on this."

Before heading back to the scene, he said, "My team would tell me it's all science. But my gut tells me this was a crime of passion."

Red agreed.

She was on the porch of the mansion when the BCA van emerged from the path to the summerhouse. Geraldine stood next to her with her hand on her mouth as it slowly drove by. "Where are they going?"

"Our medical examiner is in St. Paul. They'll take the body there for an autopsy."

"My God." The anger and the brusqueness Red had experienced from Geraldine disappeared as tears slipped down the woman's cheeks. "I didn't know her well—but no one deserves that."

The way she said it caused Red to wonder if Geraldine had been a victim of abuse. "You're right. We'll find who did this."

As the van disappeared down the long treelined drive, she thought for a moment about the expense of the autopsy. Would it screw up her budget?

"Oh, God," she mumbled to herself. "I've turned into a bureaucrat." She could almost hear Will's chuckle. "Ah, Red," he would have said, "I knew that a bottom line lurked somewhere inside you."

Jason walked up the wooden steps to the porch. "They've located Jimmy Crea. One of his parishioners has gone to pick him up in Duluth. The officer who talked with him said he didn't handle the news well."

"What do you mean?"

"Said he collapsed, slid right off the chair and hit his head. They had to take him to the emergency room over at St. Luke's."

Red wiped her brow, pushing back a curl that kept drooping into her eye. "I guess it would be a shock."

She would join Waltz for the interview with Jimmy. Perhaps she could learn from him. Right now, she wanted the burning question answered. How did the victim end up out here in a summerhouse in the middle of the woods?

Derek Grandgeorge's pickup inched around the vehicles lining the driveway. Even in the heat of the afternoon, he wore a green army jacket, which rested loosely on his shoulders. As he walked from the vehicle, his gaunt face registered a combination of anger and puzzlement.

"What is this, Sheriff?" He stood straight with his arms folded.

"We found a body in the summerhouse."

"What? Who?" He stared at her. "A drifter? We've had them tramping through the woods before."

Behind her, the door to the house opened. She turned long enough to see Caddie and Angela emerge from the house. She watched the color rise in Derek's face.

"We found Joanie Crea's body in your summerhouse. She was strangled."

He blinked hard. "Joanie?"

Red nodded.

"What the hell was she doing here?" He spoke to himself, his fists suddenly clenched at his sides.

"I wanted to ask you the same thing," Red said calmly.

From inside the house, a tremulous voice rose faintly. "Girl, I think I'd like my tea now. Clyde should be here soon."

Derek stared at the house, his dark eyes narrowing. "This is bullshit!" He strode onto the porch and into the house.

God, what kind of secrets held these people together? Red moved around the back of Derek's pickup. The bed of the truck was empty. It looked like it had been swept out.

6

JOANIE'S HOUSE

Jason stood in the driveway of Joanie Crea's house, touching the handle on his holstered gun. His slightly pudgy face and dancing eyes belied the fact that he was almost thirty years old. The first time Red had met Jason, she had thought, *This is what a grown-up Beaver Cleaver would look like*.

"Want me to break down the door, Sheriff?" Jason grinned.

It broke the tension that had seized both of them. "Only if we can get it on video." The concrete drive emitted late afternoon heat. She was tired, hungry, hot, and battling an angry headache. She'd missed an important meeting with the county commissioners, who were determining the public safety budget for next year. Her clothes still held the odor of Joanie's body even though she'd hardly been exposed to it. Worse, she couldn't get the image of Joanie Crea's sightless eyes out of her brain. What she really wanted right now was a cold beer and perhaps a different profession.

Neighbors stood in the street in clumps of two or three, watching. The news had traveled quickly.

They had not recovered keys or any personal possessions from the body, and the doors to the house were all locked. She called the only locksmith in town.

He answered after the third ring.

"Sheriff Hammergren here."

"Oh, hi, Sheriff. The wife was just telling me about Mrs. Crea. This'll keep me busy for the next two weeks. Everyone is going to want their old locks fixed or changed."

"Did you work on her locks?"

He chuckled. "I knew you'd be calling. I just pulled the work order. I changed that lock, front and back, first week in May. She said Jimmy was moving out and she needed new locks."

"Was she trying to keep Jimmy out?"

"I don't think so. She told me now that she was living alone, she wanted to make sure no one got in because she kept her work computer at home."

"How many keys did she have made?"

"She only wanted two."

"How fast can you get over here and open up the lock on the house?"

"I'll be over in five."

"Thanks."

"Any time, Sheriff."

Red doubted Joanie was afraid of break-ins. Most people in Lykkins Lake didn't lock their doors.

After the locksmith arrived and unlocked the door, she stepped gingerly through the doorway, then beckoned Jason. The inside of the house was shadowy with the curtains pulled. The air had the hot summer staleness of a house shut tight against the sun and humidity. It smelled slightly of a woodsy perfume. Red took a deep breath but couldn't identify it.

"Do you smell that?" she asked Jason.

Jason sniffed and shrugged. "Shampoo, maybe?"

The two of them quickly searched the house. The living room was furnished with a love seat in a flower pattern and two easy chairs. The walls were bare, and other than an array of books in a bookcase, little in the room seemed personal.

"I'm told they bought this house eight years ago. It hardly looks lived in."

Jason agreed. "You'd think they would have hung some pictures, at least."

"It looks like whatever they had on the walls has been taken down."

The Pines Were Watching

One of the bedrooms contained a computer desk with pens and note-books but no computer. Several packed cardboard boxes lined the walls.

"It looks like she was getting ready to move." Red made a mental note to ask Lynne at the nursing office about the computer.

A night light in the bathroom emitted a sickly yellow glow in the dark-ened hallway. In the main bedroom, the queen-sized bed was rumpled and unmade. A pile of clothes lay heaped on a chair. Joanie was not a very tidy housekeeper.

As Red scanned the room, she noticed the timer plugged into the wall by the bedside table. It was connected to the lamp on the table.

Red squatted down and examined the pegs on the timer. It was set to turn on at seven in the evening and off at ten.

She found a set of keys dangling from a hook screwed into a cupboard in the kitchen. Red slipped them into a plastic bag, guessing they were the spare set.

Nothing in the house indicated that the crime had happened here.

The door to the unattached garage was unlocked. The inside was empty except for an old power lawn mower and a few yard tools. As she looked around, Red couldn't help but look up at the beam that had held the rope all those years ago. If she recalled right, Mrs. Skoglund was still alive but living in an adult family home.

"Where is her car, and how did she get to the Grandgeorge Place?"

"I'll bet we'll find that car hidden somewhere on the Grandgeorge prop-erty. Probably ditched her purse and phone there, too."

"And the shoes?"

Jason nodded. "Grandgeorge has got them stashed somewhere, too."

"Why are you so sure Grandgeorge did it?"

"Just seems logical. Body on the property. Probably having an affair with her. Maybe that's what broke up the Crea marriage."

"Have you heard something about an affair?" Jason spent a certain number of off hours at Cuttery's, the bar on the edge of town. Like the Town Talk, it was a small-town rumor mill.

"Well," he mumbled. "Somebody made them split."

"Are you guessing, or do you know something was going on between Derek Grandgeorge and Joanie Crea?"

Jason looked down at his feet. "Just a hunch."

Red held back a sigh. "Let's try to keep an open mind and stick to what we know." She made a mental note to ask the poker club about any connection between Grandgeorge and Joanie.

When she interviewed the neighbors, the story was the same. Joanie Crea appeared to be a creature of routine. Home most nights, lights off by ten. No visitors, no activity. The next-door neighbor on the east did note that in the last couple of weeks, Joanie had been coming home later than usual.

"I know because sometimes her car would pull up after dark. The lights shine into my front window. Like last night, it was probably around midnight."

"You saw her car pull in here at midnight?"

The neighbor kicked at a small pebble. "I think so. At least I saw headlights and heard a car door close."

"Do you know where her car is?"

He shook his head. "It was gone when I got up this morning."

The neighbors all said she was "nice," but their voices tended to fall away after using the word. The young couple on the south called her "nice, but different." The widow on the north termed her "nice but standoffish." Red sensed that although they were deeply affected by the tragedy, no one in the neighborhood would miss her.

7

THE GRANDGEORGE GOSSIP

At eight p.m., as Red headed back to her office in the courthouse, she noticed the light on in the back room of Georgia's Antiques. Fifteen minutes with Georgia might help settle her thoughts.

When she walked in, the entire poker club sat around the old oak table. Scotty glanced up as she passed a plate of chocolate chip cookies.

"Finally. We thought you'd never get here."

Red scratched her head. "As I recall, we had our poker night last night. What are you doing here?"

Georgia looked at her with a serious expression. "Support. We're pretty devastated."

Red pulled up a chair and sat down. Scotty placed the cookies in front of her. "Have a couple. I think you've earned them."

Tentatively, Red picked one up and took a bite. To her surprise, it tasted good. "You didn't bake these, did you?" She winked at Scotty. "They're edible."

Scotty grinned back at her. "I only put the ground-up carrots and spinach in for my customers. Most of them haven't seen a vegetable since their mothers made them eat their peas because of all the starving children in Africa."

"Your customers are onto you. I happen to know they shop at the Quick

Stop for donuts before they come in for your coffee." Lou still wore her crisp white lab coat from the clinic with her name embroidered in red on the pocket.

All eyes stayed on Red.

"You look like hell," Georgia finally said.

"Hmmm. That bad?" Red surveyed the downcast look of the group. "So, what's the talk?"

"Drug-crazed gangs from down on the border. Maybe some Islamist terrorists," Scotty said. "No one from around here would do such a thing. Not even the spooky Derek Grandgeorge. He's a veteran, you know. As one of my customers put it, 'He came back with that pasta thing.' I think he meant PTSD, but I didn't want to interfere with their discussion about all the marauding gangs."

"Been seeing a lot of gangs at the Town Talk lately?" Red asked.

"Only if you consider the senior citizen brigade from the Manor. They come tripping in every Tuesday for the meatloaf special. I think they like it because I use oatmeal. Keeps 'em regular." She paused. "Come to think of it, I've heard that Madge, down at the filling station, got a tattoo on her butt. Does that count?"

The laughter that followed was strained.

"What's the story, Red?" Lou asked.

"You know I can't tell you anything other than what you already know."

They talked among themselves for a while but could come up with nothing more interesting than Joanie Crea had been spending an increasing amount of time at the Town Talk in the last year.

"She used to come in on Thursday nights before I decided to close down at four thirty. She was always one of my only customers. Said Jimmy ran a Gamblers Anonymous group somewhere up north and didn't get home until real late. Always sat by herself." Scotty's blue eyes narrowed as she thought. "You know, I once accidentally splashed coffee on some of her papers. She grabbed them up so quickly, it was embarrassing..." Her voice trailed off.

"What?" Georgia prompted her.

"Well, they had lots of figures on them."

"What's so strange about that?" Lou asked.

Scotty shrugged. "I don't know. People around here usually do all their financial work in private. I wonder if she was trying to keep information away from Jimmy."

Red fingered the napkin on the table in front of her. "Any gossip about Derek Grandgeorge breaking up the Creas' marriage?"

Scotty shook her head. "Boy, that one would have gone through the Town Talk faster than the salmonella at the Garden Club picnic last year. I haven't heard a whisper."

Red took another bite of her cookie. Unable to disguise the tension in her voice, she tore a piece from the paper napkin and rolled it into a little ball. "I need your help on this one. Keep your ears open. Much as I hate 'they say,' sometimes gossip has a ring of truth."

"Oh, I don't know about that." Scotty smiled. "Ever heard the town businessmen at my back table during morning coffee? Last week they went on and on about the great Covid conspiracy. You know, Big Pharma backed by the Chinese letting the virus out in the world so they could make money on vaccines that don't work."

"Don't tell that to Doc Hanson. He lost several patients to Covid and still battles with some about getting the vaccine." Lou grimaced. "And now we're getting parents who don't want to vaccinate against measles."

"Boy, we're a fun group tonight—murder and the plague." Georgia turned to Red. "We'll do what we can to help."

"One thing," Lou interrupted. "And don't tell anyone where you got it— patient privacy and all that. Joanie Crea was coming into the clinic on a regular basis for dermatitis."

Georgia looked at Lou with a puzzled expression. "So what?"

Folding her arms, Lou said, "It's often stress related. I think she was under a lot of pressure."

"Well, duh, she was in the middle of a divorce." Scotty raised her hands.

"Maybe. But it didn't start until after Jimmy moved out. I think something else was going on."

"What about the Grandgeorges? Did she have a connection with them?" Red rubbed her temples.

Everyone shrugged except Lou, who looked at the table thoughtfully.

"Well, I heard she used to see Derek's mother, and I think she went out there a couple of times when Caddie had some trouble."

Red took another cookie. "Do you know what that was all about?"

Lou's cheeks colored. "I'm on some shaky ground here, Red. The Church clinic wouldn't survive if people thought I was talking about the patients."

Red agreed. "I won't pump you for confidential information, but keep your eyes open." She paused. "And be careful."

Red insisted that they each call her in a half hour to make sure they'd arrived home safely.

As they walked through the clutter of old furniture to the door, Georgia touched Red's shoulder. "You're scared this isn't an isolated thing, aren't you?"

Red rubbed her eyes, feeling as if someone had poured grit in them. "Scared is putting it mildly."

8

THE VISITOR

Red stood in her kitchen, speaking into the phone with carefully chosen words. "Yes, we have discovered the body of a woman in rural Pearsal County. We are notifying relatives at this time."

"Was she murdered?" The reporter on the other end had the voice and excitability of a twelve-year-old.

"We are handling the death as suspicious." Red thought about how Joanie Crea had been dumped on the bed. Suspicious was hardly the word for it—more like horrendous. "I'll issue a statement tomorrow. Sorry I don't have more information to release yet."

Red hoped tomorrow would be a big news day somewhere else in Minnesota. She would be happy if Joanie Crea's murder turned into four lines in the back of the Metro section. She did not look forward to news crews trampling through the Grandgeorge property.

Georgia, who'd navigated many a press conference during her days as the Minnesota Commissioner of Health, once told her, "You can do one of two things—either be witty enough to catch their attention, or dull enough to make them go away. Witty when you want something from them, boring when you don't. But watch your step. There's a fine line between sounding witty, boring, or just plain stupid."

Blue sat on the floor, looking up at her with curious eyes. "Well, I hope I bored that reporter." She reached down and patted his head.

She was finishing a note on her laptop when a knock on the door startled her. It was after ten, and most of her constituents had settled in for the night. Blue let out a one-syllable bark and trotted to the back door.

Waltz stood under the outdoor light, holding up a six-pack of beer. "I thought we could talk."

Although she was dead tired, she knew she wasn't ready for bed. Why not have a beer?

"It's a nice night. Let's sit on the patio."

They settled into the lawn chairs as the stars twinkled overhead. Blue nestled in her lap.

"Nice patio," Waltz commented, opening a beer and handing it to her.

"Good beer, too. If you'd brought me something that said 'Lite,' I would have had to arrest you."

He laughed, but Red felt tension in his tone. She rubbed at a knot in her neck, unsure why Waltz had shown up.

Below them, the lake lapped against the shore, and a chorus of cicadas trilled.

Waltz sat forward. "I'll bet you are wondering why I'm here?"

She stroked Blue. "The thought did cross my mind."

He held the beer in one hand and with the other he drummed his fingers on the arm of the lawn chair. "The truth is, I've never worked with you. I knew Will, and he was a good sheriff, and I'm guessing you are, too. However..." He paused to find the right words. "If we are to catch this person and convict him—or her, we need to trust each other."

Red stopped stroking Blue to peer at Waltz. "And you're not sure we do?"

Waltz set his beer on the patio table. "Okay, I need to backpedal a bit. It's not that I don't trust you, it's that I don't *know* you and you don't know me."

Red admired the honesty in his voice. This was probably why he was so good at interviewing people. He didn't pose a threat.

"Please don't tell me you want to teach me a good cop, bad cop routine before we talk with the husband."

The Pines Were Watching

Waltz tilted his head back and laughed. "Hardly. I myself flunked that class. Not good at the 'bad cop' part."

She smiled. "I never even took it. Too hard to figure out whether I wanted to be good or bad."

Something disturbed the leaves in the woods, and Blue pricked up his ears at the rustling sound. He yipped once, then settled again.

"He's my guard dog. Please don't tell the citizens of Pearsal County that I rely on him for protection."

More relaxed, she made a few obligatory comments about the weather before they settled into exchanging life stories. Waltz was a widower whose wife had died ten years ago from breast cancer. He had two grown children and had never remarried.

"Marilyn was a unique person. Not always easy to live with, a little OCD and a little bossy. But somehow, we fit. She's the reason everyone calls me Waltz instead of my first name, Maynard. She said Maynard reminded her too much of an old farmer."

Red laughed. "I have to agree with her."

"And what's the story about your name?"

"You might notice I don't have red hair like you'd expect."

"I did notice."

"My mother was a fan of Loretta Lynn, and she loved the movie *Coal Miner's Daughter*. She insisted on naming me after her, except she spelled my name wrong on the birth certificate. Instead of Loretta, she put down Loredda, with two *D*s. From the time I was a baby, I was called Red."

"Bet you never got teased just like I never got teased about being Maynard."

"Ha! What I wouldn't have given for a name like Amy or Amanda or even Mary."

Waltz's eyes shone with amusement. "I said I was named after Maynard G. Krebs, except no one my age watched reruns of *Dobie Gillis*."

Red felt a warmth from the beer relax her. She gazed toward the lake and after a few moments asked, "How long did it take for you to feel normal again after Marilyn died?"

He rubbed his chin. "I still don't. Sometimes I see her disappearing into a crowd, and for that moment, I think, good, now it's back to the way it was, crazy as it was sometimes."

Red stayed quiet, surprised she'd asked the question. A heaviness filled her, and she realized she wasn't ready to talk about Will—especially not to a stranger.

The moon rose above the tree line. Red stared at it. "Damn, almost a full moon. Do you believe there's more energy in the air when it's full? Will did."

Waltz followed her gaze. "Intuitively, maybe. Scientifically—it's unproven."

"I taught middle school science and math, but I do believe in gut feelings."

"And?"

"Well, I hate to bring up work, but a couple of people have me worried. I know you didn't see him, but Derek Grandgeorge's reaction to the murder was odd. He didn't ask questions, he simply stormed into the house."

She told him about seeing the tarp in the back of the pickup.

"And the nurse on the scene—Angela Driver? She was close to hysteria. In my experience, nurses are the people who stay calm in the middle of a crisis. I think the two of them are holding something back."

"Good information. We'll need to bring this Grandgeorge in as well as the husband." He glanced at his phone. "I guess I should head back to the motel. We'll talk with the husband tomorrow."

She walked with him around the house to the driveway. "Thanks for the beer. Next time it will be my treat."

It was after midnight, and she needed to be up early to face the morning, knowing the citizens of Pearsal County expected answers. They shook hands at his car.

As he drove away, she wondered why this impromptu meeting left her feeling off-kilter. Will would have told her it was because she didn't like surprises. She wasn't sure that was what bothered her. Perhaps Waltz was a little too good to be true.

9

A FLASH OF LIGHT

In the early hours of the morning, Red woke up with a groan. Slowly she opened her eyes as the images of a nightmare disappeared. The green digits on her clock registered 2:00 a.m. She blinked, and it seemed like a shadow disappeared into her closet.

"Now what?" The dream left her with an uneasy feeling like she had a monster lurking under her bed. The nightmares where she saw Will as a skeletal wraith had subsided in the last year, but an overall uneasiness hadn't gone away. Perhaps talking with Waltz about his wife had stirred up her subconscious.

The sleeping poodle on the pillow beside her lifted his head and looked at her with a slow yawn.

"You know, Blue, you're never very reassuring when I wake up like this."

Blue sighed, shifting until he was nestled up to Red's face. His fur smelled of old dog.

"Ugh. You're not that old! Time for a poodle shampoo." Red threw the sheet off while remnants of the dream floated through her brain. Something dark, something suffocating. But what? She knew she needed to take some ibuprofen, but she hated to move. The half-open closet door drew her attention. For a moment, she thought she felt a movement. She held her breath, then let it out with a contemptuous sigh.

"What is wrong with me?" Blue pricked up his ears at the sound of her voice. She remembered as a teenager sitting with her brother, Lad, when he had night terrors. Little did she or her parents know this was the beginning of the mental illness that caused him to disappear years ago to the streets.

Blue stood, his head cocked in alertness.

"You hear something, old boy?"

What would Waltz think about the ghosts in her closet? She immediately blinked the image of him sitting on the patio out of her head. Worse, what would the citizens of Pearsal County think of a sheriff who held conversations with her dog in the middle of the night?

She reminded herself that a certain number of Pearsal County voters still checked the name "Hammergren" on the ballot because they thought they were voting for Will or Will's father before him. In the darkness of the night, she remembered Will talking to her in a voice hoarsened by the cancer and too many years of cigarettes. "Promise me, Red, that when I die, you'll run for sheriff. I need to know the county is in good hands." She'd kept her promise, and to her surprise, and the surprise of several of the county commissioners, she'd won the next election.

Blue let out a half-hearted bark before jumping off the bed.

Darkness surrounded her as she walked barefoot to the bathroom wearing one of Will's oversized T-shirts. She leaned against the vanity, fumbling with the child-proof cap on the ibuprofen bottle. Blue's toenails clicked on the tile as he trailed behind her.

In the mirror, she saw the lines in her forehead. A curl of black hair fell over her left eye. She pushed it back, thinking absently of the surprised looks people gave her when she introduced herself as "Red." She had a dark complexion, which tanned easily, and light, almost gray eyes.

Red closed her eyes as she finally pried the ibuprofen bottle open and shook the caplets out onto the hard marble surface of the vanity. The medicine would dull the pain in her head but not erase the foreboding.

With a cool washcloth pressed to her forehead, Red padded to the patio door to let Blue out. The little poodle sauntered down the steps, stopping to sniff the air.

"It's the middle of the night, pal. Get on with it."

Blue's collar jingled in the darkness as he hunted just the right tree. Red whispered through the screen, "You've got thirty seconds. Any longer and you'll be tomorrow's poodle noodle soup."

The dog ignored her. The leaves on the trees shimmered in the light of the soon-to-be full moon. Red took a deep breath and leaned her head back against the doorframe. She remembered on a night when the moon cast a glow on the waters of Lykkins Lake how Will had gripped her hand for the last time and whispered, "The light's coming. I'll be fine." Scotty, Georgia, and Lou had been with her, the Nightingales who'd kept Will comfortable and at home.

While Blue trotted in and headed for the bedroom, Red continued to stare at the darkened woods leading to the lake. Will had loved this house, and she'd done little to change it since he died. At least she'd finally been able to settle his estate once Georgia and Scotty had located Will's older brother, Rolf, who had been lost in the state care system for nearly seventy years. She had plans to finally visit him in the nursing home in Minneapolis but kept putting it off.

After Red canceled a visit this summer, Georgia commented, "It's part of your grieving." Red had brushed her off. "No, it's not grief, it's the county board and all their 'emergency' meetings." In truth, Red wasn't sure what she'd say to the frail old man who had been taken from his home and placed in a state hospital at age fifteen.

She was about to turn back into the house when she thought she caught a brief flash of light beyond the trees that sloped to the lake. She blinked and saw nothing but darkness. Still, she felt like something wasn't right. Slipping back into the house, she put on a pair of sandals and grabbed a flashlight.

The light had come from the marshy shore of Lykkins Lake. This time of year, the lake tended to shrink as the water level lowered and runoff from the fields caused the algae to grow thick and green. Taking careful steps, Red moved in the direction of the flash. When she reached the boggy shore of the lake, she switched on the flashlight and looked around. Nothing moved in the still night air.

"Fireflies?" Still, as she stood listening to the sounds of the frogs and the occasional plunk of water as a fish rose to catch an insect, she sensed someone had been here. Above the stagnant odor of the swamp, she thought she smelled a faint aroma of something less natural and more artificial.

She took in a deep breath, trying to place the scent, but nothing came to her.

Back at her patio, she stared out at the lake. "Must be imagining things." A lonely mosquito landed on her forearm. She glanced at the moon and wondered if in the end, Joanie Crea had seen a flash of light and felt at peace. She hoped so.

In the distance, a car engine rumbled to life. Red turned and went back to bed, praying for a dreamless sleep.

10

ANGELA DRIVER

Just after dawn, Red settled in her office to review the notes on Joanie Crea. The sun peeked over the horizon in a hazy pink glow. Already the temperature was seventy-five degrees. The day promised to be long and hot.

She reread the notes on the computer from her deputies who had conducted interviews yesterday afternoon. One strong theme emerged. While no one had much to say about the deceased, they all thought Jimmy Crea was a "wonderful, wonderful man."

"Ain't it great to be so wonderful?" she said to herself. Jimmy's church, Faith Christian, was known for its strict rules and its devoted congregation. Jimmy was a deacon and the treasurer. He was also involved in the Lykkins Lake Chamber of Commerce. Red recalled a photo of him last year receiving an award at a Chamber event. In the photo, he'd had close-cropped hair and a boyish smile. He seemed a mismatch for Joanie Crea, who everyone described as serious and straitlaced.

Since Red's only encounter with him had occurred when Rose Timm had reported money missing from the church, he appeared to be an upstanding local citizen.

At eight, Ken Harrison, the county auditor, stopped by with a folder and a caramel roll. In his mid-fifties, he carried himself like a twenty-year-old. Ken ran marathons in the summer and skied in the winter. He was the only male county employee who dared wear an earring and a ponytail. Red had once had a beer with him at Cuttery's. She'd learned very quickly that Ken Harrison's main interest in life was Ken Harrison. The local women, married and unmarried, considered him very eligible. His ex-wife considered herself lucky to have gotten out of the marriage.

"The city is abuzz, Sheriff," he said, settling into the empty chair next to her desk.

"Any theories, Ken?"

He wiped a piece of caramel from his tie, licked his fingers, then flipped through the file in his lap. "Well, here's her county benefit papers."

"Life insurance?" Red pulled out her notebook and jotted down, *finances.*

"Standard county policy. Twenty-five thousand dollars. Looks like she changed the beneficiary in late May. She took Jimmy's name off and put in her parents."

"Then it doesn't look like her estranged husband would benefit from her death."

Ken shook his head. "At least not from the life insurance. As far as I know, they weren't divorced. Could be other money for him."

Red shifted in her seat. "What's the gossip, Ken? Did she have a boyfriend?"

Ken put his hands out in a gesture of surrender. "Not me. I swear."

"What about Derek Grandgeorge?"

Ken tapped his fingers on her desk. "I can't see it. Grandgeorge is like one of those PTSD vets. Twitchy, you know?"

"Capable of murder?"

He shrugged. "He stops for a beer at Cuttery's from time to time. Drinks alone. Always seemed harmless."

After Ken left, Red wrote the word *harmless* at the top of her legal pad.

By ten o'clock, five people had wandered into her office with tips and suggestions. The owner of Cathy's Salon stopped by to tell her that she'd trimmed Joanie's hair last Friday.

"Did she say she had any special plans?" Red asked.

She rubbed her cheek. "She never talked much. But she always tipped

The Pines Were Watching 47

well and always liked what I did with her hair. You know her hair was a wreck."

"What do you mean?"

"It started after she and Jimmy broke up. Her hair turned brittle, with no body to it. Nerves, I'd say."

After she left, Red shut her door and propped a chair against it. Privacy was not an understood term in the Pearsal County courthouse. Ten minutes later, Billie huffed from exertion as he pushed the door open.

"Gosh, Sheriff. I thought your door was stuck."

"It was."

"That red-haired nurse is outside. Says she needs to get on her visits and wants to know if she can talk with you now."

Red made a quick call to Waltz to be part of the interview. "I have Angela Driver in the office. She wants to give me her story."

"Hang on a minute. Crisis in the making."

She waited until he came back on the line. "Listen, I've got another case that is causing me a huge headache, plus a family problem I need to deal with. I definitely want to be in the room when you talk with the husband, but I'm guessing the nurse is not a person of interest."

Red pictured the sobbing redhead and agreed. "Okay, I'll fill you in."

Billie blushed as he showed Angela into the sheriff's office.

Red noted the smudges under the nurse's eyes.

"You look tired," she commented.

Angela blinked. "Pardon?"

"It's okay. Have a seat." Red pointed to the chair in front of her desk.

Angela sat looking at her feet, with her hands folded limply in her lap. "I don't know what I can tell you today that I didn't say yesterday."

Red ran through a list of questions, more interested in the nurse's expression than her answers. After the third question, Red stopped. Every question brought an almost imperceptible flinch, as if she expected to be hit.

"Are you all right?" Red tried not to sound impatient.

Angela looked startled. "Why?"

"You seem to be afraid of the questions."

"What?" Her pale cheeks changed to a sickly rose color.

"Angela, is there something you're not telling me?"

She replied in a soft, strained voice. "No. I'm just tired, that's all. I need to see a bunch of Joanie's patients. I have a lot of driving to do."

Red nodded. "If you think of anything, perhaps a connection between the Grandgeorges and Mrs. Crea, let me know."

Angela left without saying anything else. Red stared at her notebook, chewing on her thumbnail. The nurse seemed surrounded by a disturbing aura.

"Oh, come on, Red. Good police work is based on facts, not murky auras." She wondered what Waltz would say.

11

JIMMY CREA

It was close to noon before Waltz arrived to join her in interviewing Jimmy Crea. He wore a white polo shirt, creased khaki slacks, and brown loafers. He could have been a Gen X banker on casual day rather than a forensic expert.

He must have noticed how she looked him up and down because as soon as he sat in the chair across from Red's desk, his eyes crinkled in amusement. "You're wondering about the detective's cheap suit and tie. Am I right?"

Red felt a slight blush crawl up her neck. "Uh...okay, you got me."

"I don't like to intimidate the people I'm talking to. And I certainly don't want what they tell me to seem coerced."

They discussed the strategy for talking with Jimmy. Waltz emphasized the need to remain objective. "Leading questions get you quashed in court."

Red gave him a thumbs-up. "I got that when I took your class. I believe you had a PowerPoint slide about it."

Waltz laughed, and then his expression turned serious. "These interviews can be tricky—especially if we are dealing with someone who is either in the shock of bereavement or shock of getting caught."

They agreed to try moving back and forth between the two of them when asking questions. It was a good cop, good cop version. "If he responds better to you than to me, I will let you do most of the questioning. If it doesn't seem to matter, let's just ad-lib it."

What he didn't say, but Red was sure by his expression that he meant, was that if Red's questions became leading or inappropriate, he would take over.

They moved to the interview room, with its plain walls and basic table and chairs. Red always felt the room itself was intimidating. Years ago, she suggested to Will that they put some motel-type artwork on the walls. "What? And have a drunk crazy person rip them down and throw them at me?" She never brought it up again.

When Jimmy walked into the interview room, Red sized him at five foot eleven and two hundred pounds. He wore a limp, white short-sleeved shirt with a tiny egg stain on the front. Though his shoulders were broad, his stomach hung softly over a belted pair of wrinkled khaki pants.

Was he strong enough to strangle his soon-to-be ex-wife? She pushed the thought out of her head, remembering Waltz's mantra of not making any assumptions.

Jimmy lurched forward, off-balance as he entered the room. Quickly, both Red and Waltz guided him to the metal chair.

"Sit down, Mr. Crea. This is my colleague Maynard Waltz from the Bureau of Criminal Apprehension. He's helping with the investigation into your wife's death."

Jimmy eyes widened. "Uh...am I in trouble?"

Waltz folded his hands on the table and looked at Jimmy with a sympathetic expression. "First let me say how sorry I am for your loss. This has to be a difficult time for you."

Jimmy stared down at the table. His eyes were red and swollen. "I'm sorry. I'm not thinking real straight. They gave me some pills at the hospital. They make my head a little woozy." Little spears of hair spiked on the back of his head. He was unshaven and unshowered.

As Red studied the rounded face and the whiskered patchy skin, a vague memory flickered through her head and disappeared. She recognized him from something long ago. She readjusted the chair, noting how uncomfortable it was. What was that memory, and why did it flit through her head right now?

The Pines Were Watching   51

Waltz spoke in a low, gentle voice, as if talking with a child. "I know this is hard, Mr. Crea, but we need to ask some questions." He went on to give Jimmy a general overview of finding Joanie and calling the death suspicious. Red noted how carefully Waltz avoided providing any details other than that she had been discovered on the Grandgeorge property.

Jimmy nodded, closing his eyes. When he opened them, he looked sleepy. "You can call me Jimmy. I wish you would."

A report of the preliminary investigation last night by a Duluth detective sat in a folder in front of her. She and Waltz had reviewed it before the interview. According to the report, Jimmy said he had been home all night Sunday, the probable night of the murder. He'd left early the next morning for a two-day conference in Duluth. He had no idea why anyone would murder his estranged wife and appeared to be devastated by the news.

"Jimmy," Red said slowly, "according to what you said yesterday, you were home all Sunday night."

He looked straight at her, blinking. "Yes?" he said softly.

"And home is a set of rooms at Norma Elling's?" She turned to Waltz and spoke in a conversational tone. "Norma has a house a couple of blocks from here and rents out rooms on the second floor."

Jimmy's voice was choked as he spoke. "After we...broke up...she wanted to stay in the house, so I took rooms at Norma's." A tear slipped down his cheek. "It seemed the right thing to do."

They sat in silence for a few moments while Jimmy took out a wrinkled handkerchief and wiped his face.

Red resumed, "Do you know if anybody can verify that you spent the night at home?"

His lips pulled together into a grim line. "Sheriff and Mr. Waltz," he said, barely opening his mouth, "I didn't kill her. My God, how could you think such a thing?"

Red took a deep breath, letting it out slowly. Waltz gently tapped her foot with his to signal he'd take over. This was not the way she wanted the interview to go.

"Jimmy." Waltz continued to rest his elbows on the table. "I'm sorry. We're not trying to be confrontational, but you need to remember that your wife was a victim of homicide. We have to explore every possibility."

Red noted how Waltz's voice had changed from sympathetic to firm although the expression on his face remained the same. God, he really was good at this.

Another tear trickled down Jimmy's cheek. He blinked hard, gasped, then threw his hands up to cover his face. "I...I can't believe it!" he sobbed. "Who...who would have done this thing?"

Red looked at Waltz. "Jimmy, let's take a little break, and I'll get you some coffee."

When she left the room, he was crying quietly, the handkerchief pressed against his eyes.

Billie sat in the outer office, his eyes wide. He started to ask a question when Red cut him off with an abrupt, "Billie, would you get Mr. Crea a cup of black coffee? And put it in a mug, not one of those plastic cups."

Red walked down the hallway to the bathroom, her stomach knotted. Again, a vague memory skittered through her mind. She stopped in front of the door marked "Ladies" and tried to bring the memory to the surface. Something about her brother, Lad, and Jimmy Crea. She could picture Lad running through the backyard with a pack of boys. Then what?

The bathroom door opened, and Alma Wooster burst out, her frizzy purple-gray hair looking like a mini Afro. "Oh, hello, Mrs. Hammergren. Bad thing about Mrs. Crea, say? I prayed as soon as I heard the news. God will catch that man and strike him down." She looked piously at Red through thick wire-rimmed glasses.

"We will find the killer," Red said, emphasizing the word *we*. She turned back to her office. She did not want to spend any more seconds of her life than she had to engaged in conversation with Alma Wooster. Alma worked part-time in the Veterans Affairs office. Red had once confiscated a box full of religious tracts from Alma that claimed a Jewish conspiracy to destroy the "Christian backbone of America." Alma had tried to distribute them to all the county workers.

Red shuddered as she thought about the vile little pamphlets filled with hate and racism. She'd suspected for a long time that Alma spent her lonely evenings making anonymous phone calls.

Jimmy sat, more composed, with a mug of coffee. He apologized to the two of them. "I'm sorry. I can't seem to hold it together."

The Pines Were Watching   53

Red sat down and nodded to Waltz, who began, "Jimmy, we want to be straightforward with you. It's very rare that a murder is committed by a stranger. That's why we ask these questions. Can you tell us where you were on Sunday night and if anyone can confirm this?"

Red tensed her fingers around the pen, waiting for another emotional outburst from Jimmy. Instead, he rubbed his eyes and looked at the mirror behind her. A slight smile crept over his face.

"I was just thinking," he said in a far-off voice. "Joanie and I used to watch one of those mystery shows together on Sunday nights. She always guessed the killer. I never could." He raised his eyebrows. "It was never the husband."

Jimmy's reaction, his slightly out-of-balance response, touched a nerve with her.

He sat up straighter in his chair, his expression serious. "I was at a church board meeting until eight. Then a couple of us stopped at Cuttery's. I don't drink, but they had beer, and I had coffee. You can check with the bartender. I think I must have gotten back to my rooms by about ten thirty. I didn't leave after that until six, when I got in my car and drove to Duluth."

"Do you think Norma can verify the times?" Red asked.

Jimmy tilted his head back with a distracted smile. "Norma would verify anything I asked her to verify. I fixed her leaky toilet last week. She thinks I walk on water."

Neither she nor Waltz responded to his attempt to lighten the conversation. For a few moments, the silence built between them. Then, Jimmy cleared his throat. "Ah...I think someone might be able to tell you I was home at three in the morning, though."

"Yes?" She felt an odd sensation like a spider crawling up her neck and instinctively rubbed at it. The alibi was coming.

"Alma Wooster lives next door to Norma. Last week she told me she'd been getting crank calls in the middle of the night. Heavy breathing kind of thing. She asked me if I thought it might be one of those Arab terrorists, trying to scare the Christians."

Red fought back a smile. How nice that someone would pick on her. She wasn't surprised that Alma hadn't brought it to the sheriff's attention.

"And?" she prompted, keeping her voice neutral. Part of her really wanted to like Jimmy Crea. And part of her still saw the bloated body of Joanie splayed on the bed in the summerhouse and wondered if the estranged husband was responsible.

Glancing at Waltz, she noted he sat with his shoulders relaxed, like he was listening to someone talk about the weather.

"I told her I wasn't sleeping well at night, and if my light was on and she was frightened, she could call me."

"You talked to her on Sunday night?"

"Well, no. But I did hear her phone ring at about three in the morning. My window is very close to hers, maybe only ten feet away. I keep it open because Norma doesn't have air conditioning. I like to feel the breeze." He paused. "Joanie always wanted the windows closed..." His voice fell off.

"And?" Red prompted again.

Startled, Jimmy replied, "Oh, yes. I know she answered it. I could hear her say, 'Get thee from me, you foreign devil.'"

Red scribbled on her pad, *Check with Alma, 3 a.m. phone call.* When she looked up, Jimmy was staring at the two of them, his face a mixture of curiosity and something indefinable.

Waltz spoke this time. "I have one more question for you, Jimmy. I know you and Mrs. Crea have been estranged for a short time. Could you tell me a little about it?"

Immediately, the expression on Jimmy's face turned wary. "I wouldn't hurt her."

Red realized his reaction pushed some buttons in her. The murder-suicide that she and Will had investigated had left children orphaned. The family had covered up years of abuse from the husband. She wanted to say, "I've heard it before, and yes, husbands kill."

Waltz must have read her body language because he kept his tone even when he spoke. "I need to know as much about her as I can. For example, was there another man? That could be important."

Jimmy stuttered when he replied. "I...I don't exactly know. Maybe I spent too much time with the church and other volunteer activities. She... she just wanted to not be married."

Waltz was silent, waiting for Jimmy to continue.

The Pines Were Watching 55

Taking a deep breath, he uttered, "The divorce was her idea. I loved her."

Did she detect a glint of anger in those reddened eyes?

He lowered his head and rested it on his arms on the table.

"Jimmy, were you legally separated?"

When he looked at Red, a slight sheen of sweat formed on his forehead. He wiped his face with the handkerchief. "Young William was our—her lawyer. He was handling it for both of us."

Young William was the only lawyer in town since his father had retired. He'd inherited the practice from William, his father. Even now, at sixty with a head of silver-white hair, everyone in town called him Young William.

Waltz repositioned his chair, making a scraping noise on the floor. "Jimmy, you look exhausted. Perhaps we can talk again another time when you're more rested."

"Thank you," Jimmy whispered. "It's been hard."

Red nodded. "I'm sure it has been."

Jimmy's eyes filled with tears, but he stood straight, his handshake both warm and firm.

Ten minutes later, after refilling the coffee, Red and Waltz sat in her office. She had the same sensation she'd had when she'd turned in a C-grade essay in college. "I don't think that went well. What did we miss?"

Waltz glanced at his notes. "Were you looking for a confession?"

"It's weird, but it felt empty to me. Like we didn't find out anything substantive."

Waltz shrugged. "Maybe there wasn't anything to find out. He was out of town with an alibi, he seemed broken by the loss, and we have nothing that points to him as the killer."

Red pressed her lips together. "Glad you can be so objective."

"What's your concern?"

She thought about the questions and the answers. "He didn't ask the kinds of questions I'd expect. Like how was she killed? Or what was she doing at the Grandgeorge Place? Was she sexually assaulted? If it were me, I'd want to know the gory details."

Waltz shrugged. "I noted all of that as well. However, having done so many of these interviews, I've seen all kinds of reactions to trauma like this.

Let's keep an open mind. We'll bring him in again and see if he sticks to his story."

His phone rang, and he indicated to her that he would take the call out in the hall. When he returned, he appeared distracted. "Listen, I have a family crisis on my hands and need to get back to Minneapolis. I'm sorry. Take good notes when you bring anyone else in. Hopefully I can be back in a day or two." Before he walked out the door, he turned to her. "You did good. I think you were paying attention to my PowerPoint."

She felt so drained after talking with Jimmy that she didn't ask him about the crisis. She simply said, "Stay in touch, and I hope you get it resolved."

After he left, she stared at the door, troubled but unable to define the trouble. Behind her eyes lurked another headache, pink in color now, but soon to be a raging red if she didn't take some medicine.

12

THE BANK

As Red swallowed the Tylenol, she remembered an incident that was niggling in the back of her mind. It had to do with Lad. Until the mental illness struck full force when he was an adolescent, Lad had been an odd, friendly, outgoing kid. He was the one who always found time to play with the schoolyard outcasts. Occasionally he'd bring them home.

Red had a memory of a hot spring afternoon. She'd been reading in her bedroom with the window open. Outside, Lad played with four or five boys. They hooted and galloped through the yard, overpowering the sound of road construction behind their home. Red usually stayed away from Lad's friends because they liked to tease her about being so big and clumsy. "Red Wing boots," they used to say, pointing out her size ten shoes.

On this particular afternoon, Red remembered another sound, a whispery kind of noise coming from her parents' bedroom. Her mother had walked over to the neighbor's house, and her father had driven downtown in search of a part for the lawn mower. She'd gotten up and walked quietly toward their room. The door was closed, but she still heard the creak of the floorboards as someone walked inside the room.

"All right!" Red had yelled, pushing the door open. "Get out of there, Lad!"

Instead of Lad, she saw a fat little boy wearing a horizontally striped T-shirt, which did not cover his belly button. He stood in the middle of the bedroom, holding something wrapped in a dark scarf. When he saw her, he barreled out of the room, pushing her aside with unusual strength. Several weeks later, her mother had mentioned that her new purple scarf and a bottle of perfume were missing.

She'd never seen the boy again at their house.

"Was that Jimmy Crea?" Red asked aloud.

Billie opened the door just as the question was out. "What?"

"Nothing, Billie."

She made a note on her pad, *Check with the poker club about Crea*. She wished Lad was somewhere around so she could ask him.

Georgia called her a little after noon. "I'll bet you haven't had lunch yet. Come on over to the store. I've got sandwiches. We have something to talk to you about."

"I'll come only if you have a cold ginger beer waiting for me."

Georgia laughed and hung up. Georgia's ginger beer had something in it that never failed to settle Red's stomach. She'd once asked Georgia what she put in it.

"Maalox," Georgia had replied with a straight face.

The front room of the antiques shop was hot and dusty. Furniture, china, glass, and knickknacks crammed every open space. The store smelled of old wood and peeling varnish. A bell jingled behind her as Red closed the door.

A small air conditioner rattled ineffectively. The temperature in the shop must have been at least ninety.

Georgia walked out from the back, wearing a canvas apron stained with dark walnut varnish. Little ringlets of hair clung to her damp forehead.

"Why don't you get a bigger air conditioner? That piece of junk was made to cool a bedroom—a very small bedroom," Red said irritably. "You know the heat and the moisture warps your furniture."

Georgia smiled. "Makes the stuff more authentic. Besides, I like it hot." She stopped in front of Red, and the smile disappeared, replaced by a concerned expression. "You look worn out."

The Pines Were Watching 59

Red glanced down at the rippled wooden floor and sighed. "I'm not good at murders, Georgia. I can coordinate the staff, keep the budget, and break up a fight or two—but this is out of my league."

"Pshaw. Let me show you my newest acquisition. Scotty will be here as soon as the noon rush is over."

A fan blew a whisper of air across the oak table. Red eased into a chair as Georgia set a cold bottle of the ginger beer and a thick-sliced ham sandwich on rye in front of her. It oozed mayonnaise. Scotty eschewed all mayonnaise. "Pure saturated fat," she'd said with disgust.

The sandwich tasted remarkably tangy. "Scotty didn't make these, did she?"

"Ever heard the expression, 'Do as I say, not as I do'?" Georgia pulled a wooden canvasback duck decoy out of a shipping box. She winked. "Look at the position of the head. Ever seen anything so remarkable?"

Red shrugged. "Georgia, you know me. It looks like one of those old wooden birds Dad used to keep in the shed. As far as I know, they never lured a single duck over to Dad."

Georgia sighed as she stroked the head of the decoy. "It's a John Tax. He's the only well-known Minnesota decoy maker. They called him the last of the prairie carvers. There are less than one hundred of his decoys known to exist."

Scotty walked in as Georgia recited the John Tax history. "A new one!" she exclaimed. "Is it a Tax?"

Red blinked at Scotty with surprise. "When did you become a wooden-bird expert?"

Scotty grinned, sitting down next to Red. She smelled of deep fryer grease and Herbal Essences shampoo. She peered up and down at Red. "Geez, woman, when was the last time you slept?"

"Seventh grade social studies, I think." Red let a faint smile cross her lips.

While she finished her sandwich, Scotty and Georgia chatted about the decoy.

"If only I could get my hands on the Gravely collection. They say the old lady might be ready to sell."

"How much money are you talking about?" Scotty looked concerned.

Red watched the two of them discuss the decoys and found that their talk irritated her. A woman had been murdered, and they sat around a table talking about useless wooden birds.

"Hey," Red interrupted. "I've got to get back. Some junior reporter from Minneapolis wants to get a statement from me this afternoon. I'm worried he's going to dig up something about that goddamn county sheriff merger proposal. I don't want my picture in the paper or any screaming headlines, 'Local sheriff fights for her job.'"

"Why does that bother you?" Scotty and Georgia asked in unison.

"Well," Red shrugged, "I'm not sure all the citizens of the county are aware that I'm not Will and that their sheriff is a woman. It could cost me the election next time around."

Georgia's eyes had a sparkle to them. "Hell, you've been in office for three years, you'd think they would have it figured out by now." Both women started to laugh. "Tell the reporter you're the spokesperson for the sheriff. Then your little secret will be safe."

"Seriously, Red," Scotty propped her elbow on the table and leaned her cheek against her hand, "I've got some Town Talk scuttlebutt for you. And Georgia has a plan."

"If it's about Islamic terrorists, I don't want to hear it."

She shook her head. "I'm serious. Two things—lots of talk about the Grandgeorge Place and," she paused for emphasis, "some interesting stuff about Joanie Crea's money."

Red raised her eyebrows. "Okay, let's start with Grandgeorge."

"Well, here's a condensed version of the Grandgeorge saga, as told by a bunch of town gossips: Carl Grandgeorge flashed around a bit of cash but didn't socialize much. The boys were sent off to boarding school, and Carl sank his money into that big house. No one remembers him being in any kind of business, so the source of his money was a big mystery. He died of a heart attack or something when the youngest, Derek, was in high school."

Red nodded, having heard the story before. "And where did all the money come from?"

Scotty laughed. "Probably not the lottery."

"What do the old Town Talk wags say?"

"Mob money, profiteering on the postwar construction boom, inheritance—no one really knew. Anyway, as the story goes, Clyde, the oldest son, came home from one of those eastern colleges and married Geraldine. Less than three months later, he took off. No one has seen him around in seventeen years. Unless you count a nebulous sighting about eight years ago."

"What about eight years ago?"

"One of the Hammer Lake boys claims he saw him walking down the road after midnight during a summer rainstorm. Says he stopped to offer him a ride, but the guy ran into the underbrush."

"Hmmm...hardly a credible story. What about Derek?"

"Not much on him. Quiet, has an occasional beer at Cuttery's. They all agreed that Derek is 'different' but 'harmless.'" Scotty shook her head. "The Town Talk club was more interested in the father. It seems that the old man was a bit of a scoundrel. Didn't hang around with the men in town, but he sure liked the women."

Red ran her hand through her damp hair. She thought about the neglected mansion and how the place had felt emptied of compassion. "Any speculation on why Joanie Crea's body was found there?"

Scotty rubbed her palms together thoughtfully. "A woman sitting in my front table told me that her daughter works next door to the public health nursing office. She said her daughter said that the secretary there said that Joanie spent more time out at the Grandgeorge Place on visits, especially when she was seeing the old lady last fall."

"Suggesting some type of liaison between Joanie and Derek?"

"Could be," Scotty said, "although no one has seen them together."

Red sighed. "Well, that's not much of a connection, but I'll check it out."

"Sorry. It's all I got on that subject, except some wild speculation that Clyde is lurking around the grounds somewhere." Scotty touched Red's wrist for just a moment. "But I do have some interesting stuff on Joanie Crea's finances. According to my source, who shall remain anonymous, Joanie had a large chunk of money in a savings account over at the National Bank. About two months ago, she started taking it out in cash withdrawals."

"Any explanation?"

"My source says she seemed real nervous the first couple of times she took money out. Said something about money for a business investment. By the third withdrawal, she didn't say anything at all."

"Did your source say how much money she took out altogether?"

Scotty nodded. "About fifty thousand dollars."

Georgia whistled. "Wonder what kind of business. That would be enough to buy a decoy or two."

"How much is left?"

"Less than two hundred dollars."

Scotty focused her eyes on Red. "Maybe she was trying to hide the money from Jimmy—you know, the divorce and all. My ex tried to do that." Scotty's ex-husband was a local pharmacist who ended up an addict. "Of course, most of it went up his nose. Never got a dime from him."

Georgia toyed with the pendant around her neck and gazed at the tapestry hanging on the wall. "Maybe she was being blackmailed. That would explain the cash."

Scotty shrugged. "Could be."

"Looks like I'd better get my hands on those bank records."

"Good idea," Scotty piped in. "One of the advantages—among the great disadvantages—of small-town living is that people pay attention. I remember last winter when Addie Malmrose toddled into the bank and tried to withdraw all her savings. Said she was going to give it all to God. The clerk asked her who God might be. She said he talked to her from the television set. The clerk called her daughter in the cities."

They all laughed. "Addie is now installed at the Lutheran Home over in Duluth."

"And God or the televangelist is out Addie's savings," Georgia noted.

Red stood up and nodded emphatically at them. "Keep your ears open, but let me do the investigating. I'll take it from here." She added, "That's why I make the big bucks."

Georgia and Scotty eyed each other.

"What?" Red asked.

Georgia stroked the head of the decoy on the table. "I talked with Clarise Manson this morning—Joanie's boss. I'm going to take a temporary position with the nursing agency. She needs someone to cover Joanie's patients. Turns out there was a reason I didn't drop my nursing license when I retired."

Red frowned. "Damn it, Georgia. I don't want you nosing around. It could be dangerous."

Georgia was quiet for a moment, then said with an intensity Red rarely heard, "Listen, Red, my main concerns are the old folks she was seeing. If I happen to run across something interesting, I'll pass it on to you. I'm not going to snoop into closets, if that's what you're thinking."

Scotty nodded. "I know Clarise Manson. If she doesn't have someone to see those patients, she'll go herself—and she's an idiot. Georgia is right, the old folks need her. Meanwhile, I'll keep my post at the Town Talk and try to throw dishwater on some of the rumors about terrorists and gangs invading the county."

"Speaking of outsiders," Georgia smiled, "I had a couple in the store just this morning. Kid with a shaved head and a girl with fluorescent pink hair. She had a little gold ball in her tongue and enough rings in her ears to tatter the cartilage." She wrinkled her nose. "They wanted to know if I had any antique fishing lures. I think they were trying to catch old fish."

"And did you sell them anything?"

"Well, Red, between the two, they hardly had enough money to buy a can of leeches, let alone something from my store. I did mention the Church, just in case."

Red smiled to herself as she stepped out of the warm back room into a wall of heat. Leave it to Georgia to be thinking about everybody's health.

She saw only one car on the road between the store and the courthouse. The windows were rolled down, and the two people inside looked hot and miserable. *Ah, summer,* Red thought. *In a few months, we'll look wistfully back at the time when we could go outside without long underwear, sweaters, parkas, and mittens.*

At three o'clock, Red received a phone call from her deputy Matt.

"The autopsy is done," he said, his voice filled with energy.

"Quick work, must have been a slow gun day in the cities."

"Huh?"

Red sighed. *Don't kid with the help,* she thought. "What did they find?"

"Strangled. Probably happened on Sunday. They couldn't pinpoint the time, of course. Said she was a healthy woman. Some evidence of a struggle."

"Anything else? Signs of sexual assault?"

"No. She had a gash on her forehead, though. They said it looked like something you'd get if you fell and hit the corner of a wooden table. They thought maybe a picnic table."

"Picnic table?"

"They found some little slivers of wood. I guess they'll take a look at them a little closer tomorrow."

Red closed her eyes and pictured the Grandgeorge Place. Had she seen a picnic table on the grounds? Nothing came to her, but she hadn't explored the areas around the mansion. But, if not there, then where?

13

DEREK

Red sat next to Derek Grandgeorge on a wooden Adirondack chair on the sagging Grandgeorge porch. It was now five o'clock, and the temperature had climbed to near ninety degrees. The air on the porch hung still and thick.

Derek wore the same green army jacket he'd had on yesterday. His blue jeans were covered with sawdust and forest dirt. His right hand was wrapped in a white handkerchief stained with dried blood.

"Looks like you rapped your knuckles pretty good."

Derek glanced at his hand with a distracted look. "Oh, I guess," he said vaguely. "I was cutting trees." He pushed up at his jacket sleeve, revealing a fresh, scabbed scratch.

Though he had a lean build, his arm appeared hard with muscle. Red guessed that he was stronger than he looked.

"Did a tree branch do that?" Red pointed toward the scratch.

"Probably."

The sun beat hard on the roof of the porch. Red wiped her arm across her wet forehead, wishing that the standard sheriff's uniform included shorts instead of stay-press khaki pants. Maybe she'd write a new dress code. It would probably be her last act before losing the next election.

Even with his jacket on, Derek did not appear to be bothered by the heat. In the spotty bright light of the porch, Red could not read his expression. He refused to meet her eyes.

"I want you to tell me what you know about Joanie Crea."

Derek rubbed his temple with his left hand. His scraped right hand remained clenched in a fist resting on the arm of the lawn chair. "I didn't kill her. If that's what you're thinking. I hardly knew her." His tone was flat, as if this question had been asked often.

"I didn't ask you if you'd killed her, but thanks for the information." Red bit back the sarcasm, wondering why both Jimmy and Derek immediately denied murdering her. "What can you tell me about her?"

Derek shrugged, still not meeting Red's eyes. "She used to see my mother for her legs. Then this spring, she made a couple of visits to see Caddie. She seemed very formal."

"Can you tell me where you were on Sunday night?"

Again, Derek shrugged. "I was here all night."

"Can anyone confirm that?"

"I doubt it. I come and go. Geraldine is usually in the kitchen until late. Caddie does her own thing. And Mother doesn't always know whether it's day or night."

"You didn't know Mrs. Crea?"

Derek shifted in his chair, keeping his gaze away from Red. "I had no reason to kill her."

"I only asked if you knew her," Red said calmly.

He shook his head. "Talk to Caddie and Gerry. They would know more about her."

"Do you know why she was seeing Caddie?" For a moment, Red wondered if she might be the connection between the Grandgeorge Place and Joanie Crea.

Derek again shifted in his chair as if his back pained him. "Caddie isn't pregnant anymore. That's all I know."

"Did Mrs. Crea help arrange an abortion?"

"Probably."

Red felt her face tighten with irritation. She guessed Waltz would not be proud of her interview technique right now. She tried to keep her voice flat. "Why do you think Joanie Crea's body was in your summerhouse?"

The Pines Were Watching 67

Derek peered at her, his face masked. "I *don't* know."

"Ah." Red let the silence build for twenty seconds, then asked, "What were you carrying in your pickup truck Monday that needed a tarp cover?"

Derek frowned. "What?"

"I saw your pickup on Monday."

Derek's mouth opened in an expression of disbelief. "You think I was hauling a body, don't you?"

Red shrugged. "A body was found on your property."

Again, a curtain of silence fell between them. Finally, Derek stood up. "I have work to do."

"What were you carrying?" Red persisted.

"Wood. I cut and haul wood for a living." Derek stepped off the porch.

Before he turned away, she asked, "Do you have a picnic table on the grounds?"

Derek stared at her. "A picnic table? Here?" He nearly spat out the words. He waved at the unkempt lawn. "Feel free to look around."

It appeared to Red that he overreacted to the question. She would have Jason look around the grounds later. Meanwhile, she changed the subject. "Do you mind if I go inside and ask them some questions?" She needed to talk with him in the interview room. She'd bring him in later, after she'd dug up more information on Joanie's visits to the Grandgeorge Place and when Waltz was available to keep her from reacting to this man in the green jacket. The house, the broken-down veranda, and the summerhouse behind it gave her the creeps.

A grim smile crossed Derek's face. "Of course I mind. Wouldn't you? But go ahead."

Red watched his hunched gait as he walked toward the pickup and wondered what haunted his soul. Murder? She felt a mix of emotions as she pushed herself out of the chair with its peeling white paint. Derek's impenetrable veneer reminded her too much of her brother Lad's teen years as he fell deeper and deeper into his darkness.

With an audible sigh, she let herself in the door, calling down the hall, "Hello? Sheriff Hammergren here. Derek said to come in."

She stood in the large foyer facing a wide hardwood staircase with a flowered runner. Off to her right, she heard someone wheezing. When she walked into the sitting room, Mrs. Grandgeorge looked up at her from her chair. "Yes?" Her voice had a patronizing quality to it, even though she seemed to struggle to catch her breath.

The elderly woman sat in a cracked red leather recliner wrapped in a beige afghan. Her face had a youthful plumpness to it, which contrasted with her thin wrists and hands.

Red scanned the room, noting the elegance of the needlework on the tapestry upholstery of the sofa. Heavy oak furnishings were placed haphazardly throughout the large room. It looked as if someone had unloaded a truck full of antiques and forgotten to arrange them. Georgia would go nuts in a place like this.

Mrs. Grandgeorge's leather recliner was an island of calm amid the chaos.

"Mrs. Grandgeorge, I'm Sheriff Red Hammergren. Could I ask you a few questions?"

"Why, you're a woman!" she exclaimed as Red approached her. "Does your husband know you're wearing those clothes?"

Red smiled and squatted down by the old woman's chair.

"Lordy, lordy." Mrs. Grandgeorge tilted her head back and closed her eyes. "What will happen next?"

Red looked at a framed fading snapshot of two teenage boys that sat on the stand by the chair. One she recognized as a younger version of Derek. He smiled broadly with an amused sparkle to his eyes. It was hard to imagine that Derek had once looked so bright and cheerful. The older boy next to him wore a green letterman's jacket decorated with pins and awards. He was shorter and stockier than his brother, and his hair was much lighter, almost a sandy color. He, too, smiled into the camera, but his look had a roguish quality to it. As Red studied the photo, she thought she noted a slightly jaded arch in his eyebrows.

"Your sons are handsome men," she commented. "Is this Clyde?" She pointed to the older boy.

Mrs. Grandgeorge nodded with a contented smile. "That's my Clyde. He's coming back now, you know."

"Oh? That's nice. Where is he?"

The old woman frowned, as if trying to remember something. Finally,

The Pines Were Watching 69

she said, "He writes to me from time to time. I can't recall where he is just now."

Red shifted her weight, leaning a little closer to the chair. "Mrs. Grandgeorge, can you tell me if Derek was home on Sunday night?"

Mrs. Grandgeorge continued to look at the photo, a faraway expression on her face. "He's a good boy. He'll be back soon."

"Mrs. Grandgeorge? What about Derek? Was he home on Sunday night?"

"She wouldn't remember."

Red turned to see Geraldine standing in the doorway. "Oh, hello, Geraldine. How are you?"

Geraldine seemed taken aback by the friendliness in Red's voice. She looked down at her bare feet. "All right, I guess."

Red stood, patted the old woman on her thin hand, and walked over to Geraldine. "Could I ask you some questions?"

Geraldine backed away from the door with a flustered expression. "Does Derek know you're here?"

"He said it was all right to come in and talk with you." Red spoke in a soothing tone, the same one she used with the skittish farm dogs she ran into on sheriff calls. "Can we go somewhere and sit down?"

Without replying, Geraldine turned and plodded down the hall into the kitchen. She had a defeated hunch to her shoulders as she walked. Silently she eased herself onto a kitchen chair. Red surveyed the room. It was designed as a spacious country kitchen. All the appliances had the early nineties look, well before the era of stainless steel. The white refrigerator door was smudged and covered with scraps of newspaper clippings held by magnets. Other than dirty dishes in the sink, the kitchen was clean.

"Sorry, I haven't washed dishes today. The dishwasher broke a couple of weeks ago, and Derek hasn't fixed it." Geraldine pointed to the appliance that sat under the counter.

Red sat in a chair across from Geraldine. The kitchen smelled of lemons. "Can you tell me anything about Joanie Crea? I know she made nursing visits here last fall and again this spring."

Geraldine pursed out her lower lip, then sucked it back in. She stared beyond Red.

"She used to see Gramma Rebecca. Then the redheaded nurse took over. In the spring, she visited a couple of times because Caddie got herself pregnant. That's all."

"What did she do for Caddie?"

"She talked to her about what would happen in the pregnancy and how she should eat and things like that."

"Did she help Caddie arrange for an abortion?"

Geraldine's cheeks flushed. Red couldn't tell if she was angry or embarrassed. "Caddie never said."

"Did Caddie seem angry or upset?"

"Not that I noticed. Caddie seemed relieved when it was over and she wasn't throwing up all the time."

Geraldine busied herself wrapping the long strand of hair around her index finger. She did not look up when Red spoke. "Do you know if Derek was home on Sunday night?"

The hair cut into Geraldine's pudgy finger. "He's always home," she said in an uneasy voice.

"Could you verify that you saw him on Sunday night?" Red leaned across the table toward Geraldine. "This is important."

Geraldine bit her lower lip, then mumbled, "I wasn't here. I went up to the Golden Deer to play the slots." Then she looked at Red, her eyes troubled. "I'm not supposed to leave Gramma Rebecca, but she seemed fine, so I went for a while. I didn't see Derek's pickup when I came back."

"What time was that?" Red jotted the information down in a small spiral notebook.

"It was dark, so it must have been after nine." She drummed her fingers on the table. "But he was down for breakfast on Monday at seven."

Rebecca Grandgeorge called from the other room. "Girl? Say, girl, I could use a little tea here."

Geraldine pushed her large body up with a heaviness that was more than the extra weight she carried. "I've got to go."

Red followed her down the hallway. While Geraldine murmured to Rebecca in the front room, Red peeked into the library on the other side. The room was paneled in light oak with a thick red carpet. Floor-to-ceiling bookcases filled one wall. A large mahogany desk was placed in front of the

The Pines Were Watching 71

three-paneled window. The desk held a laptop computer, a tray of papers, and an antique silver pen-and-pencil set.

The neatness and order to the room contrasted completely with the chaotic arrangement of the front room. Other than the laptop, it appeared to be a relic from days long ago.

Caddie's voice startled her. "Uncle Derek doesn't like anyone in his office."

Red moved away from the door. "It's a beautiful room. Lots of books to explore."

Caddie shrugged. "I wouldn't know. Derek gets real mad if I go in there."

Red noted the heavy makeup and the cropped top that exposed the girl's flat belly. Would she become soft like her mother?

"Just a quick question, Caddie. When Mrs. Crea came out to see you this spring, did anything happen between the two of you?"

The girl bit her lip. "I don't know what you mean."

Red kept her voice low and gentle. "Both your mother and Derek told me you were pregnant. Did Mrs. Crea help you arrange an abortion?"

Caddie didn't meet Red's eyes. "She told me how they worked and gave me some phone numbers. That's all."

"Was the father of your baby upset that you had the abortion?"

Slowly Caddie stared at her with a dawning awareness. "He didn't care. He was such a jerk, anyway."

"Did he know Mrs. Crea gave you information about the abortion?"

"No," she exclaimed, her eyes flashing with defiance. "I told him it was my body and my decision."

Red nodded sympathetically. "You're right. It was your decision." She paused for a moment to let Caddie calm down. "Who was the father?"

Caddie spoke in a sharp tone. "Buddy Harrison, if you have to know. But he wouldn't kill anybody, if that's what you're thinking. He's too dumb for that."

"You two broke up?"

She nodded.

"Caddie?" Geraldine's voice carried across the hall. "Come help me with your grandmother."

"Shit!" Caddie mumbled. "Gotta go."

Back in her car, Red sat in the thick heat of the front seat and thought about the Grandgeorge women. Rebecca, old and senile, waiting for a son to come home. Geraldine, fat and bored with nothing much ahead of her. And Caddie, too experienced in the worldly ways for her seventeen years. She put the car into drive and turned around, glancing in her rearview mirror as the unfinished house receded. This was not the grand mansion that Carl envisioned for his bride. This was a house of despair.

14

LAD

Red didn't reach the lawyer, Young William, until almost eight in the evening. He'd spent the day out on the new eighteen-hole Golden Deer Casino golf course, fifty miles north of Lykkins Lake. The growth of American Indian–owned casinos in the state had been a boon to the tribes and a nightmare for local law enforcement. The sheriff to the north was constantly complaining about the increase in traffic, drunk driving, and theft. Red was grateful that the casino was not located within her county.

Young William had built a reputation as a reliable, if dull, small-town lawyer. Judges found him to be long-winded and plodding in court. He settled many cases out of court simply because people dreaded going to trial with him.

It took him forty-five minutes to answer ten minutes' worth of questions from Red. By the time she put down the phone, she was yawning into the receiver.

She jotted down a few notes. The Crea proposed settlement included equal division of all property except the cash inheritance from Joanie's grandfather in the amount of about $50,000. The house was to be sold with proceeds divided equally between the Creas. Current equity in the house was less than $10,000.

If Jimmy killed his estranged wife, it probably wasn't for money—

unless he thought she had left his name on her life insurance policy. Red considered other motives for murder besides money. Two years ago, a man in a neighboring county had shot his ex-wife and her boyfriend out of jealousy. But Red had not turned up any lovers. Her intuition told her this wasn't a simple case of spousal rage. This was a well-plotted-out killing. But who and why?

Perhaps the townspeople were right—a random psychotic killing by someone from the outside.

Red stretched the tension out of her back before studying her notes one more time. Her telephone interview this afternoon with Joanie's parents had revealed that they did not like Jimmy much. Joanie was an only child, and Red had sensed an attitude that said, "No one would have been good enough for our little girl."

Yet they had been unable to provide any clues. They expressed puzzlement at the divorce and some anger with Jimmy.

"I never believed in his jolly face around us. I knew he was more interested in his church and volunteering than in our daughter," Joanie's father had said with contempt. "All the money she earned went to him. I know it."

They were puzzled when Red asked about the inheritance and what might have happened to it. "Did your daughter tell you she was withdrawing the money in cash?"

The silence on the line told her they had no idea about it. Finally, her father spit out, "He probably found a way to wrangle it from her."

They also alluded to feeling abandoned because their daughter had chosen to stay in Lykkins Lake rather than come home to them after Jimmy moved out. "She said she owed it to her patients. But what about us?" Joanie's mother started to cry.

It was time to close the conversation. Red would talk with them again when the news wasn't so raw.

A thorough search of the Grandgeorge property had yielded no car and no picnic table. She'd sent a bulletin to the state highway department to be on the lookout for Joanie's white Ford Escort. So far, none had been found.

Damn, she thought, looking at her notes. *I've got nothing.*

. . .

The Pines Were Watching 75

Red arrived home as the sun set beyond the trees surrounding the house. She peeled off the limp cotton-polyester-blend white shirt and khaki pants and left them heaped on the bedroom floor. She pulled on a comfortable pair of shorts and a T-shirt. Blue sniffed disdainfully at the crumpled uniform, then trotted behind her to the kitchen for his evening meal.

Out on her patio, Red sank into the cushioned redwood chair with a groan. Blue jumped up on her lap and took a quick lick at her chin.

"Yuck! Blue, your dog breath could bring a dead carp back to life."

Blue burped once, then settled comfortably on her lap.

Thoughts jangled through her head as she sipped slowly on her beer. She knew she was missing something, some connection between Crea and Grandgeorge. Her neck felt tight, as if someone had gathered up the muscles between her shoulder blades and started to twist.

Her rambling thoughts turned to Lad and the incident with the fat kid all those years ago. Lad, the lost brother. She remembered, with lingering shame, how at age eighteen she'd been so angry with her parents over him. One spring evening in her senior year in high school, she'd come home from a movie to find her father sitting at the kitchen table with Sheriff Will Hammergren. Her mother had stood leaning against the sink, her eyes reddened from crying.

"What?" she'd hissed. "What is it this time?" She'd stopped herself from yelling, "Did he kill someone?"

Her father had looked at her with a sadness so deep she'd sat down immediately. "They're taking him to a home for disturbed boys. He's gotten into trouble—breaking things." His voice dropped as he gestured helplessly.

Her gaze had moved from her father to her mother, then back to her father. The anger boiled over. "Why didn't you stop him?" she'd spit out at her parents. "You could have stopped him!"

If only she could call back the years and apologize to her parents. Lad's illness was not theirs to control.

A fish jumped out on Lykkins Lake. Red watched the twilight sparkle off the water as it lapped in circles outward from the fish. Absently she stroked Blue's soft, kinky fur.

"You know, Blue, I was terrible to Mom and Dad those years. I thought they could fix Lad."

Blue shifted and sighed.

"Will took me outside that night and read me the riot act about being so nasty. He said, 'You're too young to understand this yet, but you'll find that we don't have control over a lot of things in this life.' I was so embarrassed. Years later he claimed he didn't remember anything about it."

"Chatting with that miserable creature again?"

Red looked up in surprise as Georgia walked around the corner of the house. Recovering, she smiled. "No one else will listen to me."

"Just let me know when he starts talking back. That would make a nice juicy piece of information to pass on at the Town Talk." Georgia stood in front of her, arms akimbo, a smile crinkling the skin around her eyes.

"What brings you here after dark?" Georgia didn't like to drive at night.

"Your neighbor had some decoys he thought I should buy."

"And?"

Georgia shook her head. "Manufactured junk. When I told him I wasn't interested, he insisted on showing me his salt-and-pepper-shaker collection. He thought it might be worth thousands of dollars. Who needs five hundred salt and pepper shakers?"

"Who needs a house full of wooden ducks?" Red spoke with a straight face.

"Decoys," Georgia corrected. "Someday, I'll make you a believer. You need to come with me to the Chesapeake Bay area, where people understand my obsession."

Red brought Georgia a beer. Blue tried to jump onto Georgia's lap, but he missed.

Red shook her head. "You've got to practice that a little more, Blue. Georgia already thinks you're a poor excuse for a living creature."

A slight breeze rose from the lake, whispering through the trees as they sat in comfortable silence. Across the lake, a dog barked, the noise echoing off the calm water.

Red swatted at a mosquito. "They'll drive us indoors in a minute." She flicked the carcass off her arm.

Georgia chuckled. "Imagine the power those little insects have. We

The Pines Were Watching

human beings think we're so strong, yet something so small and insignificant as a mosquito can send us into complete retreat."

"Perhaps we could train them and use them in our next war."

Georgia grinned at her, smacking a mosquito that had landed on her cheek. "I'm sure someone has already thought of that." She settled more comfortably in the chair. "What's this conversation you've been having with that piece of shag carpet you call a dog?"

Red stretched her arms over her head as she yawned. "Oh, I don't know. Between crazy dreams, murder, mayhem, and Derek Grandgeorge, I've been thinking about my brother a lot."

"The black sheep?"

"He's every parent's nightmare." Georgia already knew the story, but Red told her again about Lad's gradual slip into darkness, the diagnosis of schizophrenia, the drinking and drugs as an adult. "He disappeared one day..." Her voice dropped. "I haven't seen him in over twenty years."

Georgia reached down and absently scratched Blue on the head. "Mental illness. It's so problematic. I saw it all the time in my work. Families torn apart by it. After years of trying to hold families together, I finally figured out that the sane ones usually had to flee." She looked at Red with a grim smile. "We emptied out the institutions and then refused to support the former inmates."

"Now they're all camping under the freeway or sitting in our county jails and our hospital emergency rooms."

"Ah yes, the progress of man and the cry of 'no new taxes.'"

Red set the beer bottle on the redwood patio table next to her chair. She gazed absently up at the starry sky. "Until the dementia took Mom, she hoped every day to hear from Lad. We talk a lot about closure in the death of someone. She never got that closure because we never found him. Still, I hold out hope that someday he'll miraculously show up at my door. At least I've stopped having nightmares about a coroner's call in the middle of the night. I guess I've built up some immunity."

Georgia nodded. "We have a nursing phrase for that immunity. It's called 'wearing the spit shield.'"

"I love medical terminology."

Blue pricked up his ears as the neighbor's cat crept around the side of the house. He let out one brief, shrill yip, which the cat ignored.

"Go get him," Red urged.

Blue remained sitting with an expression that said, "What? Me?"

"That dog has a killer instinct." Georgia reached over and patted him on the head. He yipped one more time, then lapsed into silence. Her expression turned serious as she studied Red. "Tell me. How are you doing?"

Red took a deep breath. "Every time I close my eyes, I see that body. Part of me feels so helpless. Part of me is damn angry. And the rest—guilty. Like I should have prevented this."

"Any leads?" Georgia's voice was soft and gentle.

Red shrugged, finishing her beer. "Jimmy Crea is clean. Good alibi. No motive. Derek Grandgeorge is a complete mystery. But I have no reason to bring him in. I'm stumped." She told Georgia about the visit to the Grandgeorge Place today.

"What does your gut say?"

"That I need a refill on my Maalox." Red smiled.

They sat in comfortable silence until Red's phone rang. When she picked up the call, the relief dispatcher said calmly, "We've got a situation over at Rose Timm's house. She thinks someone is in her basement."

Red remembered Rose's call about the missing church money. She was a middle-aged divorcée who lived alone. Did Red have a killer who preyed on divorcées?

"Do you still have her on the line?"

"Yes, I do."

"Tell her to keep talking. It'll take me about three minutes to get there."

Red hurried into the house, calling to Georgia, "I've got to check something out. Will you take charge of Blue and try to keep him from peeing on my recliner?"

"Serious, eh?"

Red nodded, strapping on her gun. She hated carrying it. She hated having it in the same house with her. She hated the thought that someday she might have to use it.

She could handle the gun adequately. She had a good marksman's sense, but she was slow. She'd once told the poker club, "This is a secret,

The Pines Were Watching

but even dead, Clint Eastwood could outdraw me. But if you give me a few minutes, I'll hit the target every time."

Fortunately, the only time she'd ever used her gun in the line of duty was to shoot a rabid skunk weaving through a yard over in White Cross Township.

Once in her car, Red took a deep breath, centered her thoughts, and pushed the gas pedal to the floor. The sound of her vehicle echoed through the quiet streets of Lykkins Lake.

15

ROSE

As Red pulled up in front of Rose's house, her eyes swept the neighborhood. The house stood next to a weedy vacant lot on one side and a ramshackle two-story clapboard house on the other side. The clapboard had been empty for at least six months—since Red had helped escort the ninety-four-year-old owner to the nursing home.

Swiftly she stepped out of the car, her flashlight on high beam. Around her, the town had settled into its twilight quiet. Two houses down, a flicker of the television escaped through a crack in the drawn drapes. Rose's little ranch-style house was dark except for a dim light coming through a curtained window on the west side. Probably the bedroom.

Red walked up to the front door, radio in hand. She said to the dispatcher, "Do you still have Rose on the line? Tell her I'm at the front door. I'm going to ring the bell." Red tried the door. It appeared to be securely locked.

She spoke into the radio. "Tell Rose to answer the door. It's locked."

For a moment, the only sound in the neighborhood was the static from the radio. Red closed her eyes and listened, blocking out the static and the distant noise of trucks on the highway. Something very faint registered—an almost imperceptible whimpering. It sounded like it came from the back of the house.

The Pines Were Watching

"Rose," Red broke the silence. "Come on, Rose, open the door."

From inside the house, hesitant footsteps approached. Suddenly the radio crackled. "Sheriff, Jason just radioed in. He's on his way."

"Tell him to approach as quietly as possible. I don't want to scare the whole neighborhood."

Before the door opened, Red again heard the faint whimpering.

Rose stood at the door, pale and disheveled. She smelled of whiskey.

"Hi, Rose. Can you let me in?"

"Someone's in my basement," Rose whispered. "I think he wants to kill me like he did Jimmy's wife." She undid the hook lock on the screen and opened the door. As she stepped back, she stumbled.

Red took her firmly by the arm and steadied her. "Okay, Rose. I'm going to check this out. First, though, I'm going to have you go sit in my car."

She pointed Rose in the direction of the Subaru. "I'll walk with you, Rose. You can lock the car door once you're inside."

Red helped the woman as she half stumbled toward the vehicle.

Once Rose was safely inside, Red walked slowly around to the back of the house, sweeping the yard with her flashlight. All the windows appeared to be closed and secured on the west side of the house. As she turned the corner to the back of the house, she heard a scraping noise. Quietly she crept toward the sound.

"Rose, you may be intoxicated, but you're not imagining things." Red squatted to inspect the open basement window just below the bedroom. It appeared that the glass had been broken by something the size of a baseball. The window rattled slightly in the light evening breeze.

Red stayed at the window for a long moment, listening, letting her senses work. Someone was definitely in the basement, but she didn't have a feel for the danger. Was the intruder armed? Did he strangle lone women?

A car screeched to a halt in front of the house. Jason's voice boomed out into the night. "Sheriff, I'm here."

Again, the scraping noise.

"So much for the quiet approach. There goes any element of surprise," Red muttered. She stood up. "Around back, Jason," she called.

When Jason turned the corner, he sounded like a parade horse, all the equipment on his belt jangling. He stared at her, his mouth open, until she realized that she had run out of her house in shorts. The gun looked ridiculous strapped over a pair of white cutoff Levi's.

He spoke in a harsh whisper. "I hear Rose tends to drink a bit. Is she tipsy, Sheriff? Like maybe hearing things?"

"Never jump to conclusions." Red pointed to the broken window. "Someone is down there."

"For sure?"

Red nodded. "I want you to stay right here by the window. I'm going inside."

Jason's eyes burned with excitement. "I can go if you want."

Red took a deep breath and let it out slowly. The idea of going into the basement caused sweat to break out on her palms. "Keep your radio on, Jason."

She moved around to the front of the house, noting that all the windows on the east side of the house were closed. In less than fifteen seconds, she was inside the Timm house. A fan in the living room circulated stale air. It smelled like the house had not been aired out in months. The odor of cooking grease mingled with old cigarette smoke. As Red made her way toward the basement steps, she beamed the flashlight through the living room and small dining area. A thick layer of dust covered the dining room table. A plant, long dead, its leaves turning to a powdery brown, sat next to the window.

This was a house of grief. Red remembered how Jack Timm had abruptly left his wife for a male companion six months ago. Rose's religion would not console her on this.

Her shoes squeaked on the vinyl kitchen floor. At the head of the basement staircase, she spoke softly into the radio. "I'm going into the basement. Stay by the window." She switched off the radio.

Abruptly she flicked on the basement light and yelled, "It's the sheriff. Come on out."

Glass crashed to the cement floor. Red took the steps two at a time, holding her flashlight securely in her hand. "Come on out," she called again.

Silence.

She stopped at the bottom of the stairs, breathing hard, listening for

The Pines Were Watching

movement. For ten seconds, she heard nothing. Then it came again, a child-like whimpering on her right. In the light of the bare forty-watt bulbs that hung from the ceiling, Red could see the gray furnace.

Someone was hiding behind it.

"It's okay," she said in a controlled voice. "Come out from behind the furnace. No one will hurt you."

With the crack of a gun, Red felt the whisper of the pellet zing past her right ear. She dropped to her stomach, drawing her gun. "Damn it!" she yelled. "Put that thing down and come out! I don't like this!" The anger in her words reverberated throughout the basement. Behind her, Jason came crashing down the steps.

"He's got a pellet gun, for God's sake."

Suddenly a sound of wailing erupted from behind the furnace. "I wanna go home! I wanna go home!"

Red, still on her stomach, said firmly, "Throw out the gun. We won't hurt you, but you have to put the gun down."

Something clattered to the floor. Red stood up slowly. "Thank God I didn't have my Sunday clothes on," she muttered, brushing years of basement dirt off her T-shirt. "Okay, son. Come on out."

A small, grimy boy stepped out from behind the furnace. Tears streaked down his cheeks.

"I want my mom."

"I know you do, Tommy." Red squatted in front of Tommy Henley. He wore baggy shorts and an oversized T-shirt advertising Cuttery's Bar.

"I want my mom. I was supposed to see my mom today." He continued to cry. "But she didn't come."

"Why did you come here, Tommy?" Red pulled out a handkerchief and wiped his nose.

"'Cause."

"Why, Tommy?"

A look of sudden terror crossed his face. "I can't tell."

Very gently, Red touched the boy's shoulder. He flinched. "Why can't you tell me?"

He opened his mouth, then his face dissolved into tears. "I want my mom. I want my mom."

It took Red a good ten minutes to calm the boy. She would talk with him again when he felt safer.

Rose Timm sat slumped in the car, her whiskey breath seeping into the front seat. Red leaned close to her. "Do you know why Tommy Henley would sneak into your house?"

Rose blinked in a slow, drunken way. She shook her head.

"Do you know his mother, Arlis?" Again she shook her head. Then she pulled herself up into a straight sitting position. "I am a Christian. I keep the church's books. I don't associate with people like that."

Hurray for Christianity, Red thought, escorting Rose back to her house. No room for the Mary Magdalenes of the world in her church.

It was well after midnight before Red returned home. Georgia had locked everything up and left her a little note. *Sorry, I couldn't wait up for you. I've got to see some of Joanie's patients tomorrow morning.*

Red sank into her easy chair with a groan. Tommy Henley had shaken her. She felt he knew something important. Why would he look for his mother in Rose Timm's house?

Blue jumped up on her lap and quickly licked her cheek before settling in. "Maybe it was a coincidence, Blue," she said without conviction.

She remembered when she took the job as sheriff's deputy before she and Will realized they loved each other. He'd mentored her in a way that no law enforcement classroom could do.

"It's not 'just the facts,' Red. It's the ability to put the puzzle pieces together. If I learned anything from my father when he was sheriff, it was that coincidence doesn't exist. The pieces are connected."

"I can't see the connections, Blue." He nestled into her lap but offered no wisdom.

16

A SCRAP OF PAPER

On Thursday morning, Harv Smith, county commissioner from the Hammer Lake district, sauntered into the office while Red studied the emailed autopsy report on Joanie Crea. He was hardly through the doorway when she smelled his drugstore cologne and quickly turned the screen off on her computer.

"Harv. What can I do for you?" *You sneaky bastard.*

"How are you, Sheriff?" He wore navy blue polyester pants and a short-sleeved white perma-pressed shirt. On top of the cologne he smelled of bacon grease and cigars.

"I guess you've been meeting with your constituents, Harv."

He looked at her in surprise. "How did you know?"

"It's my sixth sense. Remember how Will used to talk about it?" Red flashed a large, insincere smile.

Harv shuffled a bit. "Ah, they're just wondering about the investigation. Have you arrested that Grandgeorge yet?"

Red pointed at the folder in front of her and said in a confidential voice, "Well, Harv, other than the fact that she was found on his property, we don't have any reason to arrest him." Her voice was unnaturally sharp. Harv drew back. Rubbing her hands together, she softened her voice. "Sorry. I'm tired and worried."

Harv blushed, screwing up his face as if he was about to say something profound. Instead, he said, "Ah...um..."

Red rescued him from any more two-letter words. "Listen, Harv, you might be able to help me. Next time you see the boys up in Hammer Lake, ask them if they've noticed anything unusual about the summer folks. Joanie used to do a blood pressure screening up there and also saw a number of patients."

He brightened considerably. "I'll see what I can find out. You betcha."

After he walked out the door, Red rested the back of her head against the chair and closed her eyes. Why, she wondered, had she just played into the provincial notion that nobody who actually lives around here could possibly commit a crime? Harv would pass it through his good ol' boys network that the sheriff thought it was a tourist who killed Joanie Crea.

Even though she didn't report to Harv or the other county commissioners, she was dependent on them for the public safety budget. As Will had once explained, "I'm elected, so I report directly to my constituents. However, the commissioners still hold the purse strings. Whether I agree with them or not, I keep a cordial relationship with them."

Red sighed. She tried to be diplomatic with the Harv Smiths of the world, but she wasn't Will.

As she turned the screen back on to look at the report, she was reminded that Waltz hadn't contacted her. She wanted to review with him her talk with Derek Grandgeorge. Would he advise that she bring him in for an interview?

"I'm missing something big." She massaged her temples. Picking up the phone, she dialed her friend Rob, a psychologist in Minneapolis. During her time as a middle school science teacher, Rob had worked with some of her more troubled students. He had a calm manner and a way with teenagers.

Rob answered his own phone. He housed himself in a storefront near the Uptown area, where he served a largely gay male clientele.

"Rob, Red here."

"Well, Sheriff, how are things in Nowhere County?"

"Not so fine, Rob." Red knew the strain in her voice carried across the 150 miles of telephone lines to Rob.

The Pines Were Watching 87

"Easy, my friend. I read about the murder this morning. Domestic?" Rob's voice had a soothing quality, which contrasted with his shock of wiry black hair. His looks reminded Red of a caricature of the mad scientist.

Red outlined the details. Since this wasn't a formal consultation, she didn't reveal the missing shoes or the wood splinters the autopsy found. She did, however, describe how the body was positioned.

"It was so undignified, like the killer simply dumped the victim."

"Sexual assault?"

"That's a curious part of it. No. And she was fully clothed." She paused long enough to take a deep, shuddering breath. "So, what's your read? I'm guessing you must have some ideas." Red drummed her fingers on the desk. "I need to know where to look. I have a creepy feeling this person isn't done yet."

Rob paused for a long time. "You know I don't work on criminal cases much anymore. I got tired of depositions and hanging around the court-house, waiting to testify. I spend most of my time helping Harry pick up the pieces after Tom leaves and before Dick arrives. Here's a largely amateur opinion. Take it for what it's worth. The person you are looking for has some deep-seated problems. I doubt it's a random murder, and I'd bet your victim knew the person. Look for connections, Red."

Connections. That was what Will used to say.

"I'm trying, for God's sake." Exasperated, Red picked up a pencil and snapped it in two. She closed her eyes to the snapping sound of the wood. "Sorry, Rob."

"Red, I have confidence in you. After all, you managed a classroom of fourteen-year-olds who had nothing better on their minds than how to get to you."

"Thanks, but that's hardly reassuring. They might have been on the edge of delinquency, but I don't think they were plotting murder."

He laughed. "I'll check with some colleagues and see if they have any suggestions."

Red tossed the broken pencil pieces into the wastebasket. "Thanks."

Thirty minutes later, Jimmy Crea called her. "Um...I'm sorry I was so emotional yesterday. I hope I answered your questions."

Red listened, puzzled that he would call. "I'm sure it's been difficult, Jimmy."

"Well...uh...I was wondering if I could go to the house. I still have some clothes and things there. I'd like to...uh...get them." His voice faded.

Red thought about it for a few moments and decided a walk-through of Joanie's house with Jimmy might yield something.

"Sure. Maybe you can tell me if anything is out of place."

"I haven't been inside since I moved out, but if it helps..."

They met outside Joanie's house. The neighborhood was quiet, although Red noted someone peeking through the blinds across the street.

Jimmy wore a pink knit polo shirt and a pair of pressed khaki pants. His face was clean-shaven, and he looked rested.

"How are you doing?"

Jimmy slowly shook his head. "Sometimes I think it was all a dream. Then I wake up." He looked directly at Red, his brown eyes clouded. "It was God's will. That's the only thing I can think to say."

Red scratched the back of her head, turning away from his clichéd remark. She did not believe that God willed anyone to be strangled and dumped in a summerhouse to bloat in the heat and humidity. "We checked here on Tuesday and didn't see any evidence of robbery or that she'd been forcibly taken from the house."

Jimmy let out a huff of air followed by an abbreviated snuffle. "This is so hard, Sheriff. So hard."

Red smiled sympathetically.

The deadbolt slid open with a click. Jimmy stared at the lock as Red pulled out the key. "She had a new lock installed. We only found one key in the house," she explained.

"She always kept our house locked. When I was growing up, we didn't have locks for the doors."

Red pushed the door open and turned to Jimmy. "Was she afraid of something?"

He shook his head. "Habit. That's all. She just never adjusted to living in Lykkins Lake." He looked at Red with a soft expression. "Who would break into our house? It's not like we looked rich."

Red found his remark to be a little odd but did not reply. Inside, the air

The Pines Were Watching

hung heavy and stale. Dust motes floated lethargically in the stream of light let in by the partially opened drapes. The absolute emptiness of the house sent a shiver down Red's forearms. Her parents' house had felt like this after her mother's funeral.

"Jimmy, I need you to look carefully through the house and let me know if anything has been taken or disturbed."

"Um...I'm not sure I'll be of much help." He paused. "Joanie wanted her space."

At first, Jimmy walked delicately, hands in his pockets, gazing at the furniture and the bookcases. He scrutinized the books and pulled out a leather-bound Bible. "This is mine. Is it all right if I take it?"

"Why don't you leave it for now. Once we get things settled, I'm sure you can have it."

Jimmy quickly flipped through the pages before shoving it back in the bookcase.

"Are you looking for something?"

"What? No. I like the feel of the pages, that's all."

Odd thing to say.

As they made their way through the living room to the hallway, he shuddered. "Nothing," he whispered.

"What do you mean?" Red noticed a droplet of sweat rolling down the side of Jimmy's face.

He stopped by the door to the bathroom, wiping the sweat with the back of his hand. "Nothing has been changed since I was last here in June. Nothing. She didn't even move the pillows on the sofa. It's like she didn't live here."

A pale yellow light illuminated the bathroom. Jimmy peeked in but did not cross the threshold. "She never turned that light out. I think she was afraid of the dark." He turned away from the bathroom with a shake of his head.

Red kept her distance as the back of his shoulders hunched up and he coughed away a gasping snuffle. She peeked into the bathroom, again noting a lingering fragrance, almost covered by the smell of dust and heat.

"Did Joanie wear perfume?" Red asked.

He turned to her, wiping his hands with a folded white handkerchief. "Pardon?"

"The bathroom smells like perfume."

Jimmy stood staring back into the bathroom, his feet planted, toes out like an overgrown child. For a second, the image of that fat child in her parents' room flashed through Red's mind. She blinked it away.

"I'm allergic to perfume. Makes me wheeze something awful. Gives me trouble when I have clients who wear it." He frowned. "We only used Ivory soap."

Red allowed Jimmy to continue into the bedroom. She walked into the bathroom and closed her eyes. For a split second, the color green flashed behind her eyelids. A wave of dizziness washed over her, and suddenly the fragrance grew strong and invasive. She opened her eyes to gray splotches. *Great*, she thought, *Red the psychic. Let's explain that to the Hammer Lake boys. "Fellas, I solved the mystery just by closing my eyes."*

She backed out of the small room, the dark curls of her bangs plastered to her forehead.

Jimmy stood by the rumpled bed, hugging himself. "I...I can't see anything out of place. Joanie was not a neat person. You know. She wasn't a slob either, but she always had clothes and stuff lying around."

The closet yielded more clothes, mainly blouses and dark pants she probably wore for work.

"Jimmy, I don't see any of your clothes."

He stood with his hands behind his back, staring at the floor. "She must have donated them." His voice was barely above a whisper.

It struck Red that if Joanie had gotten rid of Jimmy's clothes without telling him, the rift in their marriage must have been much stronger than he was willing to admit.

He turned to Red, his eyes filled with tears. "I think I'll wait outside if you need to look around more."

After he walked out, she surveyed the bedroom one last time. She spied a scrap of paper sticking out between the bed and the bedside table. She must have missed it when they'd inched through the house on Tuesday evening.

Taking a pencil from her pocket, she eased the paper out. It appeared to

The Pines Were Watching 91

be a page that had been torn out of a spiral notebook. Listed on the paper were several phone numbers with notations by each number.

Red slipped the scrap into a baggie and tucked it into her pants pocket.

Outside, the air heated in the midmorning sun. They stood in the driveway by Red's car and talked for a few minutes. "The neighbors said Joanie used to be home by ten. Do you know what she did in the evenings?"

Jimmy thought for a moment. "Evenings were a busy time for me. I wasn't around because of church meetings and the gamblers group I ran. I think she spent a lot of time doing her paperwork." Then he smiled as if remembering something pleasant. "She loved those old people she saw through the county. She used to bake things for them."

After pausing, he added, "She was a good person. I never wanted the divorce."

Red locked up the house with an uncomfortable feeling that she'd missed something important.

Jimmy climbed into his dark green SUV. The vehicle looked new. Idly she wondered how he could afford a truck like that. After Jimmy drove away, Red stood leaning against her car. Her uniform clung to her body like plastic wrap. She looked at the empty house for a long time before she drove away.

17

A MISSING MOTHER

Red called Herman Winstead, the child protection worker. Not surprisingly, she found him at his desk. Herman rarely left his office unless it was for a trip to the Town Talk for coffee. She remembered Scotty calling him a burnout.

"Back in the early days when I worked with him, he really cared about the kids. But the system doesn't always work. I saw the light go out in his eyes the day he had to take a baby back to a mother who was smart enough to get herself a good lawyer. Two months later, she suffocated the baby to death. You can only see so much of the crap that goes on with the kids and you either quit, lose your compassion, or you go into hiding. Herman's hiding."

Red listened to a slurping sound as Herman picked up the receiver and swallowed something before he answered. "Yeah, hello."

"Herman, this is Sheriff Hammergren. Did you locate Arlis Henley?" She'd left him a message this morning to look for her after last night's incident with Tommy.

The slurping sound filled her ears again. "Well, she didn't answer the phone when I called out there. I tried the Golden Deer, where she works. She didn't show up for her shift last night. They said that wasn't unusual."

The Pines Were Watching 93

Red pressed her lips together. In a tight voice, she asked, "Did you go out to her trailer?"

"Too busy this morning."

I'll bet, she muttered to herself. "Listen, Herman, I'm going to head to her trailer. If she's not there, do you have any suggestions?"

"You might try Cuttery's," he chuckled. "I'll help you look there, if you want me to. I could use a beer."

"No, thanks." Red hung up without saying good-bye.

The child protection worker before the county hired Herman had been a sturdy, no-nonsense woman who'd visited Red's parents when Lad was slipping into his mental illness. Unlike Herman, she was gung-ho to put him in a home for wayward boys. Back then, no one had evaluated him for mental illness. The assumption was that he was a delinquent on his way to jail.

Red remembered how her mother stood up to the woman, her voice trembling with emotion. "My boy isn't a criminal. He's sick."

Sadly, the sickness eventually turned him into a criminal.

Red rubbed her eyes, wishing away the image of her mother pointing a shaking finger at the woman.

Ed, the janitor, swept the steps of the courthouse. She greeted him and he replied, "Hot enough for you, Sheriff? It's going to be a corker."

"You got that right, Ed."

The courthouse lawn was baking to a crisp brown hue. When Red stepped into the Subaru, the steering wheel was so hot from the direct sunlight that she could only touch it with her fingertips. Quickly she started it and turned the air conditioner on full blast.

"How did we ever survive in the olden days without automobile air conditioning?" She wiped her brow before driving to Arlis Henley's trailer. She would have just enough time to check out her place before meeting with Clarise Manson of the public health nursing office.

As Red drove up to the Henley trailer, she noted that the rusted red Henley van, with its smashed passenger window, was still parked on the dirt patch off the driveway. It didn't look like it had changed positions since Monday when she'd come to talk with Arlis about Tommy.

Before Red climbed the two metal steps to the trailer, she paused, took a deep breath, and closed her eyes. She listened for the small sounds of life inside the trailer. Sure enough, she heard applause. "*Family Feud* must be on."

Despite the sounds inside, no one answered her insistent knock. "Arlis? It's Sheriff Hammergren." Red repeated herself, pounding harder on the door. No one answered.

"Come on," she muttered under her breath. "Open up. Tommy is worried about you!"

After a minute of pounding, Red tried the door, and it creaked as she opened it. "Arlis?"

No answer.

The kitchen area smelled like ripe garbage. Unlike her visit the other day, the kitchen was a mess of dirty dishes and leftover food. A fat housefly crawled over a half-eaten bologna sandwich sitting on the kitchen table. Beside the sandwich stood two empty beer bottles and an ashtray with a half-smoked cigarette.

"Arlis? Sheriff Hammergren." Red raised her voice. "I'm coming in."

On the large-screen television, a bare-chested man with six-pack abs demonstrated an exercise device that attached to the wall.

She called again, "Arlis?"

The bathroom and Tommy's bedroom were empty. Tommy's bed was neatly made, as if Arlis was getting ready for him to come home.

"Arlis?" she called out one more time as she pushed open the door to the back bedroom.

Clothes lay strewn over the floor and the dresser. The sheets were wrinkled with the top sheet thrown aside. Over the pervasive smell of sweat and dirty laundry, she detected a lingering fragrance of some sort.

As Red walked out the door, she stopped to survey the room once again. With the mess on the kitchen table and the dishes in the sink, something struck her as being off. She looked down at the floor. It looked like it had been recently swept. Why had Arlis cleaned the floor but not the table?

"Arlis, where are you?" For a moment, a pressure like two hands pushing on her temples caused Red to draw in a sharp breath. The moment passed.

.   .   .

The Pines Were Watching   95

Back at the courthouse, she sent out an alert to look for Arlis Henley. After several tries, she located Arlis's supervisor at the Golden Deer. The woman spoke with a nasal whine. "Nope, she didn't show up for her shift. I decided the next time she came in, I would fire her."

"Can you tell me anything else about her?"

The woman hesitated. "Well. One of the other kitchen girls told me that Arlis told her she was going to quit. Said she'd gotten into some kind of a sweet deal and wouldn't need to work anymore."

Red sat up straighter. "Do you know anything more about it?"

"Naw. I hear this kind of stuff all the time. Mostly they go on about how they've figured out the slots and are going to make their fortune. Me? I wouldn't spend a penny on those machines. Waste of money."

Before Red hung up, she took down the name and the phone number of the kitchen help who'd talked with Arlis.

Her next call was to Debbi Taft, Tommy's foster mother. She let Debbi know that she was trying to locate Arlis. "How's Tommy doing?"

"He's quiet and sad. I know he misses his mother. He told me he had a stomachache and didn't want breakfast this morning. Poor kid. I'm sure it's from worry. I wish I could get him to talk."

Picturing the fear on Tommy's face when she'd found him in Rose's basement, Red wasn't surprised. "I'll see if Herman can arrange for a counselor for him."

Red was sure Debbi said, "Fat chance," before she ended the call.

As soon as she was off the phone, Ken Harrison, the auditor, bounced into her office, his ponytail swinging.

"Heard you are on the lookout for Arlis Henley."

"Word travels fast around here."

He grinned at her. "I have friends." Ken was known to spend a lot of time with Red's summer temp filing clerk.

She pursed her lips. "Ken, she's just out of high school. Shame on you."

He continued to grin. "She's my pitcher. We only talk strategy."

Ken coached the Lykkins Lake women's slow-pitch softball team.

"Anyway, I stopped by to tell you that I just thought of something else about Joanie Crea. You remember that Saturday in May, when we had the softball tournament?"

Red nodded, only because she had picked up a carload of women on a DWI after celebrating their victory at Cuttery's.

"I think I saw Joanie at Cuttery's that night with Derek Grandgeorge."

Quickly, Red pulled out her notepad. "Tell me what you saw."

"Well," Ken tugged at a strand of hair that had loosened from his ponytail, "the place was packed that night, including the men's room. I decided to step outside."

Red nodded noncommittally.

"You know Ralph Cuttery is a cheapskate. That parking lot is one of the darkest places in town. I walked over to the edge of the lot for some privacy."

"And?" Red prompted.

"As a car pulled out, I saw two people in the headlights about fifty feet from me. One was Derek Grandgeorge, and I think the other was Joanie Crea. They were talking by his truck."

"Are you sure?"

Ken looked down at the floor, then back up. "The guy was wearing a jacket, even though it was hotter than hell that night. If you remember, May was a bitch for heat."

"Was the jacket like the one Derek Grandgeorge wears? Army type?"

Squinting at the window, Ken shrugged. "Probably." He paused. "You know, it was dark, and I was a little tanked. I just remember walking away thinking it was Grandgeorge. I didn't see his face."

Red set the notebook down on her desk, folded her arms, and said, "Ken, why didn't you tell me this when I talked with you the other day?"

Ken looked a little sheepish. "I didn't remember until this afternoon when I saw Grandgeorge's truck in town. I guess I pretty much tied one on that night. Some of it is real blurry."

"Can you think of anyone else who might have seen them?"

"You might try Ralph Cuttery. He usually remembers his customers."

Red thought about her conversation with Caddie about the pregnancy and the boyfriend. "Ken, don't you have a boy who's a senior?"

He shook his head. "Nope. No kids. Why do you ask?"

"A kid named Harrison came up in…a conversation." She let her voice

The Pines Were Watching 97

drop into vagueness. She didn't want Caddie's ex-boyfriend to become part of the rumor mill.

Ken raised his eyebrows. "Oh, you mean Buddy. He's my brother's boy. Used to date that Grandgeorge kid. I heard they got in trouble."

"In what way?"

Ken grimaced. "You know, like pregnant. My brother was furious about it."

"Because of the pregnancy?"

Ken tugged at his earlobe. "Probably because she was pregnant and then she wasn't. He married a strict Catholic and bought all that crap about abortion."

Red wondered if in a convoluted way, the brother had blamed Joanie for the abortion. "I might need to talk with him."

"That could be hard. He's been up in Alaska working the oil fields all summer. Won't be back for another month."

"Thanks, Ken."

There went a possible lead.

After Ken left, Red called Cuttery's. Ralph remembered the night because of the softball tournament. "Hell of a lot of people that night. Good clean crowd, though." He couldn't recollect seeing either Joanie Crea or Derek Grandgeorge that night. In fact, he seemed puzzled by Red's question. "I only saw Jimmy Crea's wife in my bar once, maybe a month ago. She ordered lemonade and sat by herself."

Before walking over to the public health nursing office, she left a message for Jason to see if he could dig up anyone who might have seen Joanie and Derek together that night.

"Well, at least I might have a connection," she said without much conviction.

18

THE MISSING VISIT

Red waited for Clarise Manson. Lynne sat behind her orderly desk, tapping the computer keyboard. She talked as her fingers clicked in a staccato cadence.

"Like I said the other day, Joanie stayed out of the office as much as possible." Lynne looked disdainfully toward the closed door with a brown nameplate that said, *Clarise Manson, MPH, Director*.

"Bad blood?" Red thought back to how nervous Clarise had appeared when she'd first talked with her. What was behind it?

Lynne stopped tapping out the numbers, her cheeks suddenly pink. "Oh," she said vaguely, "I don't know. It's just that Joanie thought nurses should be out seeing patients, not spending all day writing reports. She once said, 'Lynne, this is a one-horse agency. Manson should be out visiting like the rest of us.'"

"How long did Joanie work here?"

"Eight years this fall. I remember when she came. Scotty hired her. So skinny. I thought all the coffee and rolls we had around here would fatten her up. Never did." Lynne's voice had a disapproving tone to it—as if Joanie had not done her part when she hadn't "fattened up."

"Lynne, what can you tell me about Mrs. Crea's involvement with the Grandgeorge family?" She asked the question using her "let's be conspira-

The Pines Were Watching 99

tors together" tone. People who lived their lives through the misfortune of others often responded well to it.

Lynne's eyes registered suspicion, then a short, intense light. "Nothing," she said in a low voice. "She saw Mrs. Grandgeorge for a while until Angela took over. Then she went out there for Caddie a few times. She never talked about it."

Red kept her eyes on Lynne. "But?"

The dusky pink on her cheeks deepened. She accidentally bumped a coffee mug filled with pens, sending it skittering across the desk. "Listen, Sheriff. Derek Grandgeorge is a good person. He wouldn't hurt anyone." She looked down at her lap, her voice barely audible. "I just know it."

Red was about to ask why she was so sure when the door to Clarise Manson's office banged open. She swept out, her black blazer slightly askew on her shoulders. A yellow Post-it note clung to her long black skirt.

"Please come in," she said in a raised voice. Red looked at Lynne with a slight smile. Lynne shrugged, her lips forming a straight line.

Today Clarise wore heavy makeup and red lipstick that was too dark for her complexion. Brown hair cascaded to her shoulders, giving her face a pinched look. She smelled of coffee.

Red followed her back into her office, cleared off a pile of papers on a chair in front of the desk, and sat down.

"As you can see, I'm very busy. We're quite short-handed." Clarise's hands swept the room like a model pointing out the goods.

"Yes, I understand that Georgia is helping you out."

Clarise furrowed her brow. "Yes. Highly irregular, though. I had to make exceptions in order to hire her as a temp because the process is very strict." She sighed. "It was quite complex."

"I'll bet." Red nodded. "All the rules we have to follow."

"What more can I tell you?" The woman's shoulders twitched with tension. "I want to make it clear that whatever happened had nothing to do with any lapses on our part. We always follow policy and procedure."

Red kept her voice even. "I am not questioning your use of policy and procedure. I'm sure you are very good at seeing that the rules are followed."

Clarise pushed at a hank of hair, nodding slightly.

"I want to know if there was anything unusual with Mrs. Crea's patients, especially with the Grandgeorge family."

Clarise blinked almost as if Red had thrown something at her. "Uh... well, I don't know if I can let any of the information out of the chart. Data privacy, you know."

"This is a murder investigation." Red's jaw tightened. "I would hate to see one county office pitted against another over this. The county board would not be happy to find out that you slowed down the investigation. People are anxious and worried."

Clarise suddenly hugged herself, her lips forming an O.

"Well," she said, again in a loud voice. "Well." After making some throaty noises, she tapped the keys on her laptop and turned the screen to Red. "I'm not sure this is okay to show you..." Her voice trailed off.

Red scanned through the notes. Two visits had been charted from April. In both of them, Joanie had offered to provide information on the termination of Caddie's pregnancy. The notes were stiff and brief.

"Is there a way I can verify the dates on these visits? Perhaps Mrs. Crea made a follow-up visit that wasn't charted?"

Clarise sat up very straight in her chair. "My nurses chart all their visits."

Red let the irritation rise in her voice. "Do you have logs?"

"Of course, it's all on the computer."

"Let's look."

Clarise turned the laptop back. She fumbled with windows and commands. Finally, her face flushed, she dialed Lynne. "I'm having some difficulty with the log program, Lynne. Could you come in here, please."

Lynne walked in with her noticeable limp. She used the cluttered desk for support as she squeezed into the space next to her boss. "Remember, you have to use 'Control F' to get into the log file."

"You don't have to remind me," Clarise snapped.

Red watched the interplay with amusement. Like two dogs staring each other down. Of the two, her sentiments were with Lynne.

The screen filled with names and dates. "You can sort it by patient name," Lynne said, punching in some more keys. Clarise sat back, obviously deflated.

The Pines Were Watching 101

"See, she visited Caddie Grandgeorge on April twelfth, again on April nineteenth, then a third time on May twentieth."

Red stood up and walked around the desk to the computer. "The chart only has two visits documented."

Lynne shrugged, eyeing her boss. "The nurses enter their own logs."

"Would the notes be somewhere else?" Red asked.

"I don't think so, unless Joanie got so far behind in her charting. But she was very efficient. Perhaps a computer glitch?" Lynne shrugged again.

"Well." Clarise huffed. "Well. We'll have to check her laptop."

Red guessed that at this moment, Clarise Manson was praying for the resurrection of Joanie Crea to explain the gap in the record.

"Did Mrs. Crea discuss her cases with anyone else?" Red directed her question at Clarise.

Clarise answered in a tight voice, "You'd have to talk with Angela Driver."

"I have," Red said dryly. "She wasn't helpful."

Clarise glared at Lynne. "You have her laptop, don't you?"

"No."

"Well then, where is it? If it's lost, it could be a privacy breach." Her cheeks colored. She pursed her lips as she looked at Red. "Do *you* have it?"

They hadn't recovered either her computer or her phone. "I'm sorry, we're still searching for it."

"Humph. This could be a privacy breach. I'll have to report it." Her tone said this was one problem too much.

After a few more fruitless questions, Red left the woman to her fussing about privacy breaches. She remembered hearing the saying, "Those who can, do. Those who can't, administrate."

Lynne sat at her desk with a faraway expression on her face. For a moment, she looked young. Red sat down on the yellow plastic chair. She remembered the Town Talk gossip about Joanie making too many visits to the Grandgeorges.

"Was something going on between Mrs. Crea and Derek Grandgeorge?"

Lynne looked at her with a startled expression. "No."

"Someone told me that you had made a comment about Mrs. Crea making too many visits out there."

An orangish flush rose from Lynne's neck, spotting her cheeks. "I...I didn't mean anything by it."

"What did you mean?" Red kept her voice quiet and neutral.

"I was just mad at her, I guess."

"Why?"

"Derek is so nice, and Joanie is...was so strange."

"In what way was she strange?"

Lynne squirmed in her chair like an uncomfortable second-grader. "Oh," she said vaguely. "She made more money than Clarise Manson because she's been here so long. But she never had any money. Bought a lot of her clothes at garage sales." She stopped.

Red studied the way Lynne clasped her hands and twisted her fingers. "There's something else, isn't there?"

Lynne hugged herself.

"Why did you say that Derek Grandgeorge wouldn't hurt anyone?" Red's tone was gentle.

Lynne gazed beyond the barrack-green walls of the office.

"He's so nice," she said slowly.

"What do you mean?"

"When I was in high school, he once gave me a ride to school. My legs aren't right. It's a congenital hip thing they can't fix. Kids used to tease me. It was in the winter, and I was having a real hard time walking through the snow. He stopped and rolled down the car window. 'Could you use a ride?' he asked. I remember his car smelled like pine."

"And?"

"No other guy has ever been that nice to me."

Red sat back in the chair. "Do you know anything more about him?"

Lynne looked at Red as if she'd just awakened from a dream. "What?"

"Can you tell me anything else about Derek Grandgeorge?"

She shook her head, tinkering with a pencil on her desk. "Geraldine says he's nice." Her voice dropped off.

"Geraldine Grandgeorge?"

Lynne put the pencil down and looked directly at Red. "Geraldine is a friend. We talk sometimes. Derek was real nice to her when that creep of a husband ran out on her."

The Pines Were Watching   103

Manson's door opened with the whoosh of cheap plywood. "Lynne, I need my reports." She looked disdainfully at Red. "Now."

Red stood up. "Thank you for your help." She resisted the urge to walk over to Clarise and straighten her jacket and pull the Post-it note off her skirt.

Red walked back to the courthouse. By the time she reached the front door, her shirt already stuck to her. Ed stood beside a little power mower, his John Deere hat in hand. "Hot enough for you, Sheriff?"

"I'm glad this old building has air conditioning. Wish my house did."

Ed scratched his head, squinting up at the sky. "You know that poor nurse that was killed?"

"Yes?"

"I just remembered it was last Saturday...no, the Saturday before that I saw her with someone. Wouldn't have noticed except no one is ever in that office on the weekend."

Red wiped her brow. "What did you see?"

"She was with a redheaded gal. You know the one that came into your office the other day?"

A car drove by with the hum of an electric vehicle. Not a common sight in Lykkins Lake. Ed watched it go by. "Who ever thought you'd plug in a car?"

"You were saying about Mrs. Crea and the other nurse?"

Ed nodded. "Oh yeah, they got in a car and drove off together. I remember because the car had a bad muffler." He frowned like he was thinking hard. "Just wondering if that's a clue."

Red smiled at him. "Thanks, Ed. I'll make a note of it."

As she walked in, she wondered why Angela hadn't mentioned meeting Joanie on the weekend.

Back in her office, she called the clinic, asking for Lou. "Do you think you could do something for me?"

"Is it legal?"

"Definitely." Red could picture the amusement on Lou's face. "Look up

Joanie's record and tell me when she started getting treated for the skin rash."

Red waited on hold while an orchestral version of the Rolling Stones' "Let's Spend the Night Together" assaulted her ears.

The song clicked off, replaced by Lou's quiet voice. "May twenty-eighth."

"Thanks," Red said. "By the way, I checked with the county attorney about the data privacy stuff. The dead no longer have the same rights to privacy."

Lou tsked. "Well, where's the law when you need it?" Her voice turned serious. "By the way, I accidentally pulled up Jimmy's chart before I found Joanie's. Isn't that a coincidence? He came into the clinic today."

"Why was he in?"

Lou cleared her throat. "He came in with hematuria."

"Translate, please."

"Blood in the urine. Probably a urinary tract infection."

Red interrupted. "It could also be due to sexually transmitted diseases, right?"

"God, you are a smart law officer," Lou said.

After she hung up, Red added under Jimmy: *Blood in urine. Check with the Doc.* She reviewed the rest of her notes. Joanie had possibly been sighted at Cuttery's on the fifteenth and had made an uncharted visit to the Grandgeorge Place on May twentieth. Eight days later she'd developed severe dermatitis. She remembered the advice of her psychologist friend, Rob. "Look for connections."

Red called the bank. The head teller pulled up the information and then said, "I was never comfortable with giving her all that cash. But it was her money."

Joanie made her first savings account withdrawal on May twentieth. Was her visit to the Grandgeorge Place a payoff visit for something that happened the night of the fifteenth? What could have been so bad that Joanie broke out in a rash and started withdrawing all her money?

19

POKER CLUB INTEL

At seven in the evening, Georgia called Red at the office. "I'm inviting you to an emergency meeting of the Florence Nightingale Memorial Poker Club. We've got more information for you."

Red rubbed her temple with her right hand. "I think I'm on information overload. Can it wait?"

"Nope." Georgia's voice was emphatic. "Lou is bringing over her cashew chicken salad, and I have fresh vegetables and dip. Besides, Scotty just cleaned out the supply of Summit Pale Ale from the liquor store."

"You're trying to lure me with liquor?"

"We nurses of the poker club have no shame."

Red stretched her legs out. "Okay." She'd gotten nowhere trying to make connections in the investigation, and she'd heard nothing from Waltz. The family crisis must have been a big one.

As Red walked into the back room of Georgia's Antiques, she realized that she'd forgotten to eat lunch. A light-headed, hypoglycemic sheriff was just what the county needed right now, with one woman dead and one woman missing. No one had seen Arlis Henley, and she hadn't shown up to pick up her paycheck.

Putting all her manners aside, she sat down and helped herself to the chicken salad. "Better than the frozen pizza I had planned for this evening."

Georgia nodded at Lou. "See, didn't I tell you our sheriff needs a mother?"

Scotty laughed from across the table. "She doesn't need a mother, she needs a boyfriend." She looked directly at Red. "Georgia tells me you've been spending your evenings talking to your dog. Seems to me you could use someone in bed beside you who doesn't lift a leg to pee."

For a second, Red thought about Waltz on the patio with a beer and was glad she hadn't mentioned it to Georgia last night. Even though it had been three years since Will died, she wasn't ready to entertain a dating life. Will was the only person she ever wanted to share her bed. Before glowering at Scotty, however, she took a breath and held her hands up. "Any suggestions?"

"Well, no. Although I'll bet the unattached ladies of Pearsal County are going to start courting Jimmy Crea. They'll give him a month, six weeks tops, to grieve. He won't lack for home-cooked meals for the next year."

After they finished eating, Georgia winked at Red. "We're gathered here tonight to supply our eminently capable sheriff with further clues in this crime." She glanced at Scotty. "Though I'm afraid of what you might say whenever you open your mouth, let's hear from you first."

Scotty glared back at Georgia. "Here's the latest from the Town Talk. Rumor has it that Joanie's coworker, that redheaded nurse, moved here after getting into some kind of trouble with a patient down in the cities. Apparently, Lynne, the secretary, overheard her boss checking references when she hired the nurse. She didn't hear the details but got the impression that the hospital had conducted some type of investigation."

Red pictured Angela Driver and wondered what secrets she carried.

"More importantly," Scotty added, "Derek Grandgeorge has been seen at Cuttery's with the redhead on a couple of occasions."

"Hardly any kind of motive there for anyone to kill Joanie," Lou said.

Scotty held her hand up. "But what if Joanie found out somehow about the redhead's past and threatened to tell Grandgeorge? Or better yet, what if Grandgeorge was trying to protect his new love?"

Red took a sip of the beer and tilted back in her chair. "Maybe it would make sense if Joanie was somehow blackmailing Angela Driver. Except it's Joanie's money that seems to be disappearing."

The Pines Were Watching 107

Scotty looked up at the ceiling, her lips moving silently as she tried to sort it out. Finally, she shrugged. "It doesn't make much sense, does it?"

"Here's another piece that doesn't make much sense," Red said, letting down her investigative privacy guard. "Joanie might have been spotted in the parking lot of Cuttery's with Derek Grandgeorge. I can't confirm any of it."

Scotty wrinkled her brow. "I would really question that sighting. As I said once before, the talk would have started long ago if Jimmy's ex had been hanging around with Derek Grandgeorge. For weeks my tables were filled with people speculating on why she and Jimmy were going to divorce." She shook her head. "Grandgeorge was never mentioned."

Red drummed her fingers on the table. "What do you know about Arlis Henley? Any connection with either Grandgeorge or Joanie?"

"I heard she's disappeared," Scotty replied.

"Are there no secrets in this town?"

"Not in my diner."

They were silent for a few moments. Then Lou said, "I went to school with a bunch of Henleys. There must have been eight or nine kids in that family. Bruce, the one in my class, was loud and dirty. Whenever I'd complain about him at home, my mom would say, 'Lou, not everyone gets the best start in this world. Life for the Henleys isn't easy. Have patience. Bruce will find his way.'"

"Did he?" Georgia asked.

Lou shrugged. "I think he went into the army. The rest of them have scattered over the years. Arlis is the only one still living in Lykkins Lake. Her dad died a few years ago, and I think her mom moved to the cities to live with a daughter."

"I've heard some twittering from time to time at the Town Talk about Arlis and her side business entertaining men," Scotty said. "I don't think anyone was sure who Tommy's father might be." She tsked. "What a sad way to live."

Red picked at the label on the beer bottle. "She had a steady job at the Golden Deer Casino, and she told me she had money for a lawyer to get Tommy back. I don't have a good feeling about this."

The old building housing Georgia's Antiques seemed to sense the apprehension in the room, its walls shuddering with the evening breeze. The poker club sat in silence until Georgia pulled out a black spiral-bound organizer and set it in front of Red.

"Let's change the topic. I've got Joanie's calendar. Looks like she kept her schedule on paper instead of on the computer. Clarise Manson gave it to me and said, 'Here, this should help you figure out what the patients need.'"

Red carefully paged through the recent entries, stopping on Tuesday's. Most had a last name and a first initial and some type of code—*mc, ma, ew, mch, pp*. Some included notes, such as *renew rx, draw blood*. She looked at Georgia. "Do you know what these codes mean?"

Georgia shrugged. "Clarise was so desperate to get someone out to see patients that she didn't explain much to me."

Scotty leaned over to study the book. "They look like billing codes. *Mc* for Medicare, *ma* for Medicaid, *ew* for elderly waiver, *pp* for private pay..."

"Hold it." Red wrinkled her brow. "What's an elderly waiver?"

Georgia looked at Scotty. "See if you can explain it."

Scotty opened another bottle of beer, took a sip, and said, "I'll need a flip chart, please."

"I'd rather have the CliffsNotes version," Red responded dryly.

"Minnesota has a number of programs that pay for care in order to keep people in their own homes and out of the nursing home. Somewhere along the line, some smart people at the state figured out that paying an aide to bathe a person in their home twice a week was a lot cheaper than paying for someone to be in the nursing home. Elderly waiver is one of those programs. People who receive services generally have a little money, but not enough to pay for a bath aide. Elderly waivers helps them pay."

Red raised her hand. "Okay, that's enough. If I need to know more, I'll ask you to bring your flip chart."

Scotty frowned. "But I was just getting to the good part. You know, where I take the opportunity to bash the Republicans and their antigovernment, throw-out-the-taxes-and-bring-back-the-good-ol'-days stupidity."

Outside, the ten o'clock whistle blew. Red noted the puzzled look on Georgia's face. "Something wrong?"

The Pines Were Watching   109

"I'm not sure." She was leaning over Joanie's calendar. "I'm going to study this a little more. Something isn't quite right."

Red peered over Georgia's shoulder. "I should probably take it in as evidence."

Georgia looked up at her. "Not on your life. I wouldn't have a clue who to see or what they needed without it."

"Bring it in tomorrow. I'll get it copied for you."

"Yes, ma'am."

Red stretched. "I'm pooped. I think I'll go home and talk with my dog about elderly waivers." She winked at Scotty. "Despite what you might think, he's a very good listener."

On her way home, she pulled into Cuttery's dirt parking lot. Five cars and two pickups were parked close to the entrance. The rest of the lot stood empty and dark. Red walked over to the spot where Ken Harrison had chosen to relieve himself the night he thought he saw Joanie and Grandgeorge together.

Peering into the darkness, she tried to re-create the incident in her mind. Ken had claimed Grandgeorge's truck was on the other side of the lot, near the edge of the woods. Red squinted. According to Ken, the man had been wearing a jacket. At this distance, with the brief brightness of a passing headlight, could he identify the type of jacket and color? She shook her head.

"Not likely," she said to herself.

In bed that night, Red wrestled with the tangled sheets as lights exploded behind her eyes. She felt as if something was being held over her mouth and nose. With a grunt, she sat up. Her breath came in gasps as she forced her eyes open to the darkness in her room. Blue sighed and stood up.

"Sorry, pal," she said, patting him on the head. "I've got another headache. I hope to hell it's nothing more than tension."

Pulling on Will's old green corduroy robe, Red shuffled to the bathroom for some ibuprofen. As she uncapped the bottle, she glanced into the darkened mirror. Lad looked out at her with deep, troubled eyes. Blinking, she looked again, only to see her shadowed face.

Blue trotted behind her as she made her way to the living room. She eased herself into the recliner, trying not to move her head. Outside, the lake rested, quiet in the night heat. At her feet, Blue whined until she picked him up. After fifteen minutes, the throbbing began to subside. Weak lightning illuminated the darkness for a moment.

"I used to understand the principle behind heat lightning," she told Blue. He licked her forearm. "For the life of me, I can't remember anything about it now. It's a good thing I'm not teaching science to junior high kids anymore."

Blue snuggled into the crook of her arm and closed his eyes. She looked at the dog, remembering what Georgia had once told her.

"Why, Red. You have the perfect dog. It's like having a baby without needing a babysitter. That dog will love you whether you feed him steak or dried cat food."

The sky lit up again with a slightly green hue, then closed into rank darkness.

"What is it about green these days? Green sky, green jacket?"

Blue nestled a little deeper into the crook of Red's arm without replying. His fur felt hot against her skin. She shifted slightly in her chair. He lifted his head in irritation.

"Hey, I wasn't placed on this earth to be your pillow, young pup."

With her index finger, Red lightly stroked the top of the dog's head, marveling at the softness of his hair. The pain in her head dulled. Every once in a while, she glanced at the phone, half expecting it to ring. After a long time, she carefully stood up, cradling the sleeping dog, and walked slowly back to bed.

God, she thought as she gently placed Blue on the pillow beside her. *I do handle him like a baby.* Harv Smith would love to take that information to the Hammer Lake boys. Two more years before the next election, and if she didn't find out who murdered Joanie Crea, she wasn't sure Pearsal County would forgive her.

20

THE WAKE

Joanie's wake was scheduled from six to eight Friday evening at the funeral home. Her parents then planned to bring the body back to Southern Minnesota for a memorial service and burial. Red suspected that the Iversons, who did not like Jimmy much, bypassed his church to make as loud a statement as they could about him to the community.

When they walked into Red's office, she noted immediately the resemblance between Joanie and her father. He was tall and slim with sharp features. Mrs. Iverson, on the other hand, had a plump face and carried fifty pounds extra weight.

They sat stiffly across from Red and refused her offer of coffee. Mrs. Iverson fought hard to keep her face from crumbling as she talked about her daughter.

"She wanted to be a nurse from the time she was a little girl. All through high school she worked as an aide at St. Mary's Care Center. She'd come home some evenings so tired that she fell asleep without taking her uniform off. But she loved those old folks." Her eyes misted over.

Red let the silence fill the room, then she asked softly, "Did you talk with her in the last couple of months?"

Mr. Iverson leaned forward on his chair. "She called us every Sunday night. Said everything was fine." His voice dropped off.

Red waited.

"But I could tell something was wrong." He looked up at her, his eyes flashing. "I know it was that Crea who was the problem."

"What do you mean?"

Mrs. Iverson placed her hand on her husband's thigh. Red wasn't sure if it was for support or to quiet him.

"Oh, just little hints. She'd start to say something about Jimmy, then she'd stop."

Mrs. Iverson looked at Red. "He's just talking nonsense. Joanie never said a bad thing about Jimmy. We just sort of sensed it." She took a deep breath. "We thought everything was going to be okay with our little girl. Last Sunday she called and said she was ready to move on. She was going to find a new job and come back to us. She sounded real happy—like she'd finally worked some things out."

"Do you know what kind of things she'd worked out?"

They both shook their heads.

"If only we'd come to visit..." Mrs. Iverson dabbed at her eyes with a tissue.

When Red walked them to the door, she knew little more about Joanie than when they'd sat down. She did sense, however, that some change had occurred very recently. She agreed with Mr. Iverson that Joanie had "worked something out." She wondered if that was the key to who killed her.

The parking lot at the Larsen-Nord Funeral Home was full. Cars lined the street for a block in each direction. Joanie's wake had become a community affair.

Down the street, parked in the early evening shadows under a dying elm, away from the streetlights, Red watched, wondering how many of the visitors truly cared about Joanie or her family.

She noted who walked in the oak double doors of the funeral home. Large portions of the people attending the wake were elderly. It appeared that Joanie was well liked by the senior citizens of Pearsal County. Funny she was able to connect with them but not with anyone else.

The Pines Were Watching 113

As Red watched a frail woman struggle with her walker to reach the entrance, a red pickup pulled onto a side street not far from where Red was parked. Derek Grandgeorge, dressed in a white shirt tucked neatly into his blue jeans, stepped out of the truck, took several tentative steps toward the funeral home, then stopped. He looked back at his truck, turned to it, then turned again toward the funeral home.

Red was reminded of a squirrel dashing onto the street, changing its mind, then suddenly dashing out again in front of a car.

Grandgeorge walked quickly to the double doors, held them while Clarise Manson emerged, then stepped inside. Less than five minutes later, he hurried out the door and back to his truck. Red could not read the expression on his face in the twilight, but his hunched gait indicated distress.

A few minutes after Grandgeorge returned to his truck, Angela Driver walked out the door. She stood at the edge of the parking lot until Derek's pickup pulled up beside her. She looked in both directions, then stepped inside the vehicle.

As the truck pulled away from the curb, Red's eyes felt like someone had dumped sand into them, and the tips of her fingers itched from the heat inside the car.

"What are you two up to?"

"Sheriff?" The radio beside her crackled to life.

Red answered, keeping her eyes on the pickup as it drove down the street. "I'm here. What is it?"

"Some kids fooling around near Fire Tower Road found a body. Sherm thinks it might be that Henley woman."

The Grandgeorge pickup rolled out of sight as Red slapped her fist into the palm of her hand with a stinging *whap*.

"Get me the directions. I'm on my way." Her stomach twisted into a hard knot. "God almighty, what is happening in this county?"

21

FIRE TOWER ROAD

Sherm Walker's RV partially blocked Fire Tower Road. Red yanked up the parking brake on her car and rolled down the window.

"Goddamn it, Sherm. Move that pig of yours, or I swear I'll get my crew to impound it."

Sherm stood beside the old Winnebago, grinning like the Cheshire Cat.

"Beat you again, didn't I, Sheriff?"

They always said in Hammer Lake Township that if Sherm didn't know about something first, it must not have happened. Red pressed her lips together.

"You middle-aged fart. Don't you have anything better to do?" she growled, trying to keep the smile off her face. Despite the fact that Sherm was fat, lazy, and dependent on a disability check for a hazy "back injury," Red counted on him as her eyes and ears for this part of the county. If someone was breaking into the summer cabins around Hammer Lake, Sherm probably could find out who it was, what they did with the loot, and everything anyone would need to know about their ancestry.

Sherm sidled up to her window.

"What's the scoop?" she asked.

"Just them Townsend boys out with a couple of girls. Thought they'd have a little campfire and drink some peppermint schnapps. Seems when

The Pines Were Watching

they got settled in, they noticed a hell of a rotten smell just down the road. Petey Townsend ain't done puking yet. One of the girls called a friend whose mother called me and asked me to check it out."

He mopped sweat off his forehead. "Didn't even bother to try to bury her. Just dumped her in a little hollow and kicked some leaves over her. 'Course, it's been real hot and humid the last couple of days. But I'm damned sure it's the Henley woman—the one you've been looking for."

"Not pretty, I guess." Red shook her head. "I suppose I'd better look for myself." The adrenaline that surged through her was offset by the thought of viewing yet another dead body.

"Sure thing. You're the sheriff."

Beyond Sherm's RV, the road narrowed to a rutted track. Her Subaru bounced and jolted like an old school bus. Red pulled to a halt behind the Townsend boys' rusty Chevy truck. As she stepped out of the car, she noticed immediately the faint, sickly sweet smell of decomposing flesh masked by the acrid smoke of a dying campfire. She wanted to go directly to the body and confirm what Sherm had told her. She wanted to get that part over with, but her instincts told her to talk with the teens first.

The teenagers huddled silently by the side of the road, staring down at their phones. Red approached them with her arms loosely at her sides. She didn't want to spook them.

"Didn't turn into such a good weenie roast, did it?"

The four of them shrugged in unison but did not look at her. Pete Townsend kicked at a clump of dried grass, his face bluish white in the twilight.

"Thanks, Pete, for not running after you found the body. I appreciate that you all stuck around." Red did not have to mention that all four of them would have hell to pay from their folks when they got back home. "Discovering bodies is not what I call a fun night."

"For sure," Pete said, mumbling to his shoes.

"Can you all tell me about it?"

At first, all four of them concentrated on the phones and the grass beneath their feet. Red stayed silent. Her teaching experience told her that kids like to talk when given a chance, especially about gruesome things.

Finally, one of the girls looked at her and said, "I smelled something as soon as we started the fire. I told Pete he'd sure lit up some rotten wood."

"We couldn't figure out what it was," the other girl said, looking at Pete's brother, Joe. "At first, we just kidded that someone had really let one go."

"Yeah, Joe can really stink up the place when he feels like it." The two girls giggled nervously.

Ah, the feminist revolution, Red thought. Now girls can talk farts as easily as the boys. Red redirected the conversation. "So, Pete, you were the one to go looking?"

The boy looked at her with wide eyes. "It smelled a lot like our woods the summer someone dumped a dead dog by the ditch. I thought it might be a dog or a deer." His voice dropped off. "But not a lady."

After that, they all started talking at once. Within five minutes, Red had all the details she needed about the discovery.

"Did you move anything?"

Pete shook his head. "I just kicked some leaves away with my foot. When I seen that face, with those eyes just staring, it made me puke."

"How about the rest of you?"

"We were all behind Pete. When he came running back, gagging, we didn't go any further."

I'll bet, Red thought. Wild horses wouldn't keep those kids from seeing what it was that sent Pete on the run.

She bet that if she confiscated their phones, she'd find photos. In fact, she was sure the photos were already out in cyberspace.

"Do you come up here a lot?"

Collectively they shook their heads.

"When was the last time you were here?"

Collectively they shuffled their feet.

"A week? Two weeks?"

Silence.

"Come on, I may be a sheriff, but I'm not dumb. That campfire setup you've got looks pretty cozy and pretty well used. Who else comes by here?"

One of the girls finally spoke up. "Well, lots of kids do. You know, it's just a place where people go."

The Pines Were Watching

And if you dump a body here, someone is likely to find it, Red thought. The killer wanted Arlis found. Interesting.

Red took down the names and phone numbers of the teenagers and had the dispatcher contact their parents. Mentally she listed what needed to be done. First a quick look at the body before Waltz's team arrived. She shuddered, thinking about Joanie's body in the summerhouse. What kind of nightmares would this body give her?

She closed her eyes for a moment and massaged her forehead, remembering the little Henley boy.

With her teeth gritted, she walked slowly to the hollow where the body lay.

"Blue, I wish you could answer the phone, so I could tell you I'll be late. More pee for my recliner, I guess."

Her phone rang with Waltz on the other end. "I hear you've got more troubles."

"A missing mother has been found."

"We'll be there within the hour."

She gave him directions and said she'd have one of her deputies meet the team in town and escort them out. "We're in a pretty remote spot."

"I'll bring mosquito dope."

She pictured the amusement on his face. Right now, she didn't feel it as she trudged to the spot that held the body of Arlis.

22

SHERM

Red waited next to her car, talking with Jason. Waltz and team were about ten minutes away. Jason asked the question that was gnawing at her.

"Do you think we have a serial killer? You know the rumors are going to fly and the true crime podcasters will be all over it."

Wearily she answered, "Let's hope we solve it before they show up."

It was nearly midnight when Waltz and his crew arrived. In the glow of the flashlight, she noted the deep circles under his eyes.

"You look exhausted."

"I'll look even worse by morning."

Red led him to the body, holding a handkerchief over her nose.

"Weak stomach," she confessed.

Waltz squatted down with a tired stoop to his shoulders. Pulling on latex gloves, he gingerly examined the body while Red held the flashlight.

"Damn," he sighed. "Strangled, just like the other one. I'm betting it's the same type of rope."

Red winced. It looked like she did have a serial killer on the loose.

In death, Arlis Henley's jaw had dropped slack, the defiant mouth now held open in a perpetual scream. Waltz squinted, moving closer to the body. "Something isn't right here." He shined a penlight into the mouth.

Red held herself back, letting Waltz do the work.

The Pines Were Watching

"What is that?" Turning to his kit, he picked out long needle-nosed tweezers. Delicately he inserted it into the mouth of the dead woman. Grunting and poking, he worked the tweezers. "If only I had a little more light."

Red squatted down and aimed her powerful flashlight directly at the mouth. "Does that help?"

With one more jabbing maneuver, he pulled the tweezers out. A key fell onto the torso.

"Jesus," Red exclaimed. "Someone stuffed a key in her mouth?"

"Or she was trying to swallow it."

She stared at the key. It was new, and it was familiar. "Oh, shit," she uttered. "That looks like the missing key from Joanie Crea's house."

Connections.

Waltz put the key in an evidence bag. "I'm thinking this was a crime of passion and anger."

Red coughed, fighting off the nausea that was building.

Waltz turned to her, pointing to the evidence bag. "Let's agree to keep it among ourselves. Things like this have a way of getting out."

Red wanted to disagree but knew he was right. "Okay. You, me, and your crew."

He nodded, continuing to examine the body. "When we get the lights up, we'll get a better sense of what happened here."

Gingerly he brushed the leaves and debris from the body, exposing her arm. Red recognized the Cuttery's T-shirt. "Waltz, check to see if she has a gold bracelet. She was wearing one the other day."

"I will let you know if I find one. Why don't you take a break?"

Red nodded and walked quickly away from the hollow, holding her breath until she reached fresher air. Her phone crackled as she connected with the dispatcher.

"I'm going to be here for a while. Let's try to keep as much of a lid on this as possible."

"No problem."

"Damn it!" Red kicked at a clump of dirt. "Will, if you're watching from heaven, send me something to work with—a footprint, a confession. I'm not fussy."

As if on cue, Sherm waddled up to her and placed a hand lightly on her shoulder. "Why don't you step inside and have a root beer with me?"

"Guess it couldn't hurt at this point. They'll be here for a while. God, I hope we didn't trample all the evidence." Red wondered if she'd ever laugh again.

"Hey, no one is blaming you for this." They walked under the twinkling stars to the RV. The night smelled of dry pine needles and a faint, lingering odor of rot.

Red looked up at the stars, remembering the late-night walks with Will before she realized that she was in love with him. Will would point out the constellations, and Red would strain to try to see what he was talking about.

She turned her attention back to the present. "Sherm, no matter what happens, I'll be blamed. It's our culture. Fix the blame, not the problem."

"Too deep for me, Sheriff," Sherm grunted as he stepped up into the RV.

As an eighth grader, Red had been taller than most of the boys and fully developed. That was the year Sherm and the high school football team made it to the state tournament. He had been a square, muscular kid with a jaw a bit too big for his face and a terrible case of acne.

He hung around with the popular crowd. She had to walk by his locker every morning to get to her first-hour class. One day as she walked by, he'd whistled and called out, "Hey, what a babe. How big are those things, anyway?"

Red never forgot the sound of the boys cackling. Her embarrassment quickly turned to rage. Instead of hurrying down the hall, she'd stopped, turned to them, planted her feet firmly on the scuffed wooden floor, and said, "Are you talking to me?"

In those days, boys were not used to being confronted by girls, especially sturdy eighth graders.

They'd looked at each other, laughing nervously. "Talking pretty tough, aren't you?"

"I am pretty tough."

She'd stared hard at Sherm until he finally looked down. The bell rang, rescuing them from a standoff. Sherm and the boys had never bothered her again.

How we change. She leaned her back up against the aluminum sink in the RV, sipping the cold can of root beer. Sherm sat on the bench behind his little kitchen table. The muscles of high school had turned to flab. He now carried a clear complexion and two extra chins that moved with his good-natured smile. She could no longer picture him as an athlete.

"So, Sherm, what have we got here in Pearsal County? What's your theory?" The root beer soothed her stomach.

Sherm belched. "It's local, Red. How would an outsider find Fire Tower Road? It's just two ruts off a county road. No one uses it other than some loggers and the kids."

She didn't share the discovery of the key, but she felt Sherm was right. Whatever was going on was local. And she was damn sure now that it connected with Joanie Crea.

She took another drink of the root beer. This time it tasted a little too sweet. "What do you know about Arlis Henley?"

Sherm raised his hands in mock surrender. "Nothing firsthand—honest. The wife would kill me and throw me in the swamp if she thought I was messing around with her."

Red smiled as she pictured Sherm's wife, a tiny woman with the softest brown eyes, trying to hoist Sherm into the swamp. "But you do know her reputation?"

"Everyone does. Steady stream of traffic out to her trailer on Saturday nights, they say." He paused, wrinkling his brow. "My little brother was in her class in high school. If I recall, she wasn't so wild in those days. He once told me he thought maybe something was happening to her at home. Came to school one day with a black eye and said she fell. I don't think she ever graduated."

"What do you know about her customers? Local boys? Loggers? Truckers?"

"Hell, Red, I keep track of Hammer Lake, but she was a townie. No one up here really talked much about her. We've got our own trailer trash to keep us busy." Sherm looked up at the ceiling. "Someone did say they'd seen her van a while back up in our part of the county." He paused for emphasis. "Except some guy in a green jacket was driving."

Red straightened from her slouch. "Green jacket? Who?"

Sherm shrugged. "Didn't say he knew the guy."

"Can you check it out?"

"Sure. You betcha." Sherm yawned. "Better get home to the wife. She worked the swing shift at the nursing home. Bound to wonder where I am."

"Thanks for the root beer." Red stepped over to the door, then turned back to Sherm. "Did Derek Grandgeorge have any connection with Arlis Henley?"

Sherm shook his head. "You got me. I never really knew him. I knew his brother better when I worked down at the garage. Drove that fancy Mustang. Said it used to belong to his dad. God, that car was a beaut." He knit his brow. "Seems to me there was something about him, but it slips right by me now."

Before she left, he added, "Arlis and Geraldine are cousins. That's the only connection I know."

Red stayed at the site until they removed the body. The medical examiner was going to wonder what was happening in Pearsal County. She let Waltz know she was headed home.

"Say hello to your guard dog for me."

As she drove back to town, she thought about Arlis. It was as if she'd been born with a cloud hanging over her—poverty, probable abuse, and all of it medicated with alcohol and men who paid for her services.

And what about the mysterious guy in the green jacket. Tommy had mentioned a green jacket. Was it the same person? Arlis told her she had friends with money or influence and would get Tommy back. Was all of this connected? And what about Grandgeorge? If so, why didn't anyone identify him? Was she looking in the wrong direction?

By the time she reached home and let Blue out, Red's head pounded. Sick green and yellow lights flashed in her peripheral vision. As Blue trotted back into the house, Red said, "There's got to be a better way to make a living. I need to find myself a rich man who likes smelly little poodles."

23

ANOTHER SCRAP OF PAPER

Light from the rising sun sparkled gently off the dewy grass-blades growing between the ruts of Fire Tower Road. Blue snuffled in the grass ahead of her. He was headed directly for the spot where Arlis Henley had been found. A heaviness hung in the humid air. Red breathed it in, trying to remove the lingering stench of death.

Waltz and his team had packed up at about three in the morning. As she watched the crime scene tape fluttering in the cool dawn breeze, she called Waltz. "I'm at the site. Do you mind if I look around the periphery?"

Waltz's voice was raspy with sleep. "Stay out of the marked area." His tone was abrupt, which took her by surprise. "Tramping through it could screw up the investigation. I hate when people mess with my crime scenes."

Red stared at the phone. She felt like she was being berated by the principal.

"I won't disturb anything. I need to get a sense of the place in daylight." She hated the tentativeness in her voice. Waltz had pushed that button that lurked behind all her decisions. Was she competent to do the job?

He sighed audibly. "Okay. Let me know if you find anything. I have to get back to the city—still dealing with a family matter."

She watched the light on her phone go out when the call ended. "What happened to the chatty Waltz who sat on my patio with a beer and a smile?"

His response to her fit with what she'd been told. Waltz could be companionable, but he was all business when it came to a case. She guessed her lone trip to the site was not within his protocols.

Blue strained at the leash.

"Well, Blue, do you see anything that I've missed?"

Carefully Red circled the hollow, staying outside the taped-off area. She picked up the wet dog and carried him further away from the site. "I'm looking for footprints or some indication of how the body got here. Go find them!" When she set him down, Blue gazed up at her as if to say, "You want me to do what?"

Between the teenagers, the forensic crew, and the medical examiner's van, any tire tracks had been obliterated. The area outside of the police tape looked like it had been trampled by a crowd of rock concert goers. Her thoughts turned to Will. Would he have handled the site differently?

Georgia would tell her to stop making comparisons. "You're every bit as competent as Will. He handled authority well but wasn't great on details. You know that."

Red gazed up at the sky for a moment. "Sorry, Will. It was late and dark and a wild scene." Still no excuse.

Rays of the early sunlight stabbed through the canopy of pines that appeared to watch over the site where Arlis had been found.

Blue trotted comfortably by her side. The further they moved from the death site, the more Red thought about the child's game of hiding something. "Blue, I think we're getting colder, not warmer."

He gazed up at the sound of her voice and then wandered over to a large dying oak. She watched as he sniffed the ground before lifting his leg. Near where he stood, she saw something white.

"What's that?"

She squatted down to see a crumpled scrap of paper. It had been torn from a spiral notebook like the one she'd found in Joanie's bedroom. Holding it by its edge, she picked it up. One side was blank, but when she turned it over, the words *green jacket* followed by *Grandgeorge* were printed

The Pines Were Watching

in faint pencil. The letters had a precision to them, like they'd been written by someone who was meticulous. Below the name were several question marks.

Was this the same handwriting? She carefully placed the paper in a baggie she had in her pocket. She'd compare it with the other scrap of paper before sharing with Waltz. His attitude on the phone had unnerved her, and at the moment she wasn't feeling particularly collegial.

For the next ten minutes, she explored the area around the tree but found only a few empty beer cans and liquor bottles that had been thrown into the woods from the campsite. The forest floor was late-summer thick with undergrowth and contained no footprints.

"Well, Blue, if only you were a bloodhound instead of a poodle, maybe you could track where this came from."

By now, Blue's paws were soaked with the dew, and he shivered as he stood by her. Time to get him home and settled on the recliner and time for her to face the rest of the day.

In the office by 7:30, she checked the tipline that had been installed under Will's administration. As she listened to the female voice intone, "You have eight new messages," she remembered Will's discussion some years ago with the county board over the tipline. He had laughed when he told her Harv Smith's reaction to the proposal.

"Hell, Sheriff, this county has gotten on without it for one hundred years. It's them big city telephone people trying to take away our jobs. Besides, folks here in Pearsal County don't want to call the sheriff to talk with some damn machine."

Wisely, Will had expected the resistance. He had gone to the meeting prepared with figures on cost and cost savings.

She remembered her own difficulties getting the website for the sheriff's department. Will would have enjoyed helping her with that one.

God, she missed him.

A high, muffled voice on the phone whispered, "Grandgeorge killed them all." Red pressed the save button, then listened to the message again. Whoever spoke held the phone at a distance. By the third listen, Red was sure that despite the effort to disguise it, the intonation was masculine.

In the next call, a childish voice wondered if this was part of a terrorist conspiracy. Red erased it, muttering, "Alma Wooster, don't you have better things to do than leave me dumb messages?" Two more calls offered anonymous tips about strangers seen lurking in several parts of the county. Red recognized both voices and wrote their names down on her legal pad.

Before she reached the last couple of tipline messages, her regular phone rang. "Sheriff, this is Jimmy Crea. I just heard the terrible news about Arlis Henley." He paused. Red heard religious music in the background. His voice softened. "I...I know from my own tragedy how hard this will be on little Tommy. He was just starting the youth group at the church, and maybe I could talk with him. Grief is so hard..." His voice trailed away.

"That's kind of you, Jimmy. Did you know Arlis?"

He cleared his throat. "Only to say hello to her when she dropped Tommy off a couple of weeks ago. We were taking the kids hiking that day, and I remember that she forgot to pack him a lunch."

"Oh?"

"He's a good kid."

She thanked him but said the social worker from the county would work with Tommy.

Why was Jimmy so eager to help a little boy who had lost his mother? On the other hand, if Jimmy had a relationship with Tommy, maybe he could get him to talk more about the man who had hit him. The man in the green jacket.

She shook her head. "No. Tommy has enough to deal with."

Red took out the plastic bag with the scrap of paper and compared it with the scrap she'd found at Joanie's. While she wasn't an expert on handwriting, it appeared to be from the same person. Had Joanie written this? Or had someone else written it?

"Okay, okay," she sighed aloud. "I'll turn this over to Waltz's crew to figure out."

At nine o'clock, Lou called. "You must be under siege. I've been trying to get through for the last ten minutes."

"Just working through a slew of anonymous tips. Maybe Will wasn't so smart getting the line up and going." She was unable to disguise the worry in her voice.

The Pines Were Watching   127

Lou paused. "I heard about Arlis in the clinic today. I'm so sorry."

"So am I. For me and for Tommy." Immediately, Red felt ashamed of her self-pitying tone. "Sorry," she added. "Not enough sleep."

Lou lowered her voice. "That's okay. I just called to tell you that a certain urine specimen was negative for any STD."

Red pulled out her notebook and flipped back a few pages to make a note under Jimmy Crea. *Urine spec neg for sexually transmitted disease.*

"So why the blood?"

"Well, Doc also noted no known injury, if that helps."

Blood in the urine triggered a memory. For a millisecond, a snapshot of Lad's face flashed behind her eyes. She blinked, and it disappeared. After she hung up the phone, she looked down at her notes while her thoughts strayed to Lad.

She remembered that at fourteen, struggling to fit in, he'd signed up for junior varsity wrestling. He proudly showed off his wrestling uniform to Mom and Dad. Red remembered how skinny he looked in the singlet. Through January and February, Lad had lifted weights for hours in the basement, using a crude weight set cast off by the school.

One day, Red had walked into the bathroom after Lad had used it. He'd forgotten to flush the toilet. The water in the bowl had been tinged pink. When she'd confronted him, he'd shrugged and said, "Weight lifters and wrestlers pee blood all the time, sis."

Lad's career as a junior varsity wrestler had been cut short when he abruptly skidded into a deep darkness. The weight set had collected dust in the basement until the auction after her mother's death.

The ringing phone pulled Red out of her musings.

"Red, it's Scotty. You need to come down to the Town Talk. Georgia and I have some new theories. Come and have brunch with us." She paused, lowering her voice. "I bought some cinnamon rolls from the bakery for the occasion."

Red chuckled. "What happened to your own homemade low-fat granola muffins?" She had been suggesting for five years that Scotty contract with the bakery. So far, Scotty insisted that she could bake her own, thank you.

Scotty cleared her throat. "I, ah, accidentally dumped the whole bottle of vanilla in the dough."

"Hmmm. Tasty. I'll be there in a few minutes. Could you send out for a decent cup of coffee, too?"

24

CRYPTIC NOTES

The Town Talk was unusually quiet for a late Saturday morning. The decor inside the café had not changed from the earth-tone colors of the seventies. All the tabletops were done in orange Formica. Light yellow walls offset the dark brown wood-paneled wainscoting. The café was filled with the warm, humid smells of eggs, toast, and fried bacon.

Scotty beckoned her to the back table. Georgia sat next to her, wearing a T-shirt that said, "Behind every successful woman is herself."

Red pulled up a chair as Scotty set a steaming mug of coffee in front of her. It tasted weak and slightly metallic, forcing Red to doctor it with cream and sugar.

"Well," she said, looking at the sparse crowd. "They've finally tired of the bad food."

Scotty shook her head. "Nope. They're sticking close to home. Too many murders in Pearsal County."

Absently, Red stared at a framed Georgia O'Keeffe poster hanging on the back wall. The red petals of a flower opened sensuously against the green-leaf background. "Wonder when they'll want my head on a stick?"

Scotty grinned. "Monday. It's no good getting riled up on a weekend."

Red sipped at her coffee. "So, you two think you are masters of the criminal element. What are your theories?"

Leaning over the table toward Red, Georgia lowered her voice. "I've been studying Joanie Crea's date book. I think I found an interesting pattern."

Red frowned. She'd been over the date book twice and hadn't seen anything unusual. "What did you find?"

Georgia pulled the date book out of her bag, opening it to January. "See here? Agatha Fuller?" She pointed to an entry. The penciled mark beside Agatha was a *pp*.

"Okay? Remind me what *pp* means?" Red took a slow sip of the murky coffee.

"Private pay. Agatha was paying for nurse's aide service from the county out of her own pocket."

"And?"

Georgia leafed through the book until she reached May 21st. "See, Joanie made another visit to her on the twenty-first. Notice she didn't make any notation about payment. I checked back in the book. As I told you before, Joanie was meticulous and always made payment notation."

Red looked at Georgia with a puzzled expression. "Maybe I'm dense, but I don't understand what you are getting at."

A smile swept across Georgia's face. Scotty joined her. "Just this—I checked all the *pp* notations in her book. Beginning after May twenty-first, Joanie made visits to every one of those people."

The door to the café swung open. A middle-aged man with a belly that hung precariously over his blue jeans walked in accompanied by a woman who looked like she wore a barrel under her polyester shorts and T-shirt. They sat down at the table by the door.

Scotty glanced up. "Ah, Mr. and Mrs. High Cholesterol Heart Attack in Waiting. Excuse me, I'll be back as soon as I take their order for bacon, eggs, sausage, fried potatoes, and diet Pepsi."

Red wrinkled her brow, looking at Georgia. "I still don't understand."

Georgia sat back in her chair with her arms folded. "I checked the files in the public health nursing office. Joanie closed the case on Agatha in mid-March. She wasn't her patient anymore. Neither were four other *pp* patients she saw in late May, June, and July."

The Pines Were Watching

A pan clanged in the kitchen as the sound of frying sausage filled the still quiet café.

"You think these patients have something to do with the disappearance of Joanie's money?"

Georgia nodded. "My nursing intuition tells me it's all related."

"They were blackmailing Joanie?"

Scotty reappeared from the kitchen with two steaming plates of food. She set them down in front of the couple by the door with a loud admonishment. "Karl, next time, why don't the two of you order the oatmeal? It's good for you."

Karl and his wife smiled tolerantly at Scotty. "Next time, for sure."

When she returned, Scotty looked at Red with raised eyebrows. "Pretty good sleuthing, huh?"

"I don't know. Why don't you give me a list of patients, and I'll have someone check it out. I'm having a hard time making a connection. I know Agatha Fuller did not strangle Joanie. She's nearly a hundred years old and doesn't weigh more than ninety-five pounds. Plus, she uses a walker to get around."

The three sat in silence for a few minutes. Scotty broke it by saying, "Okay, so you're not convinced that we've stumbled onto something yet. However, I have another idea."

Red pressed her lips together in a tight line before speaking. "Oh boy, I can't wait. What?"

"Well," Scotty looked smug, "what if we investigate this from a different angle."

"Oh? Who's 'we'?"

Scotty waved the remark away. "Think about it, Red." Her eyes danced. "Someone now has a pile of new money. What was in that account? Fifty thousand dollars?"

Red stirred more cream into the coffee but said nothing.

"Here's the thing." Georgia put a thick slab of butter on her cinnamon roll. "I've spent a certain amount of my life dealing with people. The killer is damn arrogant—and too confident. The money is a trophy for his work. He'll want to show it off."

Scotty interrupted. "All we have to do is find out who has been spending a lot of money around town lately."

"Or," Georgia added, "who has recently gotten out of money trouble."

Red's voice was tight when she spoke. "I don't know. If someone had a secret debt, how would anyone know it had been paid off? Remember the school secretary down south who embezzled all the money from the school district to pay off her gambling debts? No one even suspected she had a problem with the casinos."

Scotty reached across the table and squeezed Red's wrist. "Gambling, that's a great idea. I have some sources up at the casino. I can find out if any locals have been throwing money around lately." She beamed at Georgia. "You chat with the cronies from the chamber of commerce, and I'll call a few people from the Golden Deer Casino."

Red pushed her chair back and regarded the two women with growing apprehension. "I don't think it would be a good idea."

They smiled back at her in unison. Then Georgia's expression turned serious. "Red, we aren't going to do anything stupid—just put a few feelers out. People talk to us who would be afraid to talk to someone official."

"Besides," Scotty joined in, "it's a free country. You can't stop us from asking questions."

"Humph, next thing you know, you two will be doing a true crime podcast." Red tried to fix a glare at them, but a smile crept across her lips.

When she walked out of the restaurant, Georgia and Scotty were deep in conversation, much to the irritation of one of the customers. As the door closed behind her, she heard a low grumble from the booth by the window. "Don't we get a refill on the coffee around here?"

Not if you're lucky, she thought.

25

THE RED PICKUP

The courthouse was Saturday-afternoon quiet despite the activities of last night. Red's stomach roiled, and she felt a weight that was not related to the cinnamon rolls. Two women were now dead in her county. Both strangled and somehow connected by a house key and a scrap of paper.

"Boy," Billie sat at his computer. "I expected a lot of calls today about the Henley woman—like when Mrs. Crea was found. But all I've gotten is a dog-barking call and a nine-one-one for chest pains."

"I had a few on the tipline this morning but nothing useful."

Billie nodded. "Same people who always call it—right?"

As she sat at her desk with her notepad in front of her, she thought about the response to Arlis Henley's death. She guessed that for the most part, the citizens of Pearsal County probably felt that Arlis got what she deserved.

"No one," Red said out loud, "deserves to be murdered."

Billie buzzed her as she was jotting a new list of people to talk to. Derek Grandgeorge remained at the top. She reached over to the computer and replayed the tipline message on him. Something about it bothered her. Either it was the tone, the effort to disguise the voice, or maybe a certain urgency in it. Whatever the case, she needed to talk with Grandgeorge again.

"Someone is here to see you. He says it can't wait." Billie's voice oozed with sarcasm.

Red walked out to the dispatch area to find a man standing with his thumbs hooked over the pockets of his dirty jeans. He wore a graying T-shirt that said in faded red letters, *Shit Happens*.

"Well, Bud Campbell, I'm surprised to see you here on a Saturday afternoon." Red stood so close to the man that he backed away just a bit. She noted his unwashed odor.

Bud's thinning dishwater-blond hair rested on his shoulders in greasy clumps. Though he was in his late twenties, he already looked like he had lived too long. Will used to say that the Campbells were good examples of why cousins shouldn't marry. Red couldn't argue with his logic.

Bud spent a few days every year in her jail, usually for drunk driving or passing bad checks. He had an ingratiating puppy dog manner, which always irritated the hell out of her.

She sat down at her desk, motioning Bud to take a chair. An oily, acrid smell permeated the room. "What brings you here?"

He scratched his ear. "I can't stay long. Gotta go soon." He glanced back at the door. "My ride is coming back in a half an hour." His voice had a childish whine to it. "You know I can't drive now. Gotta count on my brother for everything."

Bud's brother was one conviction away from losing his license, too. Then they'd both whine at her. Red said nothing but kept a steady gaze on Bud.

He fidgeted, shifting his eyes from his feet to Red and back to his feet. "Well, if I told you something would you put in a good word for me with the judge? I could get off probation earlier if you put in a good word."

Red sighed heavily. "Bud, I haven't got a good word for you. Last time you were out driving drunk, you killed a jogger's dog and almost took her out too."

Bud fidgeted some more. "It wasn't my fault. I was trying to miss the dog. I told you that before. Besides, I haven't had a drink in two weeks. I'm done with that, you know."

Red leaned back in her chair and folded her arms. She only struck this quasi-masculine pose with people like Bud.

The Pines Were Watching 135

"Give me the story, Bud. Otherwise, I can haul your ass in for violating your probation. I know you've been out drinking in the last week."

"Shit."

Red stared him down.

"Okay, okay. You know the road that goes out by my place ends at Arlis's trailer?"

Red nodded. Bud lived in the old family homestead on the same dirt road as the Henley trailer. Most of the windows in the house had been boarded up long ago, and the yard was strewn with old junk cars.

"Well, last Tuesday, I was working on my car in the front yard. I saw a pickup go by. It was red, and the springs on it are just about shot. Made noise—you know?"

"And?"

"I only saw one other car go out there. She usually had two or three people out there every night when she wasn't working at the casino." He looked up at Red with a you-know-what-I'm-talking-about grin.

Red sat up straight and unfolded her arms. "Bud, Jason saw you at Cuttery's on Tuesday night. How would you know?"

Bud squirmed in his chair. "I know Grandgeorge was there. That's for sure. Everyone knows his pickup."

Red looked up at the ceiling of her office, noticing for the first time the dangling gray threads from the web of a long-dead spider. "Tell me about the other car."

Bud squinted at his hands. "Nothing much to tell. A little white car, I think."

"When did you see it?"

"Middle of the night, maybe."

"Could you see whose car it was?"

"Naw. It was going pretty fast."

"How long was it there?"

Bud shrugged.

Red placed her feet firmly on the floor and pushed herself up. "Okay, Bud. I might have some other questions for you. I'll mention to the county attorney that you volunteered this information. It's up to him and the judge to decide if they want to be nice to you."

After Bud walked out, Red pulled up her notes on the computer. Joanie drove a white Ford Escort. If Bud saw her car, someone else was driving it. And what the hell was Derek Grandgeorge doing at Arlis Henley's?

26

A HIGH ROLLER

Jason walked into Red's office. His white shirt was drenched with sweat and his face reddened from searching the woods around Fire Tower Road.

"Anything?" Red took a bottled water out of her desk drawer and handed it to him.

"We found a lot more empty beer cans, lots of cigarette butts, and a bong. Does that help?" He grinned. "Plus a couple of used condoms."

She pointed to the plastic evidence bag with the scrap of paper in it. "Nothing to match this?"

Jason drank from the bottle, stopping only to wipe his brow. "Sorry."

"I checked with Petey Townsend and his friends. No one knew anything about the paper. Said it wasn't theirs." Red knew before she'd called the boy that the paper didn't belong to them. But she wanted Waltz to know she'd done her follow-up. Internally she berated herself for being so concerned about what Waltz thought.

Jason set the empty water bottle on the desk before speaking. "Not a surprise. What kid these days uses pencil and paper? It's all on their phones."

"Good point. Take a break at your desk to cool down. I'd like you to call a few people who left 'anonymous' tips. If they ask you how I knew they called, just tell them their sheriff is psychic and would they please identify themselves next time."

Jason chuckled as he walked out the door, his equipment jangling on his belt.

Next, she talked with the foster mother taking care of Tommy. "Hi, Debbi. Red Hammergren here. How is our boy doing?"

Debbi had the low growl of someone who had a twenty-year, three-pack-a-day smoking habit. She and her husband had been taking in foster children for the last fifteen years. Of the sixty or so kids that had passed through their home, they'd adopted seven. To Red, the Tafts were near the top of her Good People list.

"He's pretty quiet." Debbi's voice was muffled as she called to someone, "Hey, out of the cookie dough." When she came back, she said, "Sorry. I've got a little one who has the devil in her."

"Sounds like Tommy is taking it kind of hard. I'm sure he's feeling like somehow this was all his fault. Little kids do."

Debbi coughed, cleared her throat, and replied, "You know, that's exactly what Jimmy Crea said this morning when he was over here."

Red gripped the phone a little bit harder. "Jimmy talked to Tommy?"

"He's got that magic touch. At least with the other kids here. Some guys do."

Red willed her grip on the phone to relax. "Did you call him over?"

"No. He came on his own. Said Tommy was in his youth group at church, and he wanted to be helpful."

Red felt the heat rise up her neck. She had specifically told Jimmy not to get involved. Why had he ignored her? She played with a pencil, rolling it back and forth across her desktop. "Did Tommy talk to him?"

"No. As far as I could see, he didn't say a word."

"What's Tommy doing now?"

"That's just it. He's not doing anything. He won't talk. He's not eating. Right now he's sitting in front of the computer playing some game over and over." Her voice dropped to a whisper. "My heart tells me that he's scared."

Red picked up the pencil. "What do you mean?"

"I walked over to him a little while ago and just touched him on the

The Pines Were Watching 139

shoulder. He jumped. I could tell he was close to tears, but he wouldn't talk to me."

"I wonder if he knows something about his mother that he isn't telling," Red said, more to herself than to Debbi. "Maybe I should stop by this afternoon and talk with him."

Debbi kept her husky voice to a whisper. "Could it wait until tomorrow? The kid's had enough for now."

Red agreed to call back in the morning and set up a time to meet with Tommy.

Billie ambled in with a cup of coffee.

"You look beat," he said, setting it down in front of her. Red nodded but made no eye contact, hoping he'd go away.

Billie hung by the front of her desk until she finally said, "Did you have something else to say?"

"Well," he looked down at his scuffed shoes, "Matt called a few minutes ago. He sprained his wrist last night playing softball. He thinks he can still patrol tonight, but he was hoping you could get a replacement."

Red closed her eyes and grimaced. Twenty-four-hour staffing was one of the biggest headaches of running her department. Part of her goal in working with the other county sheriffs on the federal grant was to investigate sharing some of the night duty responsibilities for the tri-county area. She'd put that plan on the back burner Tuesday when Joanie Crea had turned up dead. As Will had told her in the days when he was still lucid, "Part of being a sheriff is prioritizing. You have to decide the difference between the need to do, nice to do, and nuts to do."

Right now, staffing the night patrol was in the category of "need," collaborating on a federal grant was under "nice," and just about anything else could be called "nuts."

She looked at Billie with a shrug. "There is no one else. Call him and let him know that I'll pick up his shift tonight."

At other times, Red would have welcomed the solitude of patrolling the northern part of the county. Not today. As she watched Billie walk out the door, she was tempted to shout, "And what other goddamn thing needs to happen now?"

Her phone rang.

"Red, it's Scotty, your ace financial detective." She sounded excited.

"Didn't I leave you to serving food to your poor customers?"

"They can wait. I've dug up a puzzling piece of evidence for you."

Red found herself smiling. "Let me guess. Someone confessed to the crime in exchange for not having to clean his plate."

"Oh, you are so cruel." She paused. "I'm serious. This is big."

"Okay, I'm listening." In the background, Red heard the low roar of voices and the tinkle of silverware against plates, indicating a number of customers at the café.

Scotty's voice dropped. "I can't talk here. Can you stop by Georgia's in an hour?"

Red agreed, muttering as she hung up the phone, "This better be worth it. I'm a busy woman."

A haziness hung in the air as Red walked down the street to Georgia's. The clerk from the drugstore waved at her as she passed. She made a note to stop in on her way back to the courthouse to buy another bottle of ibuprofen. A headache lurked just behind her eyes. She made a second note to talk with the pharmacist about how much of the drug she could take in a day. The empty bottles were accumulating in her recycling basket at home.

The air in the antiques store was warmer than the air outside. By the time she reached the back room, Red's polyester-blend short-sleeved shirt clung to her damp back.

Scotty sat at the table with an animated expression, drinking a beer. She held it up to Red. "Like a sip?"

Red shook her head. "Sorry. Tempting, but I'm on duty. Where's Georgia?"

"Out making some kind of a buy. I think she found another of those decoys."

"And she left her shop open?"

Scotty shrugged. "It's a small town."

"Where women are being murdered," Red quickly interjected.

They sat in silence for a moment, then Scotty put the drink down, her eyes sparkling with excitement.

The Pines Were Watching 141

"I called my source at the casino and told him we were looking for someone local who might be high-rolling. At first, no one came to mind. Then he said some big chunks of money had been dropped by a guy from the cities a couple of weeks ago—like ten grand in one sitting at a blackjack table."

"Phew, that's a lot of money to throw away."

Scotty smiled, the lazy light from the back window highlighting her cheekbones. Scotty, in her rough way, was a very beautiful woman. "By the expression on your face, Red, I'd say you're about to tell me that gambling is a sin."

Red shrugged. "Maybe not a sin, but certainly a waste."

Scotty laughed. "Interesting comment from a charter member of the poker club."

"Maybe." Red waved a hand in dismissal. "But we're not losing our life savings by mindlessly plunking coins into a machine."

"Mindless." Scotty repeated the word. "I've heard that said before. Jimmy Crea and three of the downtown boys were having lunch one day when they got into a pretty interesting discussion about gambling. The downtown boys were looking at it in terms of the money a little casino in Pearsal County might bring in."

Red groaned.

"Jimmy, on the other hand, called gambling a mindless waste of time and money."

"I don't find that surprising. Especially since he's an accountant and understands money."

"No." Scotty shook her head. "I didn't either. What surprised me was the passion of his reaction. Jimmy actually stood up as he spoke. Suddenly the whole Town Talk was getting a sermon. He said something like, 'Watch the hands of the dealer, quick, inviting, seductive.' I thought about me trying to deal a poker hand, the cards flying all over the table, and I almost laughed."

She chuckled, a low rumble in her throat. "The rest of my customers didn't see the humor, though. Most of them watched him like he was God in the flesh. They applauded, for Pete's sake."

"Apparently he didn't convert you, though," Red remarked.

"Naw. But it was scary, how easy it was to listen to him."

"Jimmy doesn't strike me as a passionate orator."

"Me neither, but there was something mesmerizing about him."

Red eyed Scotty's bottle of beer with longing, remembering the night of patrol ahead of her. "I'll bet he and Joanie didn't spend much time at the Golden Deer." Inwardly she winced as she thought of the lifeless body in the Grandgeorge summerhouse. "I've got a long night ahead of me. What 'evidence' did you find?"

Scotty lifted the beer and drained it, setting it down with a flourish, reminiscent of high school drama class. She leaned forward across the table and said, "It's big, Red." She paused dramatically. "My contact at the casino did some checking. That high roller from the cities called himself Clyde."

Red stared at her. "Clyde?"

Scotty folded her arms emphatically. "Maybe he's the long-lost brother."

27

THE GRAVE

The Grandgeorge Place stood shabby and neglected in the hazy afternoon sun. The turnaround in front of the house was empty, Derek's pickup nowhere in sight.

Red stepped out into the heat, feeling its heaviness press into her. She stood listening for a moment by the rotting porch step. A very slight breeze whispered through the tall, uncut grass. She closed her eyes. For a second, she felt surrounded by an overwhelming emptiness, as if this house held nothing. It passed quickly, as a crow cackled loudly from the porch roof.

After knocking and calling for five minutes, Red decided to try the back door. Inside, she heard the faint sound of footsteps. Turning to the door, she knocked again.

"Hello? It's Sheriff Hammergren."

Caddie Grandgeorge stood with her mouth slack and her eyes puffy with sleep. She wore a large black T-shirt over a pair of frayed cutoff jeans. Her legs were pale but muscular.

Red watched her blink her eyes and push a wad of hair off her fore-head. The girl had all the features of her mother, a body softness that could easily turn to fat. Her eyes were small and brown with eyebrows that almost met over the bridge of her nose. Red saw something familiar in the set of her mouth but couldn't put her finger on it.

"Yes?" Caddie asked, a note of hesitation in her voice. The purplish-red polish on her fingernails was chipped. Black mascara gummed her eyelashes.

"I'm looking for Derek."

Caddie shook her head. "He's not here," she said cautiously.

"When will he be back?"

"Dunno. Sometimes he goes for days." She looked at her bare feet, breathing through her mouth. She smelled of cigarette smoke.

For a second, Red again saw a spark of something familiar in Caddie's face. She guessed that the mascara and the nail polish and the sullenness in her voice covered a deep unhappiness. She'd seen it before in teenage girls in Pearsal County—a sense of being forever trapped in rural Minnesota. Many of them did eventually become walled in by single parenthood and no skills—Arlis Henley was a prime example.

Before the family planning clinic had been established, she had talked with a local minister about the high rate of teen pregnancy in the county. He'd said to her with wisdom well beyond his divinity school youth, "They don't know what else to do, so they get pregnant. For a lot of girls, this is a community without hope." She was glad the local chamber of commerce hadn't heard his comments.

Fortunately, the girls in the county now had the Church.

From inside the house, she heard the soft, warbling voice of Rebecca Grandgeorge. "Clyde, honey. Could you bring me a nice glass of mint tea?"

Caddie turned her head to the voice, then back to Red. "My grandma needs me. I don't know where Uncle Derek is."

"One question before you see to your grandma." Red stood without moving. "She's calling for Clyde. Have you seen him lately?"

The girl's mouth dropped open into a surprised O. Again, she looked down at her feet, kicking away a dust ball. "I think, sometimes, that he's watching me." Her voice held a slight tremor.

"Has he been here?"

"No!" she said emphatically. "No." The door closed with a loud click.

Red walked around to the back of the house. The tall grass remained trampled from Tuesday, when Joanie's body had been discovered. Red easily found the path that led to the summerhouse.

The Pines Were Watching 145

As she moved through the sulky heat toward the building, sweat formed on her forehead. She stopped for a moment to listen to the sounds of the woods. Her ears filled with the buzz of insects, the slight whoosh of the breeze through the pines and the cawing of the crows. Closing her eyes, she took a deep breath and let it out slowly. In the heat of the afternoon, goose bumps grew on her arms as she thought about the death in the summerhouse. Once again, she wondered, why here? Why the nurse?

At the summerhouse, she again closed her eyes and took in the deep sounds of the forest. Nothing came to her. The yellow police tape was still up. Red walked as far as the doorway and peered in. As when she'd first viewed the body, she was struck by the neatness of the interior. An oak bookcase and an Adirondack chair sat in one corner. Several notebooks were stacked on the shelf of the bookcase. One of them had a spiral binding. It reminded her of the scraps of paper she'd found. She was about to enter the building to look at it when Caddie approached.

"Can I go in there yet?"

Red turned to her. "I'll check with the forensic staff and let you know. Is there something you want?"

Caddie stared at her feet, bare except for a pair of flip-flops. "Ah, no. I guess not."

They stood quietly, as if to show respect for what had occurred in the building. Caddie let out a little squeaking noise. Tears filled her eyes. "I...I should get back to Gramma Rebecca. Mom doesn't like me to be out of the house—especially now."

Underneath the mascara and sullenness, the girl looked almost child-like. Red wanted to hug her and tell her everything would be all right. Instead, she nodded as Caddie turned back.

She decided to stay out of the building until Waltz gave the all clear.

Red walked the perimeter of the little building, making wider and wider circles into the woods. Carefully she studied the ground.

She found the footprints twenty-five feet from the summerhouse, in the soft, mossy floor of the forest.

"My God," she said out loud. "Why didn't we pick these up before?"

The footprints came from deep in the forest in the direction of the bottom land that bordered County Road 6. She followed the prints until her feet sank into the marshy land and the footprints disappeared.

Closing her eyes, she pictured a map of the area. It was feasible but not likely that someone could carry or drag a body from the road. It would take extreme effort. "Is this how he got her to the summerhouse?" Red whistled, wondering at the strength the killer had to have had to carry a body through such soft, wet ground. "It would have to be someone who knew these woods."

Behind her, the crows cawed, a cacophony of irritated voices.

Back in her car, she drove slowly along County Road 6. The grass grew tall and straight in the ditch, and it looked like it had not been cut by the county road crew in at least two weeks. After her third pass up and down the stretch of road bordering the Grandgeorge property, Red decided to call it quits. She saw no evidence of a car having pulled off the road.

As she drove the stretch one more time, passing St. Joseph's Cemetery, a glimmer of sunlight reflecting off a stone caught her attention. She pulled into the cemetery. It had an air of neglect. Most of the people buried there no longer had families in the area. Some of the markers were tilted and covered with moss. Once a year, the county sent a crew to mow, but otherwise, the burial ground was slowly going back to nature.

It reminded her of Will's request before he died. "Don't fill me with chemicals and try to make me look like I'm still alive. Let me become part of the earth." Few of her constituents besides her poker club knew that Will rested under an old tree on their wooded acres north of Hammer Lake. As she surveyed the forgotten place, she was momentarily overcome with grief.

Walking through the gravestones, she approached the one that had caught her attention. The granite stone was polished and relatively new with the Grandgeorge name etched into it. The grass around the edges of the monument was brown and stunted. An empty urn leaned against the stone. This was the site where the patriarch, Carl, had been buried. The urn seemed to symbolize what he'd left behind. She wondered if anyone cared for this grave.

Her radio crackled to life as she studied the tombstone.

The Pines Were Watching 147

"Sheriff? Trouble at Eddie's on Hammer Lake. Someone just called in. Said it was a fight."

"I'm near the Grandgeorge Place. On my way." The crow landed on a nearby branch as she hurried to her car.

28

JUST KIDS

Red felt a prickling of energy surge through her. She prayed the fight involved fists and not guns or knives. She didn't need a shooting or stabbing to go with the two murders on her hands.

Eddie's Resort stood on the eastern edge of Hammer Lake, about fifteen miles north of town. Her car spit dust and gravel as she cut across a little township road to the highway. She was sorry she hadn't taken the cruiser to the Grandgeorge Place. At least she'd have all the bells and whistles.

Fifteen minutes later, she approached the roadhouse. Cars jammed the small gravel lot and spilled over into the tall grass and weeds on the north end of the lot. A yellow portable rent-a-sign announced, "Jim Newton and His Cowboys, Sat. Nite." In smaller letters, "Pull Tabs."

Jim Newton didn't usually attract a rowdy crowd. His fans were the middle-aged couples who were getting away from their kids for a few beers and a Saturday night dance.

Red pulled in front of the door. People stood at the entrance, staring at her as she approached. Several of them held plastic cups of beer.

"Sheriff's here!" someone shouted.

Mac Morris, the bar owner, lumbered up to the car. He was a muscular man who wore a pale blue T-shirt stretched over a growing belly. Red was not fond of Mac for several reasons. For one, he lived on the edge of the law.

She suspected that he made money on the side with a high school sports gambling business and high-stakes poker in the back room. In the winter, he rented out furnished fish houses and a deluxe trailer that was rumored to be a party place for wealthy men from the Twin Cities. It was also rumored Mac brought in girls of questionable age for the parties. Red had yet to catch him for it.

Even worse for Red's budget, a lot of public safety dollars went into cleaning up the brawls in his establishment. But mostly, she detested him because he had an attitude that said, "I'm above the law." She itched for an excuse to prove him otherwise.

"What have we got?" Red grabbed her flashlight as she stepped out of the car.

"It's all worked out. No need for the law, Sheriff." Mac grinned at her. "Just a little dustup with Wayne, that's all."

Wayne Crocker was Mac's bartender. He was a wiry little man with a mean streak and a quick temper. Red had heard that Mac kept him on because he was related to his wife. Red figured he kept him on because Mac was too much of a coward to fire him. Several years ago, Red had been the first one to see what Wayne had done to his then wife. She never forgot the black and swollen eyes and look of fear on her face.

"Let's try this again, Mac." Red's jaw clenched as she spoke. "What have we got here?"

"A little shoving between a couple of the boys. They shook hands and made up. Someone got excited and called it in. I tried to cancel the call."

His eyes shifted from Red to a spot just beyond her, then back again. Red studied him for a moment. He wasn't a good liar. "Was Wayne involved?"

"He keeps things calm."

She rested her hand lightly on the Sig Sauer on her hip. "Let's have a chat with him and make sure everyone is happy."

Mac turned and yelled into the bar, "Hey, Wayne. Sheriff's here."

Wayne came out, wiping his hands on a towel. He reminded Red of a bulldog ready to snap at her. "Yeah, what do you want?"

"I hear there was a little argument. I'd like to talk with the people involved to make sure no one got hurt."

When he spoke, his lips hardly moved. "No problem. All taken care of."

"Okay, then you won't mind if I talk with a few of the customers."

Mac cleared his throat, a worried expression on his face. "Hate to have you disturb them."

Red took a step toward the door, then stopped. Above the muffled *thump, thump* from the jukebox inside, she thought she heard a whimpering noise. It came from the south side of the building.

"You two." She pointed at them. "You come with me. The rest go back inside." Her voice had a hard edge to it that Red felt with every molecule in her body. She wanted nothing more than to smash her flashlight into Wayne's nasty little face.

The crowd began to file back into the bar.

"Come on." She headed toward the noise. She realized immediately that this was a dumb move on her part. Away from the crowd, Wayne might decide to defend his honor or whatever it was that kept him so angry. She felt it as she led them to the corner of the building. Red turned to Wayne.

"You'd better dial it down. I can tell you want to hit someone."

"Fuckin' dyke," he growled.

Red strode over to him, gripping the flashlight so hard her hand ached. She stopped just short of his face. Her heart pounded. "I can have you down on the gravel in two seconds flat. You know that. You touch me and you'll never work another bar again as long as you live." Her teeth were clenched hard enough to send a sharp pain up the side of her face.

A tiny voice in Red's head whispered, *He might look like a banty rooster, but he's the one who could have you down in two seconds flat. What are you doing? Get some backup.*

Mac stood with his mouth hanging open.

Ah yes, she thought. *Law enforcement is the art of negotiation, isn't it?*

Around the corner, shadows engulfed the kitchen side of the bar. A weak yellow light slipped through the greasy screen of the side door. The whimpering became a soft crying. A tiny female voice pleaded, "Please don't be dead. Please don't be dead."

Red flipped on her flashlight. She pushed at Wayne with the knuckles of her hand digging into the small of his back. She shoved him to a litter-infested spot of weeds about ten feet beyond the dumpster. In the early

The Pines Were Watching 151

evening light, she saw a skinny girl with dull pink hair cradling an equally skinny boy in her lap. Her T-shirt and raggedy shorts were covered with blood.

"What happened here?" Red called out, making sure she still had her knuckles firmly in Wayne's back. If he made a move, she'd whack him with the flashlight.

The girl blinked at the three of them with fear in her eyes. Her voice was small and scared. "He hurt my friend." A thin finger pointed shakily at Wayne.

His muscles tightened. With speed and strength she didn't know she possessed, Red whipped out the handcuffs and ripped his arms behind him. He jerked in surprise. Once cuffed, she hissed, "Down, get down on the ground. And don't move." She shoved him so hard he stumbled, then knelt.

"If you move, I'll shoot you—with pleasure."

She ran over to the girl. "It's okay. I'm the sheriff. What have we got here?"

"He...he hurt my friend!" The girl burst out in tears.

Red knelt by the boy, making sure that Wayne stayed in her line of vision. The boy's face was covered with blood that bubbled from his smashed nose. His jet-black hair was matted with more blood. Red quickly found a carotid pulse. It was strong and steady.

"He's okay. Looks like a broken nose."

"He ripped out Josh's nose ring and hit him and kicked him. We just wanted to buy some chips and stuff. Why did he do it?"

Because the nasty little bartender was an asshole. Red touched the girl on the shoulder. "Did anyone see this?"

She nodded. "Some men in the back room. They laughed."

Red pulled out her radio and called to dispatch an ambulance. She took the handkerchief out of her back pocket and showed the girl how to hold it over the bleeding nose. "We won't move him until the ambulance comes."

Red glared at Mac. "You tried to cover this up?"

Mac held his hands up as if she'd pointed a gun at him. "Wayne said he was stealing from the bar and he needed a lesson."

Red stooped beside Wayne. "Is that true?"

"Little snot with rings in his nose. What did he expect?"

"Maybe a little decency." Red itched to kick him. "Mac, I think you're going to need to hire a new bartender."

Mac's face registered relief. He could get rid of Wayne and blame it on Red. Ah, well.

Several bar patrons came timidly around the corner. One of them, a woman in tight blue jeans, walked over to the girl and put her arm around her shoulders. "It's okay, honey. We got a great hospital. They'll take care of your friend." She turned to Mac. "This kid is the same age as my Johnny. I hope they sue the pants off you."

"Hey," Mac replied. "He was stealing."

"Prove it!" she snapped back at him.

Mac had some mending to do in the community. Red worked to keep her expression neutral despite the urge to say, "Amen."

Two hours later, with Wayne locked up, Red sat in the hospital waiting area. The adrenaline of the moment had worn off. She felt shaky and exhausted. Jason, off duty and in blue jeans, sat across from her.

"Pretty gutsy, taking on that jerk alone."

Red had to agree. "Pretty stupid, actually. Some people just push my buttons. I lost my temper."

"So can we pull Mac's liquor license this time?"

"Doubtful. Mac didn't beat the kid up, his employee did."

A few minutes later, a nurse ushered in the pink-haired girl. She wore scrubs that made her look even younger.

"Your parents are on their way, Jennifer," Red said.

She nodded, close to tears.

"We have a few questions for you. If you'd like, we can wait until your parents come."

She shook her head. "I...I want to tell you what happened. Joshie wasn't stealing. He was going to pay..."

She described stopping at the bar to get some chips and snacks and how everyone stared at them and the bartender harassed them. Red easily pictured the situation.

"We were scared, so we decided to leave. Except Joshie was holding a bag of chips and that guy followed us out."

The Pines Were Watching 153

"How did you end up at Eddie's?"

"Josh's grandparents have a cabin up here."

"But they didn't know you were using it, did they?"

"No," she said in a tiny voice.

"Are you runaways?"

Jennifer's eyes grew wide. They were a deep, soft brown, like a teddy bear. "Oh no. We're going back to the Arts High School this fall. We wanted to travel a little before school, you know?"

"Uh-huh."

"We didn't think anyone would hurt us. Sometimes people would yell. But we didn't think anyone would hurt us."

Red folded her hands. "This isn't the city. Conformity holds a community like this together. People can be very intolerant." *And people who do not conform keep quiet about it*, she added to herself.

The girl's face reddened. "That's kind of what that weird guy at the park said."

Red studied the girl. "What guy?"

"The guy we saw in that little park—you know, where there used to be Indian mounds. We were sitting on the grass a couple of nights ago, looking at the stars, when he kind of walked up on us from down by the swamp. Really scared me. I jumped."

"Tell me more about him."

Jennifer wiggled in the chair. "Oh, I don't know. He kind of swayed when he walked, like he was drunk. But he didn't sound drunk. He said, 'Careful around here. You go out of bounds and bad things will happen.' It was real creepy."

"What did he look like? Short? Tall? Young? Old?"

The girl bit her lower lip. "Well, it was dark, and we didn't get too close to him. He wore one of those jock jackets. It was pretty raggy-looking. And his pants were wet and muddy up to the knees. Like he'd walked through a swamp or something."

"Did you notice anything else?" Red kept her voice calm and even. She didn't want to scare her.

Furrowing her brow, Jennifer looked up at the ceiling. "I can't think of anything..." Her face relaxed. "Oh, now I know what it was that made him even weirder—I think he was looking for something."

Red slowly let her breath out. "In the dark?"

"We decided he was maybe homeless or something and was going through the trash. You know, like how people go through the garbage looking for food and stuff to sell?"

Red tried to picture the two teenagers out in the dark with a stranger coming up from the swamp. For an instant, she saw Joanie's body as it lay shoeless on the bed in the summerhouse.

"What happened to the man after he talked to you?"

She shrugged. "We were kind of scared. You know, it's pretty creepy to have someone come out of nowhere. He said he had to go and walked over to a bunch of trees. After that, we didn't see him again."

Red let silence fill the room. Gently she said, "Close your eyes, Jennifer, and think back. Did you notice anything else?"

Jennifer closed her eyes and again wrinkled her brow. When she opened them, she blinked several times as she said, "I can't think of anything—except the front of the jacket had some kind of lettering on it. You know, kind of over the pocket." She pointed to the pocket of her scrubs.

"Do you know what the letters spelled?"

She shook her head. "Once we couldn't see him anymore, we got up and ran almost all the way back to the cabin. It was kinda like being in a movie, you know? We kept looking back to see if he was following us."

Red nodded.

The nurse came out and said they could talk with Josh now that the doctor was done.

He lay propped up on a gurney, pale with wide eyes, when Red walked in.

"Hi, Josh. You've had quite a night."

"Are you going to tell my parents?"

Red pulled up a chair. "They are on their way. You'll need to talk with them."

She went over what Jennifer had said, and his story matched. "I...I wasn't trying to steal. I just got scared, that's all."

"I get it."

"Am I in trouble?"

The Pines Were Watching 155

She smiled at him. "Probably with your parents but not with me. But I do have some questions for you about something else."

After she related what Jennifer had said about the creepy guy at the park, she asked him if he remembered anything else.

Josh closed his eyes for a moment. "It was dark, but I think the jacket was green."

"Are you sure?"

He slowly shook his head. "No, I'm not positive, but I know he smelled."

"Smelled?"

"Like perfume or something. It was weird, because he looked like those homeless guys you see sometimes but you don't think of them as smelling good. You know?"

A smelly man in a green jacket looking for something in the dark. Was any of this true?

29

THE MYSTERY MAN

Red checked her watch. It was now well past eleven on a Saturday night. Before she headed back on the road for the night patrol, she listened to her voicemail messages. She deleted seven, including one from Harv Smith asking for an update on the investigation. He could keep calling as far as she was concerned. He had no more right to an update than the general public.

The eighth one was from Sherm. "Red, I think the wife has some info for you. Give me a call."

Even though it was probably past Sherm's bedtime, she called him. "Sherm? Red Hammergren. You left a message?"

Sherm cleared his throat, sleepily. "What time is it? I left that message this afternoon. Kinda late to be getting to your messages, isn't it?"

Red declined to take the bait. "What do you have for me?"

"Well, me and the wife were talking about Arlis Henley and Joanie Crea this morning, when I remembered something." Sherm coughed.

Red waited.

"The wife is younger than me, and she went to high school with Geraldine Baker—you know, Geraldine Grandgeorge. She said that Jimmy Crea used to be very sweet on her. She thought Geraldine might have been his first girlfriend. Anyway, they went steady through senior

The Pines Were Watching   157

prom. Then, suddenly, Clyde Grandgeorge showed up, and no more Jimmy."

"Oh?"

"The wife says he was pretty broken up. Left town shortly after high school graduation for college. She was kinda surprised when he came back with that nurse wife of his."

"Hmmm." Another pebble of information to add to the bucket.

"And another thing." Sherm hacked deeply into the phone. Red held the receiver away from her ear. "The wife said she'd heard that Clyde Grandgeorge was seen around here one night last week."

"What?"

"Well, he always wore some sort of green letterman's jacket from that school out east. Wife said that one of the nurses from the rest home saw someone in a green jacket like that walking Highway 25 just north of Eddie's."

"Can you describe the jacket?"

"Well, she said it was light green in the arms and darker on the rest. You know how those jackets are."

Red nodded, thinking about the young girl's description of a "jock jacket" and the strange man at the park. Skunk Lake was just across the road from the Indian mounds. Could the man have been walking in that direction?

"Sherm, what do you know about Skunk Lake? Are there any hiking paths or unmarked roads?"

"Hmmm. Let me think. My dad used to talk about some guy he called the Swamp King who lived around there when I was a kid. Some kind of boogeyman. Supposedly he knew every inch of the place. Dad would warn me, 'You quit picking on your sister or I'll have the Swamp King come and...'" He laughed.

"The Swamp King, huh? Never heard that one."

Sherm laughed. "It was a guy thing—you know?"

Red smiled, figuring it must have been a threat to a young boy's testicles.

"Sherm, can you find out who saw the person with the jacket?"

"Sure thing." He paused. "But not tonight."

Red laughed, hanging up the phone. She didn't mind getting Sherm out of bed at all.

Red mapped out her patrol route for the night. It included swinging by some of the usual trouble spots, including Eddie's as well as Kitty's Bar on the county border.

She added a trip to Indian Mounds Park, which was on a county road not far from Kitty's.

At 1:15 a.m., the parking lot at Eddie's was empty and the neon "open" sign turned off. No after-hours Saturday night fights. Probably the earlier call had settled everyone down. Further north, Kitty's was dark other than the neon sign for Bud Light. She pulled into the parking lot, turned the patrol car off, and sat with the windows down.

The early morning air was humid and filled with the smell of the newly harvested hay in the field next to the bar. Kitty's had once been the place to go for underage drinking. At one time it was named Jukebox Alley. Will's father, the sheriff at the time, bemoaned the place and said a little arson might do the county good. As it turned out, someone did torch the place in the late 1960s. Years later, new owners from Minneapolis rebuilt it. The sheriff's office had a few calls from there, but nothing like Eddie's.

As she peered at the plain façade, she remembered her parents saying something bad had happened at the bar just before the arson. Red had seen an old file about a sixteen-year-old who died in a hit-and-run. Since the body was found across the county line, it wasn't a Pearsal case, but if she recalled correctly, the driver had never been found.

Old history. With far more pressing matters to think about, she opened a thermos of coffee and poured it into the cap. If only the walls could talk. Which reminded her of the Grandgeorge Place with its crumbling elegance and sense of emptiness.

She sifted through the information in her head about Clyde Grandgeorge, realizing how little she knew. At the time of Carl's death, when Clyde came back to Pearsal County to take over the mansion and the business, she'd been in the cities teaching science. At that point in her life, she had no thought of moving back to Pearsal County—until her mother started showing signs of dementia.

Clyde Grandgeorge was a mystery man. Near as she could tell, he hadn't connected much with the community other than Geraldine. In the last couple of days, the people she'd interviewed about the Grandgeorge family had said little about him. "Never saw much of him. Seemed kind of arrogant, driving that Mustang around."

The sheriff's office hadn't received a missing person report, and the people she talked with thought he'd simply taken off. "Probably ran out of money and didn't want Geraldine or a baby."

She stepped out of the cruiser and let the cool, moist air bathe her face and frizz her hair. It turned out that as much as she liked the energy and activity of city living, her heart had always been in the country setting. Had Clyde felt differently? Perhaps the lure of the big city?

"Red, you aren't going to get these answers at two on Sunday morning."

After the break, she drove to Indian Mounds Park. It was really nothing more than a wayside rest off the county road along the north end of Hammer Lake. It featured a couple of picnic tables and an overflowing trash bin. She parked the cruiser, took out her flashlight, and scanned the area. Closing her eyes, she pictured the large county map hanging on her office wall. This part of the county was a lowland marsh area where several underground springs eventually fed into Hammer Lake. If she recalled right, the county road skirted the marsh that eventually widened into an area called Skunk Lake.

Skunk Lake was legendary for sightings of strange lights. The office crew would tell callers, "Oh yes. We heard. It's swamp gas. Happens this time of year."

It was also legendary for being impassable. People didn't venture too far in that direction before being overtaken by mosquitoes and mucky water.

Her musings were interrupted by a clattering sound near the trash barrel. "Hello?" She pointed the flashlight at the barrel in time to see a raccoon staring back at her. It had a defiant look, and Red was too tired to challenge it.

"Time to go home and get some sleep." As she walked back to the cruiser, she thought about the teenagers seeing a man in a green jacket. Clyde Grandgeorge or some vagrant living in the swamp?

30

A MATCH FOR THE KEY

Red stood on the patio waiting for Blue to come back in. Already, at nine in the morning, the air held the promise of another hot day. For once Red didn't mind. After only four hours of sleep, she felt surprisingly refreshed.

Blue trotted by her to his food dish, his paws damp from the grass. He looked at her with hope in his soft eyes.

"Breakfast, pal?" She poured a small ration of Dog Chow into the dish. "You're lucky. I'm feeling downright perky this morning."

Blue ignored her.

"Don't worry. That will change soon, I'm sure."

Waltz called before she could check in with her staff. His voice was cordial, a contrast to the sharpness of the other day. "Hey, how are you doing?"

It was as if he'd forgotten how he'd chastised her. "I'm a little sleep-deprived but okay. And you?"

In the background, several people were talking in a low buzz. "Still trying to settle a family thing. Sorry about that. I wanted to let you know that we matched the key with the Crea house key."

"We have a connection?"

"I think we have to talk with the husband again."

"Let me know when you can be here, and I'll get it set up."

The Pines Were Watching 161

After he ended the call, she realized she'd forgotten to tell him about the scrap of paper that probably matched the paper from Joanie's house. "Freudian slip, Blue?"

The phone rang as Red stepped out of the shower. "Answer that, will you, pup?" She wrapped a towel around herself and grabbed her cell.

"Red, it's Georgia. I had an early morning epiphany and decided to bake blueberry muffins. Just thought you might like some with a cup of real coffee. Can I come over?"

"Promise Scotty didn't make any of it?"

Georgia laughed. "I've told her dozens of times that she needs to clean that coffee maker of hers out with something other than Pine-Sol."

When Georgia walked into the kitchen, she raised her eyebrow with a speculative look. "What happened to our brooding, troubled sheriff?"

Red shrugged. "Nothing like putting Wayne Crocker behind bars and a little night patrol to put things in perspective."

Georgia busied herself pouring the coffee out of a shiny silver thermos. "Okay, now tell me the truth." She handed the steaming mug to Red. "Why are you in such a good mood? It couldn't be the Prozac we put in your coffee yesterday—not enough time for it to work."

Briefly Red recounted the teenager's story about the man in the park near Skunk Lake. "I feel like some order is coming from the chaos." She buttered the warm muffin.

Georgia sipped her coffee with a smile. "I don't see much order to this. What aren't you telling me?"

Red grinned back at her. "The more I tell you, the more you want to play detective."

"You think it's that lost brother, Clyde, don't you?"

Red took another bite from the muffin. "God, these are good. Why don't you close up that dusty antiques store of yours and go to work for Scotty. She could use the help."

Georgia laughed. "Sorry, I like antiques. After thirty years of working in public health to save people from stupid lifestyle choices, I'm happy for the dust."

They sat in comfortable silence until a chipmunk skittered around the corner of the house. Blue stared at it, then made a half-hearted effort to chase it. The chipmunk stopped, sat up, and scolded him until Blue finally made a high-pitched yapping sound. The chipmunk turned away.

"The brave dog wins again." Georgia raised her mug of coffee to him.

"He's my protector."

"Speaking of protection, I did a little more sleuthing yesterday."

Red sighed loudly. "Didn't I tell you to mind your own business or something to that effect?"

Georgia grinned. "I was—minding my business. You know, my antiques business."

Red flicked a little bit of the muffin at Blue. The dog stared at it, then walked away.

"Anyway, I stopped at Agatha Fuller's yesterday afternoon."

"Agatha Fuller, the private-pay patient of Joanie Crea?"

"She had some decoys she wanted me to look at."

Red noted a sheepish expression on Georgia's face. "I suppose she just happened to call you up about them yesterday."

A pinkish blush rose up Georgia's neck. "Never mind the timing. She does have some decoys—circa Fleet Farm Supply 1987. However, I did find out that she has a very valuable Civil War coin collection left to her by her husband."

Red took another bite of muffin and ventured a guess. "And it's missing?"

"No."

"Well, don't keep me in suspense. I'll have to eat another muffin, and next thing you know, Pearsal County will have an obese sheriff just like its neighbors."

"It *was* missing." Georgia paused. "Then, suddenly it showed up again about the time Joanie made her visit in May."

Red stared at her. "Joanie was stealing from her patients?"

Georgia shrugged. "Maybe that's what the blackmail was all about. Someone—like Arlis Henley—found out about it."

Red sat back in the chair, resting her head against the wooden frame. "Interesting." She closed her eyes for a moment, trying to find the connections. Nothing came to her. "But I don't believe Joanie Crea would take anything from those old people. I don't see it."

"Gambling problem?"

Red set down her coffee. "My gut says no."

A fishing boat puttered by on the lake. A man in a white straw hat waved at Red and Georgia. They waved back.

"Even if she was stealing, why would someone kill her?"

"Maybe she stole the wrong thing."

Red sighed. "I'll have Jason talk with the private pays in her book tomorrow."

Georgia raised her hand. "Excuse me? Do you think Jason is going to get anything out of those folks? Why don't you leave it to me? It's surprising how much people trust nurses."

A faint smile crossed Red's lips. "I can't tell you who to visit and who not to visit. You're working for Clarise Manson now."

As if by a mutual understanding, Georgia changed the topic. "Gonna be a hot one today, isn't it?"

Fifteen minutes later, Red stood up. "I need to go back to Fire Tower Road. I have a hunch I've missed something."

Georgia, who was wearing baggy shorts and a hot-pink T-shirt, said, "Can I tag along? Sometimes it helps to have an outside observer."

Red considered it before answering. "I guess this will just be an unofficial trip—sort of a Sunday morning drive. But don't tell Scotty I took you along. She'll think the poker club is really useful to me."

Georgia tsked. "You are a hard woman."

The bells of the Catholic church tolled for the ten o'clock mass as Red drove out of town and up Highway 25. Blue sat, eyes wide and shining, on Georgia's lap.

"If this dog drools on me, I'll toss him out the window." Georgia smoothed out her shorts.

"Well, Georgia, if you do, I'll have to shoot you."

Blue settled his chin contentedly in the crook of Georgia's arm.

Red smiled. It was nice to have company.

As they passed Eddie's, Red told Georgia the details about last night.

"The boy is going to need some plastic surgery to repair his nose where Wayne ripped out the ring."

Georgia shuddered. "I hope you didn't let him get away with it."

"Nope. He's in jail, and I've got statements from three witnesses who were appalled—of course, not appalled enough to stop him."

They were quiet for a couple of miles until she turned onto County Road 18, the winding road adjacent to the north shore of Hammer Lake. Gravel kicked up with a rattling sound as it hit the underbelly of the vehicle. Red steered around a pothole. The roadbed was almost flush with the marshy land surrounding it.

Blue squealed with excitement as the car slowed down. His nub of a tail wiggled as he danced on Georgia's lap. Georgia pushed him away in a gesture of disgust.

"Don't you dare open that window," Red warned with a half smile as Georgia glared at the dog.

With Blue secured to a leash, she and Georgia walked over the bumpy grass to the hollow. She pointed out the spot behind the yellow tape where the teenagers had found Arlis Henley. Georgia studied it before looking around.

"Georgia, I didn't find any distinct tire marks. Of course, by the time I got here, I could have covered them up, or Sherm could have with that Winnebago."

Blue tugged at the leash, impatient to move through the wet grass. "And your bloodhound here didn't come up with anything?"

"My bloodhound has been known to walk around for half a day with a piece of onion on his nose. I think the art of smelling was bred out of him generations ago. However, he did find a scrap of paper half under some leaves by the oak." She pointed deeper in the forest.

"A clue?"

Red took out her phone and showed her a photo of the paper with its faint penciling. "I checked with the kids, and they claimed no knowledge of it. And Jason and company scoured the area yesterday. They found a lot of beer cans and potato chip bags but nothing to match this piece of paper."

Georgia wrinkled her brow. "Prim writing. Looks a lot like the notations Joanie had in her calendar."

"Yup."

Georgia peered in the direction of the tree. "So those kids looking for fishing lures in my shop saw some guy when they were at the Indian mounds?"

Red nodded.

Without saying anything more, Georgia headed west, away from the hazy sun toward Skunk Lake and the wayside rest. Red followed, her eyes sweeping the forest floor. Soon the trees gave way to highbush cranberries, hackberry bushes, and thick scrub aspens.

"How far did you look in this direction?" Georgia asked.

"Probably fifty yards. I figured something would show up within that distance. After that, the underbrush is so thick. I didn't think I'd see anything." She stopped. "You know, Georgia, I didn't look very hard in this direction because I knew I'd run into the swamp. I was thinking that the killer had to have driven up here."

The terrain grew more uneven as the land sloped downward toward the swamp. Soon the firm ground was replaced by boggy hillocks as they pushed through thicker and thicker brush. Ahead of her, Red saw Georgia's sneakers sink in the muck.

She surveyed the lowlands filled with tangled brush and tall weeds in front of her. "This is not possible, Georgia. No one could carry Arlis Henley this far. She weighed over one hundred eighty pounds. What was I thinking?"

Georgia continued her determined walk toward the swamp.

"Georgia," Red called in exasperation. "You'll get wet and then get pneumonia, and then I'll have that on my conscience. I'm not a nurse, you know." Even Blue had slowed down, unwilling to step into the increasingly boggy ground.

Suddenly Georgia stopped and squatted. Without turning, she called to Red, "What's this?"

Red picked up Blue and stepped carefully on the highest ground to reach Georgia. She squatted next to her and stared at the indentation in the ground.

"Could it be the markings of some kind of sledge? Like maybe Arlis was dragged over here?"

Red touched the cool, mucky ground. "I don't know, Georgia."

She took a few photos of the area, but her practical sense said the markings were probably from an animal resting on the edge of the swamp. *Okay,* she thought. *A very big animal.*

A mosquito landed on Red's neck. She slapped at it, then looked at her arm. Six more mosquitoes hovered over her skin. "If we're going to look any more, we've got to get ourselves doped up here."

"I guess we've made our presence known," Georgia said, slapping at the back of her head. "Let's get the hell out of here."

They hurried back to the car. Once inside, with the windows rolled up, Red began to laugh. At first it was a bitter sound. "Christ, Georgia. We probably just trampled all the evidence running from the bugs. How could we have been stupid enough not to spray ourselves down before we started? This is a swamp in Minnesota in the summer."

Georgia was quiet for a few moments. Finally, she spoke with a thoughtful tone. "You know, the more I think of it, the more it does seem impossible for someone to have dragged the body through the swamp."

"I agree. And if it had happened that way, Waltz's team would figure it out, and they haven't said anything."

"However, I do wonder about that scrap of paper. Is it possible the murderer planted it?"

"Why?"

"To point you in the wrong direction?"

Red slowly shook her head. "I don't know. It wasn't anywhere near the body."

"Or maybe he dropped it when he dumped her and the wind took it."

Red started the car. "Enough speculation. Let's get you back to your hunt for more antique ducks."

As she drove onto the county road, she wondered if Georgia had a point. Was the scrap a careless clue or a deliberate one?

31

INDIAN MOUNDS PARK

Even in the safety of the car, several mosquitoes still whined. Both Red and Georgia slapped at them.

"I read that the Ojibwe covered themselves with bear grease to keep the mosquitoes away." Georgia fanned the air in front of her. "I wonder what's worse—being eaten up by these bloodsuckers or smelling like a dead bear?"

"How do you know bear grease smells bad?"

"Hmmm. Call it intuition."

"Fortunately, we have chemicals now."

Blue settled on Georgia's lap with his wet and muddy paws. Georgia didn't appear to notice. She spoke with a thoughtful tone. "I had this eerie feeling like someone was watching us this morning."

Red maneuvered the car around a pothole. "No doubt your imagination. Maybe you have been watching too many Netflix series."

"Pah! I don't own a television."

What Red didn't say was that she had felt it too and now was totally ashamed by how she'd drawn Georgia into this mess.

"Is it possible Arlis was murdered for something she saw?"

Red shivered inwardly. "I don't know. I'm going to follow the evidence."

Except other than the key, the rope, and a slip of paper, she had no evidence. No one had seen Arlis, and no one her team interviewed had any idea why her body would have been left on Fire Tower Road.

"I'm going to drop you off so you can get out of your muddy things. Can we call this trip a secret venture? I'll send Jason back with lots of mosquito repellent to check further in the swamp. Meanwhile, I need to get back to sheriffing."

"Ah. Is that anything like adulting?"

Red didn't reply.

A troubled expression grew on Georgia's face. Red glanced at her. "Are you okay?"

"It just hit me that two women are dead in this peaceful community where I decided to spend my retirement. Are we really safe here?"

Red could have uttered some kind of platitude but instead simply nodded. "I'm worried, too."

After dropping Georgia off and checking with her staff, Red turned around and drove back north to Indian Mounds Park. The parking lot and park were deserted. It was clear this little wayside was not a priority with the county, although the grass had been recently mowed. Red surveyed the worn picnic table and wondered about the man the teenagers had spotted. Was he a vagrant squatting at one of the cabins down the road? Or the mysterious Clyde Grandgeorge?

The park stood on a slight rise with the beginnings of Skunk Lake to the west and the biggest part of the lake north across the county road. No one in Pearsal County was sure how these swampy waters got to be called a lake.

Will had once said, "It's a slough and a great backwater for raising mosquitoes and hiding things you don't want someone to find. My dad told me during Prohibition that's where the liquor was made. Called it skunk water."

Red instinctively turned as if Will were standing behind her. "Skunk water? Really?" She shaded her eyes as the sun rose higher in the cloudless sky. Despite the sunlight, Skunk Lake had a darkness about it she couldn't put her finger on. Shaking her head, she studied the picnic site. In the daylight, without the shadows of the trees and overgrowth, it appeared shabby and sparse—hardly an inviting place for stopping. The

The Pines Were Watching

rise it sat on was rumored to be an old Indian mound—a gravesite that had been raided and desecrated over a century ago. Some claimed it was haunted.

Red observed the warped planks of the picnic table. Over the years, people had carved their initials in the wooden tabletop. One of the freshest carvings said *luv suks*.

So does losing your soulmate, she thought. Shaking away the sudden melancholy, Red walked to the overflowing trash. The raccoons had tipped over the metal bin and rummaged through the wrappers and detritus. She kicked away a paper bag stained with grease, hoping she'd find another scrap of paper like the two she had and knowing it was a useless quest. The paper had been found on the other side of the road and at least a mile northeast of here.

Her watch told her it was time to get back to the office and check in. She made one more sweep of the area, looking for evidence of the man the kids claimed to have seen. The park sloped down into the less boggy parts of Skunk Lake. The crickets and birds livened the air with their chirping, and high overhead an airplane droned. Nothing appeared to be disturbed.

Before turning to head back to the car, she thought of Will's words about Skunk Lake: "Hiding things you don't want someone to find." A little breeze rippled the tall grasses and reeds at the bottom of the slope. Something white caught Red's eye. When she looked again, it was gone.

Making her way down the slope with its tall grass and bramble, she kept her focus on the place she was sure she'd seen something that shouldn't be there. Another wisp of breeze brought only the odor of swamp and decay.

"Are you losing your mind?" But Red was sure she'd seen something.

Before she could reach the spot, she heard a car door slam. Her gun was locked in the glove compartment of her car, but she'd left her laptop on the seat.

"Damn it, Red!" She was torn between finding whatever it was that had caught her attention and making sure no one stole her laptop. For a moment, she hesitated, but common sense told her to get back to the parking lot.

Sherm's camper was parked next to her car. He waddled to the picnic table, holding two cans of root beer. "We have to quit meeting like this." He held one up for her.

"Thanks, Sherm." Slightly out of breath, she asked, "Have you been tailing me?"

He grinned. "Like in those movies? Nah. I was at Eddie's checking on things, and I saw your car heading north. Didn't see it coming back, so I figured you were here."

Red wrinkled her brow. "Why here?"

"Heard those kids told you they saw something here."

Red raised her hands in surrender. "Sherm, it looks like I have to either arrest you for being a nuisance or hire you as an investigator." She sat across from him, noting how the picnic table tipped under his weight. "What else do you know?"

"I know Mac is worried the kid's parents are going to sue."

Red silently urged the parents to get a lawyer. "Anything else?"

"Oh sure. The wife gave me the name of the person who thought she saw Clyde Grandgeorge. I wouldn't get too excited. It was Millie Fillmore's mother, and she's going in next month for cataracts. Vision isn't so good."

"You're making my day." Red set the can of root beer down, where it teetered on the uneven surface of the table. She grabbed at it, and the can overturned, spilling sugary fluid onto the table.

She moved quickly but not fast enough to miss the root beer splashing on her white shirt. "Oh geez." As she dabbed at her shirt with a handkerchief, she glanced down at the wooden bench. "What's that?" It looked like a piece of wood had splintered off and... "Is that dried blood?"

With the flashlight on her phone, she studied the bench. The coroner had found wood splinters in the wound on Joanie's head. Was this her blood?

"Hey, Sheriff? You okay? You look like you've seen a ghost."

"Sherm, would you watch this area for a few minutes? I have to check something out."

Not waiting for a reply, Red hurried down the slope to where she'd spotted the white object. A warm breeze rippled through the tall grass and reeds. Had she imagined it? No. When she returned, she carried an evidence bag with a white tennis shoe.

The Pines Were Watching

Joanie Crea had been here. Why?

32

THE SHOE

Red sat at her desk, studying the evidence bag. Did this belong to Joanie, or was it something discarded by a picnicker? Her instinct told her it belonged to Joanie, but it was up to the forensic team to make that call. She hoped to get it to them as soon as possible. Her call to Waltz went to voicemail, but she marked it as urgent.

Her call to Clarise Manson to find out why Joanie might have been at the park also went directly to voicemail. Lynne, the secretary, had told her Joanie often stopped at the park to have her lunch when she was making her northern rounds. If that was the case, perhaps it was a random assault.

She shook her head. "No. No. No. If this is Joanie's shoe and the splinter in her head wound was from the picnic table, and yet she ended up at the Grandgeorge summerhouse, it was not a random act of violence."

Her next call was to Georgia, who picked up right away. "Hey, Sheriff, need your Miss Marple again?"

Red didn't laugh as she described finding the shoe and the blood on the picnic table bench. "Any idea why Joanie might have been there?"

"She had a couple of patients just off County Road 18, but none of them that close to the park. You might try Angela, who is taking some of her cases."

Her next call was to Jimmy Crea. "Jimmy, it's Sheriff Red. I'm wondering

The Pines Were Watching 173

if you could stop in my office as soon as possible. I need some information from you." In the background was the noise of dishes clattering and conversation.

"I'm over at the Town Talk. I could stop by as soon as I'm finished." He sounded surprisingly cheerful.

A half hour later, he walked in with Harv Smith. Harv's cologne overwhelmed the air in the office. Red guessed it was Brut, a favorite of a certain generation. They were both dressed in short-sleeved shirts and stay-press pants—the summer Sunday church attire.

Harv spoke as he entered the room. "I hope you got some leads on this thing. I'm getting calls from a lot of scared folks. They think it's an outsider —you know, one of them...uh...people from down at the southern border."

Red counted to ten before replying, her voice flat. "Well, Harv, have any of your folks seen someone suspicious?"

He scrunched up his face, reminding her of a little weasel. "No, but we heard they're out there."

"Make sure they call me if they see anything."

Jimmy stood next to Harv with his hands in his pockets and the hint of a smile on his face. She wasn't sure if he was smirking at Harv or agreeing with him.

She pointed to Jimmy. "Why don't you come in, and Harv, maybe you could have a seat outside my door. Help yourself to the coffee." She hoped the coffee was at least a day old and maybe moldy.

For a few moments, Harv didn't move. "I thought I could be a support to Jimmy. It's been a hard week."

Jimmy patted Harv on the sleeve. "It's okay. I'm fine. You go ahead and wait outside."

The interchange between the two of them made Red uncomfortable. Was Jimmy playing up to Harv because he was a commissioner? She shook the thought away, beckoning him to sit on the other side of her desk. Before Jimmy sat, he glanced back as the door closed. "I...uh...didn't invite him to come with me. He's worried that I'm not all right." He rubbed his eyes. "It's been hard, but I'm okay. Stopped taking the pills to help me sleep."

Red took out the shoe in the evidence bag and showed it to Jimmy. "Do you recognize this?"

A flush rose in his cheeks as he peered at the shoe. "Where...where did you find it?"

She fixed her gaze on him. He appeared to be genuinely distressed. Not the reaction of a murderer.

He moved his lips but didn't speak.

"Jimmy, are you okay?"

When he looked up at her, his eyes were moist. "She always wore Keds. Never anything fancy." He paused, biting his lip. "I thought they said she was—well, you know—dressed when she was found."

Red had said nothing to Jimmy about the state of the body but knew this kind of information had a way of slipping out. "I know this is hard, but do you know any reason she would have been at Indian Mounds Park last weekend?"

Jimmy's eyes widened. "Is that where you found the shoe?"

Red didn't reply.

"I guess some of her patients were up in that area, but she never said anything about the park." He wiped his eyes with the back of his hand. "My ma told me when I was a kid that the place was haunted by the old Indians that got dug up." He paused. "I guess it is."

Red asked Jimmy a few more questions but determined he didn't know anything else about why Joanie would have been at the park. He left, shaking his head. "Doesn't make sense."

He walked out the door, his shoulders rounded and his head bowed in defeat.

She remembered what he'd said when they'd first interviewed him. "It's never the husband."

33

CHURCH OF THE PERPETUAL SLOT MACHINE

Red checked her watch. It was nearly three, and she hadn't eaten. She walked out into the clear air and took a deep breath. Ed had mowed, and the area around the courthouse smelled of grass, reminding her of her neglected lawn. When she'd moved into Will's house, she'd had this notion that she would landscape it and do a few Earth-mother tasks. Work took over, and the lawn was as patchy and filled with dandelions as when they'd married.

She needed a cup of coffee and a basket of fries. The Town Talk would be closing soon. She hurried over to find Georgia at the back table, dangling a tea bag into a mug of hot water. The Town Talk was exceptionally busy for a Sunday afternoon. Scotty often closed down at 1:00 because the church crowd had gone home and no one was left downtown except, as she put it, "Kids on bicycles and Alma Wooster shooing them away."

Scotty sat down next to them. "Georgia tells me you went sleuthing without me."

"Did she also tell you she made me a decent cup of coffee?"

"No comment." Georgia took a sip of her tea. "At least you can't wreck a good bag of Earl Grey."

Red asked for a cheeseburger and fries.

Scotty tsked. "Sorry, the grill's closed. But I have a nice salad in the fridge with your name on it."

"Better not have brussels sprouts in it like the last one."

She brought Red a large chef's salad complete with real bacon bits. Red ate, pouring too much dressing on the salad as she thought about the shoe and where she had found it. Had the killer thrown it down the hill? Or had Joanie tried to run away and lost it in the swampy water?

Scotty broke the silence. "Georgia, Lou, and I are planning to take in the Sunday service at the Golden Deer Church of the Perpetual Slot Machine this afternoon."

"Yup," Georgia raised her voice. "We're gonna exorcise them devils from them machines and bask in the richness of heaven everlasting."

Red stared at her. "You're going to do what?"

Scotty winked at Georgia. "I think we need to send our girl to the principal for not paying attention."

"Let's take her with. She needs a break from all this sheriffing."

Red raised her eyebrows. "You two better be going to the casino because you like to lose those rolls of quarters and not because you think you're Nancy Drew and her friend George." She pointed a finger at Georgia. "Just because I took you for a Sunday walk this morning doesn't mean I expect you to meddle."

Scotty smiled sweetly at her. "Don't worry about us."

Red stood, shaking her head. "I need to get back to this sheriffing business."

On her walk to the courthouse, she observed the stores and businesses along the street. In the afternoon light, they looked like something Norman Rockwell would paint. Who would guess that two women had been murdered in this peaceful setting.

Back at her desk, Red reviewed her notes.

"I know this is coming into focus," she muttered. "I can feel it. I just can't see it." She stood up and walked over to the large county map on the wall. Outside, the Sunday afternoon calm was interrupted by the drone of a lawn mower across the street.

Why would she be at the wayside rest, assuming this is her shoe? Red surveyed the map. The wayside was on the other side of County Road 18

The Pines Were Watching 177

from Skunk Lake in a marshy, isolated area of the county. She stared at the map for a long time.

Back at her desk, Red dialed the number for the Grandgeorge Place. After seven rings, Caddie picked up. "Hullo?" she asked in a sleep-encrusted voice.

"This is Sheriff Hammergren. I'd like to talk with Derek, please."

"Not here." Caddie cleared her throat.

"Are you sure?"

Caddie paused. "The pickup is still gone."

"Can I talk with your mother?"

Again, a pause. "She always goes to the casino on Sunday."

Red thought about the man who called himself Clyde and dropped ten thousand dollars at the Golden Deer.

"Could you have either one of them call when they get in?"

Caddie hung up after saying, "Sure."

Red doubted she'd pass the message on.

Georgia picked up after two rings. "Don't tell me you broke into your piggy bank and want to ride with us to the casino."

Red had some trouble keeping the sheepishness out of her voice. "Well, actually, I was wondering if you would keep your eyes out for Geraldine Grandgeorge while you're attending the services at the Golden Deer."

"Oh?"

"Her daughter says she spends Sunday afternoon there."

"Okay."

"And," Red added, "let me know if you see anyone wearing an old green letterman's jacket."

As she flipped through her notes, Red thought about another dangling question—Angela Driver. She highlighted what she knew. Angela had visited the Grandgeorge household. She'd been present when Joanie's body had been found. She possibly had a relationship with Derek Grandgeorge. And most important, she seemed scared to death of Red.

It was time for an unannounced visit. Ten minutes later, Red pulled up in front of the little house on the edge of town that Angela rented. The house, which stood nestled in a stand of mature pines, had always intrigued Red because as a child, she had pictured it as the place Little Red

Riding Hood went to visit her grandmother. The cedar-shingle siding was now gray and washed out, but the owner had kept the trim a shiny green. The house had a reputation for short-lived tenants—usually new teachers who stayed for a year in Lykkins Lake, then moved on.

The yard looked brown and crisp from neglect. Only the crabgrass fought to stay green in the heat. A large white plastic flowerpot stood on the bottom step, thick with flourishing red geraniums.

Red rapped on the aluminum screen door. After thirty seconds of silence, she rapped again, this time banging harder on the aluminum. "It's Sheriff Hammergren," she called.

After the third round of knocking and calling, she heard a sleepy, "Just a second."

Angela opened the door, squinting, her eyes puffy. Her burnished red hair fell in a tangle around her pale cheeks.

She looked at Red with a confused expression. "Yes?"

"Hello, Angela. I have a few more questions for you. Could I come in?"

"I guess." She pulled the door open.

The house smelled of stale cigarette smoke. Red walked into the small, darkened living room, noting the sparse furnishings—a sagging beige sofa, a kitchen chair, and a coffee table. Red chose to sit on the kitchen chair. Angela sat on the edge of the sofa, rubbing the sleep out of her eyes. She wore a large purple T-shirt with *Minnesota Vikings* printed on it.

"I didn't know you smoked," Red commented pointing to the ashtray filled with cigarette butts. "I'm always surprised when nurses smoke."

Angela blinked, hugging herself. "I don't smoke much." She looked beyond Red, her pale cheeks coloring.

Red watched her for a few moments, letting the silence build.

Angela finally asked in an uneasy tone, "What can I do for you?"

Red pulled her chair a little closer to the sofa. "I'm wondering what you and Joanie Crea said to each other a week ago. She was seen leaving in your car from the nursing office."

"I..." Angela stopped, hugging herself a little harder. "I can't tell you."

"It might be important." Red peered at her.

The redheaded nurse rocked back and forth, as if a pain ground into

The Pines Were Watching 179

her belly. Quietly she began to cry. Red sat very still. Outside, a car rattled by.

Angela looked down at her bare feet and said in an almost inaudible voice, "I told her about Mr. Seldon."

Red shifted in her chair, wondering who the hell Mr. Seldon was.

"I told her how I k-killed him."

Red took a deep breath, letting it out very slowly. "Tell me." She leaned forward, almost touching the girl. "Tell me about Mr. Seldon."

"Too much insulin. I gave him too much insulin, and he died."

Red ran through a list of recent deaths in Pearsal County. Seldon was not a familiar name. "When did this happen?"

Angela wiped the tears off her cheeks with the back of her hand. "At the hospital in Minneapolis. Last year."

Reaching in her pocket, Red took out a folded handkerchief and handed it to the girl.

She dabbed absently at her eyes. "Joanie figured out that I was scared about something. I just couldn't see any of the patients at home who needed to have their insulin syringes filled. I was scared to make a mistake."

Damn, Red thought, *this isn't what I wanted to hear.*

Angela continued to talk. "I...he was in the hospital, and he grabbed at me, and I used the wrong syringe. I used the one for the woman down the hall. And he died." The words tumbled out of her mouth. She looked at Red, her eyes large even in the darkened room. "I came here. I didn't want to make any more mistakes."

Red straightened up in her chair, biting the inside of her cheek. Angela continued to hug herself. "So, Joanie wanted to talk to you about it?"

"She suspected something. She just wanted to help, I think."

"What did she tell you?"

Angela hiccupped. "She told me she once hung the wrong IV on a patient. She said the patient died, too. She told me she didn't know if it was because of the IV, but she said I had to get over it."

She pushed the hair away from her face. "Then she asked me if any of the old patients she used to see had said anything about stuff being missing. I didn't know what she was talking about."

"Did she say why?"

Angela shook her head. "Only that old people were very vulnerable, and it was our job to look out for them."

Angela's hands played absently with the fabric of her T-shirt. She reminded Red of a waif with weary, adult eyes.

"Was something going on between Joanie and Derek Grandgeorge?"

Angela stiffened. "I don't know." A tear trickled down her cheek. "Are you going to arrest me?"

"Not unless you're withholding evidence in the murders of Joanie Crea and Arlis Henley."

The girl winced. "I...I don't know who killed them."

"But you do know something. Let's backtrack a little."

"About Mr. Seldon?"

Red wished Mr. Seldon would rest in peace. She didn't want to know about him. She said nothing.

Angela started to cry again. Red waited with a sympathetic look. Finally, she stood up and walked into the kitchen. She found a tumbler in the sink, rinsed it out, and filled it with water.

"Here. Drink this."

The living room grew momentarily darker as a cloud passed overhead. Red turned to the window to watch the shadow pass through the pines.

She looked back at Angela. "Tell me about Joanie Crea and Derek Grandgeorge."

Angela untucked her legs, shifted on the sofa, and tucked them back again. When she spoke, Red detected relief in her voice. "Derek told me on Friday after the wake that Joanie thought someone was stealing from her patients."

"Who?"

"He didn't know. She asked him a couple of months ago if anyone with a green jacket had visited his mother. She also asked him if anything had been taken from their house."

"Had it?"

"He didn't say."

Red flipped the page on her notebook and sat, poised, her expression neutral.

"Angela, why did he tell you about this?"

The Pines Were Watching 181

She shook her head. "I don't know. He just said he needed to tell someone."

"But he said more than that, didn't he?"

Angela nodded, chewing on her thumbnail. "It's just that I feel like I'm betraying him if I say anything."

Red studied the smoothness of Angela's face, the creamy texture of her skin and the clarity in her green eyes. At first look, she saw a classic prettiness. However, the prettiness faded as the girl looked back at her with a slackness to her mouth that exposed her lower teeth. *She's not stupid*, Red thought, *but she's not all that bright either*.

"Angela, you need to tell me what you know. It could be important."

Angela sucked in her lower lip. "He said that he thought his brother killed Joanie."

"Clyde?"

Angela nodded. "He said, 'He destroys everything I touch.'"

Red sighed. "Have you seen his brother?"

She shook her head. "Derek hasn't either. He said, 'Sometimes I think he's a ghost haunting me.'"

"What do you think he meant?"

"He didn't say. He only said that he had a big fight with his brother over Geraldine, and his brother took off a long time ago. He said his brother had a cruel streak, and he wondered if Clyde came back sometimes to haunt him. That's all." Angela shifted on the couch, picking at some lint on the sleeve of her T-shirt. "I told him that I didn't want to hear any more. The way he talked kind of scared me."

"Were you seeing Derek? Is that why he told you these things?"

Angela continued to pick at the T-shirt. "A little. We were together just a little."

"What happened?"

Her eyes filled with tears. "He kind of scared me, and after what happened to Joanie, I broke it off with him on Friday."

"Did you ever go with him to the summerhouse?"

She covered her face with her hands and spoke in a trembling voice. "A couple of times."

"When was the last time?"

"Maybe a week before all this happened? It was on a Sunday, and he said Geraldine would be out for the afternoon. My car was being repaired, and I borrowed Joanie's and drove there." She blinked tears out of her eyes. "That was the last time, I swear."

Red scratched the back of her neck. Angela and Derek in the summerhouse a week before Joanie was found there. Was Derek setting the scene in some macabre way? And what about Derek and Clyde? Haunted by an absent brother? A man named Clyde losing money at the casino.

She had one more question for Angela. "Do you know why Joanie might have been at Indian Mounds Park last weekend?"

Angela frowned, pressing her lips together. "Um, I don't think so..." She sat up a little straighter. "Wait. She said something about meeting someone up north."

"Last weekend?" Red leaned closer. "Do you know who?"

She shook her head. "Joanie was kind of close with personal stuff, you know? I didn't even know she and Jimmy separated until Lynne told me."

After several more questions, Red stood up. The girl had no more to offer. As she let herself out, she turned. "Angela, stay away from Derek Grandgeorge. If you have to see the mother, make sure someone is with you. At least until we get this cleared up."

34

NORMA

On her way back to the courthouse, Red decided to stop and talk with Norma Elling. The former school librarian sat on the veranda of her large yellow clapboard house, fanning herself with a *People* magazine. She waved as Red walked up the sidewalk.

The house, with its wide wraparound porch, had been in the Elling family for close to one hundred years and was listed on the National Historic Register. Red suspected that all the money Norma had earned as the school librarian had gone back into the house.

"Hot enough for you?"

Red nodded, settling into a wicker chair next to Norma. The late afternoon humidity held the scent of nearby blooming roses. Norma smelled of lemons and gin.

Ten years ago, when Norma still worked as the librarian for the school district, they'd sent her to Hazelden for alcohol treatment. She'd come back looking healthy and very sad. Within a week, on a Saturday morning, they'd found her unconscious at her desk with an empty bottle of Tanqueray in the trash. Norma retired the following Monday from the school but not from the gin.

"You want to know about Jimmy." Norma's mouth crinkled into a smile. She was a small woman with a spray of light-gray curls framing her face.

From a distance, she had a rosy complexion. Close up, years of gin had mapped her face with minute, spidery red veins.

Red studied the neatly swept wooden floor of the porch. She looked at Norma, holding back a big sigh. "I'm trying to put all these people together. I guess I'm looking for connections between Jimmy and Derek Grandgeorge, Arlis Henley, Joanie Crea. It's like a big puzzle. I'm not sure I have all the pieces."

Norma patted her hand in a gesture of reassurance. "Let me get my old yearbooks. Maybe I can help you put something together."

Red waited ten minutes, eyeing the pitcher of lemonade with envy. The outside dripped with cool condensation. When Norma came back, she carried several Lykkins Lake yearbooks and a tall glass of iced tea.

"Here. It's a Shirley Temple version."

Red took the glass gratefully. The iced tea had lemon and a hint of mint in it. "Perfect," she said.

Norma opened one of the yearbooks and paged through it. "Here." She pointed to Jimmy Crea's senior picture.

Red moved over for a better glance at the photo. Jimmy's face was narrower, his hair cut much shorter than the other boys. His eyebrows were dark and thick, almost meeting over the bridge of his nose. Although he smiled broadly into the camera, his eyes held uncertainty.

Norma studied the photo before talking. When she did, she gazed beyond the rail of her porch, as if trying to put herself back in those times. "Young Jimmy...let's see. I once gave him my own copy of *A Catcher in the Rye*. You know I couldn't have it on the shelves. The school district didn't want to harm any young minds."

A middle-aged man waved from a passing car. Norma smiled and tipped her glass of lemonade at him. "Jimmy came from an odd situation. His mother was young, probably late teens or early twenties when he was born. And his father was a sly marginal character—at least twenty years older than his wife. I remember when he walked into the school one day. His clothes were dirty, his hair slick with grease, and a couple of teeth were missing. He grunted rather than talked."

Red continued to study the photo. "Come to think of it, I don't remember hearing much about Jimmy's parents."

The Pines Were Watching 185

"I think he's always been embarrassed about them. He's kept it pretty quiet since he came back to town. But even as a kid, Jimmy seemed very nice—and normal, all things considered. A loner, maybe, but a smart one. I think he rose above it all." Norma looked thoughtful. "There were some nasty rumors, though."

"About Jimmy?"

Norma poured herself more lemonade. "Would you like some more tea?"

Red smiled. "Thanks. Maybe later."

"The rumors were about his parents. People around here called Jimmy's dad the 'Swamp King.' They lived in a trailer up by Skunk Lake." Norma hesitated, a slight pinkness spreading across her cheeks. "Remember, these are just small-town rumors. But I overheard someone say, 'The Swamp King has everything for sale. Including his wife.'"

"Hard place for Jimmy to grow up, then."

Norma swatted at a wasp that was hovering near her pitcher of lemonade. "I think Jimmy's father died when he was about fourteen. He and his mother moved into town after that."

Red leaned forward. "Do you think Jimmy might be familiar with the area around Skunk Lake?"

The wasp landed on the rim of the pitcher. Norma picked up the sports section of the Sunday paper and whacked at it. Stunned, the wasp fell into the lemonade. Norma ignored it and poured herself another drink.

You may not look drunk, Red thought, *but you are.*

"Where was I?" Norma asked.

"Jimmy and Skunk Lake."

"Oh, I wouldn't know much about Skunk Lake. You should talk to Ed, the courthouse janitor. He might know." She paused. "You know, the mother wasn't a bad woman. I know that Jimmy checked out a lot of books, and I'm guessing some of them were for her." She slowly shook her head. "Some people have such a sad lot in life."

Norma turned her attention back to the yearbook. "See, now here's a connection of some sort." She pointed at a pretty girl with rounded cheeks and dark hair. "Geraldine Baker. Married Clyde Grandgeorge." The inscription beneath her picture read, *Cute, sweet. Ask Jimmy C.*

Red was looking at a photo that bore a remarkable resemblance to Caddie. "Jimmy dated her, didn't he?"

She nodded. "I remember because it was an unusual romance. Geraldine was pretty and popular. She could have gone with anybody. And Jimmy was the classic loner. The teachers used to sit around the lounge and wonder what those two had in common."

"Do you know anything about Clyde or his brother, Derek?"

Norma squinted, her lips moving in silence. "Yes," she said. "I do remember something." She paged through the yearbook until she came upon a photo of Derek. His unsmiling face looked into the camera with resentment.

Red peered at it. "He looks angry."

"If I recall right, he came back to Lykkins Lake High School midway through his junior year. His dad had died, and they ran out of money for the prep school out east. Never settled in well here."

"Do you remember him?"

Norma shook her head. "What I mostly remember is that he was called into the principal's office all the time. The teachers thought he was a hood because he wore a black leather jacket." She paused to think, then took another sip of her lemonade. "In fact, I do recall a faculty meeting where a couple of the teachers talked about banning him from graduation. They thought he was unpredictable and might do something disruptive."

"Disruptive in what way?"

Norma waved her hand in dismissal. "I don't know. A lot of dumb things are said in faculty meetings. I'd had him in the library a couple of times. I thought he was troubled but not crazy. Maybe just a lost soul."

Red finished her iced tea. "Sometimes lost souls do crazy things."

Norma smiled in a far-off way.

"One more question."

"You're wearing me out, Red." Norma set her empty glass on the table beside her.

"Have you noted anything unusual about Jimmy since he moved in?"

"Not really. He's pleasant. Gone most of the time."

"Visitors?"

Norma closed the yearbooks and set them carefully on the floor by her feet. "Just a few church people. They only come when there's a money problem."

"Financial trouble at the church?"

Norma shrugged. "All I can tell you is that they had several hush-hush meetings in his room early this summer. Then it stopped."

"Did Jimmy say anything about it to you?"

"He seemed embarrassed, that's all."

Red remembered Rose Timm's call about missing money. She made a mental note to ask around about the church's finances.

Before leaving, Red walked around the side of Norma's house. She noted the short space between the yellow clapboard and Alma Wooster's little two-story bungalow. Just as Jimmy had described it, her bedroom window looked directly into Jimmy's. His window was pulled partway closed, and the shade was drawn. Red stood there for a long time. Something niggled at her, but she couldn't bring it to the surface.

35

GERALDINE

Red stopped her car in the turnaround in front of the Grandgeorge Place. It was now six in the evening, and she was fading. Too much activity on a day with little sleep. She took out her earbuds, reluctant to leave the sweet refrain of Van Morrison's "And It Stoned Me." Derek's pickup was not in the driveway.

She knocked on the door for at least five minutes before Geraldine pulled it open. She wore a shapeless, flowered pink dress that barely came down to her knees. Caddie must have been wrong about her mother spending the afternoon at the Golden Deer.

"Derek's not here," Geraldine said before Red could open her mouth. "I haven't seen him for a couple of days."

"Could I come in?"

Geraldine sighed loudly. "I don't know what you want."

"I want to ask you about Clyde."

Geraldine blinked. "What?"

"Several people claim they have seen him."

The large woman swayed in the doorframe. Quickly, Red grabbed her arm and steadied her. She led Geraldine to a varnished wooden bench set against the wall in the foyer.

The Pines Were Watching   189

"Sit," Red commanded. "Now take a deep breath, and let it out very slowly."

After three deep breaths, Geraldine looked up at Red. "I'm okay now."

"Where can we talk?"

Geraldine led her back toward the kitchen, her plastic flip-flops smacking heavily on the wood floor. The wall of the hallway was lined with dusty old photographs. Red stopped in front of one, studying it in the dim light. Two boys, who looked to be about eight and twelve, stood together, each holding a hunting rifle. A golden retriever with a stick in its mouth sat in front of them. The younger boy was slightly built and looked stiffly into the camera. Red recognized him immediately as Derek. The older was a little overweight and grinned with a mischievous light in his eyes. Something about his smile disturbed Red.

Geraldine interrupted her thoughts. "The chubby one is Clyde. He grew out of his baby fat. God, was he strong when I met him."

Strong enough to carry a body from the road to the summerhouse?

Red sat across from Geraldine at the kitchen table. Since her last visit, the dishes had been washed and the kitchen tidied. Dust balls still swept across the floor in the languid breeze coming through the back screen door.

"Clyde isn't back," Geraldine said flatly. "He'd never come back and not tell me—or Derek."

"Someone who called himself Clyde was seen gambling at the Golden Deer."

Red watched the puzzlement grow on Geraldine's face. She shook her head. "I don't think it was the same Clyde."

"Quite a coincidence."

Geraldine rubbed her hand across her mouth, still shaking her head. "Nope. I don't believe it."

Red shifted in her chair, wiping her forehead with the back of her arm. It must have been ninety degrees in the kitchen. Apparently, the mansion had been built without air conditioning. "Geraldine, why did Clyde leave?"

The woman stared at her with her mouth open. Rivulets of sweat rolled down the sides of her face. "That's none of your business." She pressed her lips into a thin line.

Red changed her tactic in hopes that Geraldine would open up. She suspected the woman sitting before her had been abused in some way.

"Tell me about Clyde. He certainly was good-looking in that letterman's jacket."

Geraldine smiled as she tilted her head, gazing at the ceiling. "He wasn't bad-looking, that's for sure. When he breezed into town, all the girls were after him. We thought someone like him would be our ticket to exciting places."

Red nodded. "And he chose you."

The smile disappeared. "It didn't turn out like I expected."

"How do you mean?"

She scowled. "When he found out about the baby, his mother insisted we get married because she was worried about the Grandgeorge name." Her eyes flashed. "She dominated him. I should have known. And not long after that, he took off."

"Do you know where he went?"

She shrugged. "He never said."

"What about Derek. Does he know where his brother went?"

"Derek doesn't talk about his brother. Once when I brought it up while I was still pregnant, he told me to never ask again—and I haven't."

"Didn't you find that odd?"

Geraldine waved her hand around the kitchen. "Don't you think this whole place is odd?"

No kidding. Red said nothing.

"Did you ever file a report that Clyde was missing?"

Geraldine shifted in her chair. "I wanted to after he didn't come home for a couple of days, and both Derek and Rebecca said no. That was back when the old lady still had most of her marbles. She ran the show. It wasn't long after Clyde left that Derek enlisted and went off to the army."

For Red, the story didn't quite add up. "Do you know why Rebecca wasn't worried?"

Rubbing her eyes, Geraldine sighed. "She said to me, 'Honey, Clyde has a wild streak in him like his father. He'll be back.'"

"But he never showed up? Even after his daughter was born?"

The Pines Were Watching 191

A high, tinkling voice wafted back into the kitchen. "Honey, could you get me a sweater? I do believe I'm chilled."

Geraldine pushed herself away from the table. "I have to check on her."

"I got the impression that she still thinks Clyde is around."

"She also thinks that Reagan is president." The words were tinged with contempt. "But she claims she hears from him. I think it's all in her head. And I doubt the person who said he was Clyde was telling the truth."

"Why?"

Geraldine walked away without replying.

Red followed her to the front room. Rebecca Grandgeorge sat in her chair, wrapped in a blue-and-white afghan. The room was hotter than the kitchen and smelled like a strong rose-scented room deodorizer.

Geraldine pulled the afghan away and reached behind the thin cotton robe. "You're wet, Gramma Rebecca. That's why you're cold. Let's get you changed."

As Geraldine helped Rebecca to her walker, Red stepped over to the end table with the graduation picture of Clyde Grandgeorge. A smaller, faded color snapshot had been inserted into the corner of the frame. Red picked it up and brought it over to the window, where the early evening light filtered in. It pictured Clyde standing next to a Mustang. He wore a green letterman's jacket. The word *Grandgeorge* was embroidered in a small arch over the left chest.

In the bathroom off the front room, Red heard Geraldine scolding. "Now look, you've messed yourself, too. Don't you know you're supposed to call if you have to poo?"

Rebecca's voice grew shrill and childlike. "Young lady, you are not allowed to talk with me like that. I'll have you dismissed."

Red left to the sounds of Geraldine running water in the bathtub.

She thought about Geraldine's burden as a caregiver. "When I'm old and decrepit, I want someone to haul me to the roaring waters of the Temperance River and shove me in," Red spoke as she turned the key in the ignition. The Subaru sputtered once, as if in reply, then chugged to life.

36

A ROYAL FLUSH

Red left Waltz a curt message wondering when they could get the tennis shoe analyzed. For someone who was so highly respected, she was surprised that he was slow to respond. The setting sun glowed bloodred as it slipped through the courthouse oaks. She added more notes about her visits. She now knew that Joanie was planning to see someone "up north" and that Angela and Derek had been together in the summerhouse. Did that help the case? Would Angela be the next victim? She shivered. She'd ask her deputy to do extra patrolling past the nurse's house tonight.

As she glanced out the window, the corner streetlight snapped on. She stared at the light for a few moments before her phone rang.

"This is Nancy Drew, checking in. We'd like you to put on a frock, jump into your roadster, and meet us at the poker club for beer."

Red laughed. "I could use a beer, but I'm afraid my frock is at the cleaners."

"Where you dropped it off after senior prom twenty years ago, right?"

"As I recall, Jeffrey Jenson, my date and the senior class slug, threw up on it at midnight after drinking too much sloe gin."

"At least you made it until midnight. I was home by ten. My parents were so relieved." Scotty chuckled. "Of course, I was out my bedroom

The Pines Were Watching 193

window by ten thirty. Ah, prom night. I'm so glad we have better birth control now."

When Red arrived at the back room of Georgia's Antiques, the table was laden with chips, dips, and several different brands of beer.

"Are we celebrating?" Red asked as she walked in the door.

Lou sat munching on a carrot, her eyes alight with excitement.

"Don't tell me you dragged our innocent nurse practitioner to the casino, too?" Red pursed her lips as she sat down. Quickly she twisted the top off a bottle of Summit. It tasted too good after the long day. For a moment, she thought about Norma Elling and her gin, wondering if Norma still delighted in the taste.

Scotty beamed as she walked in from the front of the store. She carried an old tarnished bowling trophy, which had sat in the front window since before Georgia bought the store. The female bowler mounted on top of the trophy was poised to release the ball, her skirt nearly touching her ankles.

Scotty handed the trophy to Lou as she announced, "To the champion slot poker player. The woman who knows a royal flush when she sees one."

Lou looked down at her lap and said, "Shucks."

Georgia, Scotty, and Lou started talking at once, each eager to tell Red about Lou's royal flush worth five thousand dollars. Red lifted her hand. "Let's have some order, please, or I'll have to clear the poker room." She looked directly at Lou. "You first."

Lou's smile turned into an uncharacteristic grin. "I put in my five quarters and pushed the button, and what should come up but the queen, ten, king, jack, and ace of diamonds. I was so astounded, I just sat and stared."

Georgia interjected. "She tapped me on the shoulder and said, 'Is this what I think it is?' I told her she'd better hit all the hold buttons."

"I almost didn't," Lou answered in a meek voice. "I couldn't think."

"When Georgia started jumping up and down with her hands flapping, I came right over." Scotty winked at Georgia. "For an old, hard-core public health nurse, she sure can get worked up sometimes."

Red felt a twinge of jealousy as she pictured the three of them gathered around the slot machine.

Scotty set an empty beer bottle on the table and opened another. "Our girl here looked absolutely stunned. She kept saying, 'But I've never won anything.'"

Red sat back in her chair, relaxed for the first time in several days, and listened to the excited conversation.

"You see," Scotty said. "Jimmy Crea had it all wrong. Gambling can be good." She pointed to the check from the casino displayed on the table.

Red picked up the check and studied it. "I see Uncle Sam got his twenty-eight percent cut."

"What's left is all mine—tax-free." Lou's eyes sparkled.

Red shook her head. "Well, I hate to throw cold water on your excitement, but most people who win a jackpot eventually lose all their money and more."

"Oh, lighten up," Georgia chuckled. "You take everything too seriously. Life is short."

"And you're spewing out clichés like you were a professional baseball player," Scotty interrupted. "Next thing we know, you're going to say something about teamwork and thanking God and your mother for all your talent."

Georgia continued to chuckle. "Well, I was going to mention something about how everyone needs to give one hundred and ten percent."

"And speaking of taking things too seriously," Scotty said, cutting Georgia off, "I gathered some valuable evidence for you today, before we were so rudely interrupted by the bells and whistles."

"Oh?" Red found that she didn't really want to talk shop. She wanted to drink beer and be with her friends.

Scotty gave her a sideways glance. "Listen, Sheriff, I went out on a limb for you today. You can at least act excited."

"I am," Red said dryly.

"Just how did you go out on this limb?" Georgia asked. "I know you didn't lose any money."

A little color rose on Scotty's cheeks. She sighed. "Five years ago, I had a relationship with a, uh, gentleman who lived up by the Golden Deer. One day, he walked out on me."

The room was suddenly quiet. Scotty glanced around. "Hey, it wasn't a huge tragedy. Anyway, he's a dealer at the casino now. He was less than

The Pines Were Watching   195

enthused but finally introduced me to the dealer who claimed to have seen the guy named Clyde."

"Wow," Lou said. "You never mentioned this on the way home."

"With you singing about being 'in the money'?"

Red could not imagine quiet, reserved Lou actually singing. "Ahem? About this guy named Clyde?"

"He came in late—the night shift. Sat at one table for two hours. The dealer said he wore a green letterman's jacket that looked like it had been pulled from the ragbag. He also had a baseball cap pulled down low over his forehead and those mirrored sunglasses."

"That casino is so dark. How could he see?" Georgia asked.

"I asked the dealer the same thing. He agreed that it was all peculiar. He spent a lot of money, though, and tipped well."

"How did he know he was named Clyde?"

Scotty folded her arms, looking smug. "Two ways. First, because he told him. He didn't say much, but he dropped his name a couple of times. He would say things like, 'The next card will be a ten or my name isn't Clyde.'" She paused, the smug smile turning to a grin. "But here's the kicker. The name Grandgeorge was embroidered on the front of the jacket."

"Did he give you any other kind of a description?"

"He said he sat the whole time he dealt, so he wasn't sure how tall he was. But he had a stocky build and blond hair under the cap."

"Anything else?" Red asked, now wishing she had her notebook.

"Only that whenever he had blackjack, he would say something about being redeemed."

Georgia laughed. "The old casino redemption story."

The poker club broke up around midnight. Scotty promised to call Red in the morning with the phone number of the dealer. Red planned to send a deputy up there with some photos.

As Red drove home, she passed Norma Elling's house. Jimmy's window was dark. When she reached her house, she called the dispatcher and left the night deputy with instructions to make a couple of passes by Norma's house. "I want him there just before three a.m. Tell him to watch for any activity around Crea's room."

Before crawling into bed, she picked up Blue, who was sleeping on her pillow. "You need to go out." He opened his eyes and lifted his head off the pillow without enthusiasm. His stomach made some high-pitched rumbling sounds. She ended up carrying him to the door.

"That walk we took this morning really did you in, didn't it?"

When they were both settled back in bed, she stroked his fluffy forehead. It felt a little too warm. Her sleep was interrupted many times that night by Blue's restlessness.

37

CONNECTIONS

At six on Monday morning, Red sat on the edge of her bed, tying the laces on her walking shoes. Blue looked up at her with clouded eyes. His small body shivered. She picked him up and carried him out to the recliner. Gently, she wrapped Will's old red afghan around him. "You rest, old pup. I think I'll have to get you into the vet today. I wish you could tell me what's wrong."

Blue barely lifted his head as she shut the door behind her. A deep frown pulled tightly at her mouth. The walk seemed incomplete without Blue snuffling through the dewy grass—he never passed up the early morning hike.

A thin layer of haze turned the sunrise into a diffuse pink as a warm, damp heaviness closed in on Red. She stretched, feeling an ache on the right side of her head. She wondered if a storm front might be looming in the distance.

When she returned home, Blue, still covered by the afghan, looked up at her with an expression that said, "Can't you help me?" When she touched his belly, she could feel the tumultuous rumbling inside.

"Hang on, pup. I'll get you fixed up." Red's voice caught as she gently stroked him.

. . .

The air hung over Lykkins Lake like a wet sheet when Red walked up the courthouse stairs. Ed stood on the top landing, sweeping dirt and leaves with a slow grace.

"Going to be a corker today," he said.

"Storm might be coming in from the west," Red replied.

Ed smiled at her. "You're the sheriff, you should know."

I'm the sheriff, she thought. *I should know who's killing the women around here. Instead, I predict weather. Shit.*

"Say, Ed, I understand you know a little about Skunk Lake."

The sweeping stopped. Ed stood with the broom handle pulled close to his body. "I remember when it had more water in it. They say it's been drained to make Hammer Lake deeper. Better fishing, they say."

Red leaned up against the concrete railing of the steps. "So, Jimmy Crea's father used to know that swamp?"

"Yup."

"Anyone else?"

Ed looked up, squinting. "Not that I can remember. If my dad were still alive, he could tell you. He knew everything that happened up there—but he wouldn't set foot in the swamp. Said it was too easy to get lost. Said he heard funny things coming out of there sometimes, and he didn't think it was swamp gas."

"Any roads go through that swamp?"

Ed continued to squint, making funny little faces by working his mouth up and down. "I'd say they are long gone. The swamp's changed, you know. But there might have been at one time." He paused, repositioning the broom in his hand. "As a matter of fact, thirty-five, maybe forty years ago, my dad got called out in the middle of the night. Someone stuck his car in the swamp just north of our place. Dad had to jump-start the old tractor and pull him out. Swore the whole time."

Red waited. A mosquito dropped lazily onto the back of her hand. She flicked it away.

Ed began to sweep again, this time with a tiny smile on his face. "Yup, swore the whole time. 'Damn rich people,' he said."

"Someone from out of town?"

*The Pines Were Watching*199

"Nope. That Grandgeorge fellow. The one that built the big house where they found that nurse last week. Stuck in the swamp. Dad charged him twenty-five dollars cash money, and by God, he paid it."

Two boys, about Tommy Henley's age, came swooping down the sidewalk on their bikes. "Sucker," one called to the other. Red watched them disappear across the railroad tracks.

"Do you know why he was in the swamp?"

The smile stayed on Ed's face. "If my dad were alive, he'd belt me if I said anything."

"Then you do know why he was there."

Dust flew as Ed pushed a pile of debris off the top landing onto the next step. "Chasing after Mrs. Crea, I'd say."

Red blinked. "Jimmy's mother?"

"That's what they say."

As Red turned to the door, Ed swept another pile of dust down the step. "It's going to be a corker today, Sheriff."

"I guess." She walked into the stale coolness of the building, the side of her head aching like someone was pushing their knuckles into her jaw joint.

Billie greeted her from his desk. "Hey, one of those BCA guys stopped by about a half hour ago and got that shoe you found."

"Did he say anything?"

"Other than something about the weather, no."

Red might have put in another curt call to Waltz, but right now she was too concerned about Blue. She called the local vet as soon as she sat down at her desk. Her call was greeted by a scratchy recorded message that the office would be closed until Thursday. It suggested trying the vet in Charlesville.

Red groaned. She didn't have time to take Blue to Charlesville. Reluctantly, she dialed Georgia's Antiques. The answering machine asked her to leave a message.

"Would you consider doing me a huge favor? I need someone to take Blue to the vet in Charlesville today." Red paused. "I'll buy you your next wooden duck, or whatever it is you call them, if you'll do this."

Next, she called Georgia's cell phone. She knew Georgia hardly ever used it. Red remembered the conversation they'd had about always being available. "Red, I'm retired and not an emergency responder. No need to keep the damn thing on."

Red had countered, "You should keep it with you...in case."

"Carjacking?"

"Something like that."

"By the time I got it out and open, my car would be long gone."

She left a message on the cell phone, knowing that her voice sounded desperate. "Ah, well," she said to herself. "Georgia won't be able to say no to someone that pathetic."

Matt and Jason walked into her office at nine fifteen. Though Matt's wrist remained in the colorful sling, the pain was gone from his face.

"You're looking better today," Red commented. "Good night shift?"

Matt nodded. "Nice and quiet."

"Did the dispatcher get my message to you?"

Matt pulled out his night log. "I made three passes by Norma Elling's house. No sign of activity."

"What about your three a.m. pass?"

Matt shook his head. "Quiet and dark."

Red kept the disappointment out of her voice. "Thanks."

She filled them in on her conversation with Angela Driver. "Angela thought Joanie was going up north to meet someone. We need to find out who she was meeting. Any ideas?"

"Sherm might have noticed."

Red shook her head. "I already talked with him."

"Maybe it was Grandgeorge?" Jason grinned.

Red looked at him coldly. "There's no evidence that Derek Grandgeorge had anything more than a passing acquaintance with Mrs. Crea."

The grin dropped immediately.

"Matt, go home, get some sleep. I want you to go up to the Golden Deer Casino this evening. I'm going out to the Grandgeorge Place to see if I can get some photos of Derek and Clyde for you to show around."

She turned to Jason. "I want you to follow up on the sighting of the man in the green jacket. Check around Hammer Lake and those trailers off

The Pines Were Watching   201

County Road 18. Also try the folks around Arlis Henley's place again. Find out if she had any visitors who wore a green jacket. And," she added with emphasis, "keep your eyes open for Joanie's car."

Jason shifted uncomfortably in his chair, not meeting Red's eyes.

"Yes?" Red forced the irritation out of her voice.

"Why don't we just arrest Grandgeorge and be done with it?"

She folded her arms and leaned back in her chair. "Tell me what kind of evidence we have that Grandgeorge did it?"

Jason looked at Red with confidence. "Well, Mrs. Crea was found on his property. And..." he paused with a triumphant expression, "he logs up on Fire Tower Road sometimes."

"Tell me more." Red poised her pen.

"I checked with the DNR. You need a permit to take wood from their land. Grandgeorge got a permit this summer. They're sending me a copy."

Red studied Jason with a slight smile. Maybe he would develop into a decent investigator. "Good work. Unfortunately, it's still not enough to pull Grandgeorge in. Keep digging." She thought about her psychologist friend Rob's advice and added, "Look for connections."

Jason and Matt walked out together, both smiling. "We'll get you those connections."

After they left, Red sifted through her notes again, wondering why she hadn't thought about Derek and Fire Tower Road. "Just stupid, I guess."

At nine thirty, Red picked up the phone to leave another message for Georgia when she remembered that her friend was filling in at the public health nursing service. She called Lynne only to be told Georgia was out making visits.

"I'll have her call you as soon as she gets back," Lynne said, then cleared her throat. "Um, I was wondering..." Her voice trailed off to a loud whisper. "Clarise wouldn't like me talking with you, but I feel funny about what happened this morning. You know, like it wasn't the right thing to do or something."

Red remained silent, imagining Lynne's furtive looks toward Clarise Manson's closed door.

"It's just that Jimmy stopped in this morning, and Manson let him go through Joanie's desk. Since they were separated and all, it didn't seem right. You know?"

"What was he looking for?" Red kept her tone neutral. What the hell was Jimmy doing rooting around Joanie's desk?

"He said something about an unpaid bill."

"Did he find it?"

"He went into Clarise's office, so I don't know. Please don't tell her I told you about Jimmy. She can get mad sometimes."

"Can you put me through to Clarise? I won't say anything unless she asks."

After a few muffled clunks and some whispered words, Clarise's voice came on the phone. "Yes?"

"I understand Jimmy Crea was looking through Joanie's desk this morning."

Clarise paused, and Red suspected she was taking the time to glare at Lynne. "Well, yes. But I supervised it."

"Did he take anything?"

She cleared her throat. "I'm not sure that would be any of your business."

Red snapped back, "We're investigating a murder here. It is certainly my business. Jimmy has no legal authority to be looking through any of her things. I'll call the county attorney, if you'd like." Red took a deep breath, waiting for her temper to cool a little. The county attorney threat was meaningless because Jimmy and Joanie weren't divorced and didn't have a legal separation. Still, Clarise irritated her.

On the other end of the phone, a voice squeaked softly, "Oh."

"Did he take anything?"

Clarise hesitated, then said in a slightly trembling tone, "Only a couple of books."

Puzzled, Red said, "Books?"

"Well, they were in the drawer where she keeps, uh, kept, her personal stuff. It's not like it was county property."

Red tossed the pen across her desk. Thank God the whole county wasn't filled with idiots like Clarise Manson. As her poker club buddies said about Manson, "She gives nursing a bad name."

Slowly, enunciating carefully, Red said, "What were the books?"

"Just a couple of paperbacks on coins and antiques. He said they belonged to a friend from the church, and he would like to give them back."

After a minute more of questioning, Red hung up the phone. She sat for a long time staring out her window. She jotted down the words *coins* and *antiques*.

Connections, she thought. *Look for connections.*

38

COINS

The connection came to her fifteen minutes later, while she was mindlessly writing up the staffing schedule for October. She penciled in Matt's name along with his home phone number. The penciled phone number jumped out at her.

"Connections," she whistled. "Why didn't I look at this before?"

Standing up so abruptly she almost lost her balance, Red picked up her phone and scrolled through the photos until she came to the one she'd taken of the scrap of paper from Joanie's house. The second name on the list was *Matthew's Antiques and Coins* followed by a Duluth phone number.

Red called the number. After five rings, a deep smoker's voice answered, "Antiques and Coins, Matthew speaking."

Red introduced herself and asked Matthew if he knew anything about Joanie Crea.

After a moment's thought, he said, "I don't recall the name."

Remembering how Georgia talked about Agatha Fuller's Civil War coin collection that was missing, then not missing, she tried again. "Have you gotten any calls within the last six months or so about Civil War coin collections?"

This time Matthew did not hesitate. "Sure, you betcha. A few months ago, some woman called. She described a couple of the coins and asked me about them."

Red sat up straight in her chair. "Was she trying to sell them?"

Matthew coughed a deep, racking hack. "Excuse me a minute, gotta get my inhaler," he gasped into the phone. The phone went quiet for several moments. While she waited, Red doodled in her notebook, drawing a jacket in the middle of the paper with arrows pointing to Golden Deer Casino, Skunk Lake, and Arlis Henley.

The phone clicked back to life as Matthew picked it up. His voice was slightly hoarse. "Sorry about that. My punishment for sneaking off behind the barn to smoke when I was twelve. Quit smoking last year, but the lungs don't work like they used to."

"I'm sorry to hear that," Red said sympathetically, remembering Will's last year as he struggled to get enough air through his ravaged lungs.

"Anyway, I do remember that a woman called about a Civil War collection. It stuck with me because coin collectors are usually male."

"Was she looking for a buyer?"

"No. That's the other reason I remember it. She was looking for a seller. Wanted to buy a whole collection." He wheezed into the phone. "Mostly when women call to buy coins, it's one or two coins for a husband or brother or something. You know, birthday presents, Christmas presents."

Red drew a coin and put Joanie's name by it.

"Were you able to help her?"

Outside, the courthouse sprinklers erupted, rhythmically spraying water against one of the oak trees.

"That's not my area. I gave her the name of a dealer down in Georgia that I've worked with in the past." He paused, his breath whistling through the phone. "You know, funny thing about that. Some guy called me a month or so before this lady wanting to sell a Civil War collection. I sent him to the same dealer."

"Did you get any names?"

"They didn't leave names or phone numbers."

"Can you give me the name of the dealer in Georgia?"

The courthouse lawn sprinkler hit a tree in front of her window with a comforting *thwap, thwap* as Red took down the Georgia dealer's information. Five minutes later, she was on the phone to a man with a soothing Southern accent. He remembered a female caller but had referred her to another dealer. He was on his cell phone and would call Red back later in the afternoon when he returned to his office.

At eleven, Red stood up and stretched. Walking out of her office, she said to Billie, "I have to check on some things downtown." She didn't mention that she planned to stop home first to check on her ailing poodle.

Lykkins Lake seemed unnaturally quiet for a Monday morning. Sprinklers tossed water onto empty yards as Red drove through the side streets. Shades were already pulled against the hot morning.

Blue had not moved from his spot on the recliner. Red carried him outside. "Come on. I know you have to pee," she coaxed as he stood on wobbly legs. She waited five minutes. During that time, Blue did not move. Finally Red picked him up and brought him back inside.

"Okay, pup. You're going to be fine," she said without conviction as she tucked the afghan around him on the sofa. For a moment, she remembered Will during his last days, staring beyond her with glazed eyes. His spirit had already moved into the next world.

She turned away from Blue as her eyes filled with tears.

"Shit. The sheriff can stare at two dead women, but she falls apart at the sight of an ailing poodle."

39

JOANIE'S PATIENTS

Back in her office, Red's stomach roiled with worry over Blue. She was talking to herself as she wrote notes about the coin dealers. "Connections, Red. Joanie was into something. Was that what got her killed?"

Georgia stood at the doorway with a smile on her face. "Talking to ghosts again?"

"Geez, woman. You startled me."

Georgia walked up to the desk looking matronly in a long flowered skirt and a white top.

"I don't think I've ever seen you so dressed up," Red recovered.

"I'm a visiting nurse today. Don't want to scare the patients off."

"Did you get my message about Blue?"

Georgia smiled. "I was going to turn in my nurse costume and put on my antique-collector outfit, but it seems you need me. I've already set up an appointment to take the little ragmop to Charlesville tomorrow."

Red let out a huge sigh. "Thank you."

"Before you start blubbering and one of your constituents walks in the door, I have a couple of pieces of information for you."

"Oh?"

"I decided it was my nursely duty to stop in on a couple of Joanie's former patients to let them know, gently, of course, of her demise."

Red folded her arms and rolled her eyes. "Okay, Nancy Drew. What did you find?"

"A green jacket sighting."

"What?" How had this person in a green jacket ended up all over the county without her knowing about it?

Georgia sat down in a chair and crossed her legs demurely at the ankles. "I stopped to see Harriet Lundblad. You know, she lives in the ramshackle old farmhouse just north of Fanny Creek. Harriet was real glad to see me. She thought I was her sister Hazel. I suspect that any woman who comes by is her sister Hazel."

Red tapped her pen on the pad. "And?"

"When I told her I was the nurse, she happily led me to the dining room table, where she keeps a journal. She said I could see that she was taking her pills like she was supposed to. Most of the stuff in the notebook didn't make much sense, but she did keep a daily log of her pills—noon, bird singing outside the window, blue pill—that kind of stuff. I paged back to last spring and found a notation that read something like 'Raining, white pill, and nice man in green jacket here for glass of water.'"

Red whistled. "What did she say about the nice man in the green jacket?"

Georgia shook her head. "Couldn't remember a thing about it. I asked her if anything was missing. She assured me that she checked her coffee can in the freezer every day and all her money was still there."

"She happily tells strangers where she keeps her money?"

Georgia held her hands up in a gesture of surrender. "Looks like it. Anyway, I looked through more of her entries. Long about late May, she wrote, 'Hazel here. Nice visit. Checked my coffee can and everything is fine. Robin in the yard.'"

"I hate to even ask this, but did you look in her coffee can?"

"Of course. All good nurses visiting the elderly at home investigate the refrigerator. You'd be surprised what it can tell you. The coffee can had a rolled-up wad of money. I have no idea how much, although Harriet was happy to tell me she thought it was around five thousand or maybe fifteen thousand."

The Pines Were Watching   209

Red pushed her hand through her hair. "She seems pretty vulnerable. What else did you do?"

Georgia smiled. "I cleaned out all the moldy bread, threw away the curdled milk, and called adult protection. We had a nice chat about politics. Turns out she doesn't think much of that orange-looking fat man with the fake hair. She told me in no uncertain terms, 'He's just a damn-fool hustler.'"

Coin collections, coffee cans full of frozen dollars, and $50,000 gone from Joanie's bank account. Red rubbed her forehead. "Does all of this connect to Joanie's murder?"

Georgia looked up at the ceiling while she spoke. "I wonder if she was stealing from her patients and felt guilty, so she paid them back?"

"Everything I know about Joanie tells me no, but perhaps someone else was?"

"Grandgeorge?"

Red reflected on her conversation with Derek. "I can't place her with him. He claims he hardly knew her." She rubbed her eyes. "Maybe the money has nothing to do with her murder."

"I'll let the sheriff and her investigators figure it out. Meanwhile, Harriet did have a few other things to say."

"About fat presidents?"

Georgia laughed. "No. I told her that Joanie's death was being investigated as a murder, and she went off on the Skunk Lake Crea family."

"Jimmy?"

"Jimmy's parents and probably grandparents. Harriet said, 'My mother told me they had lots of bodies buried in the swamp. Those Creas were criminals.'"

Red remembered Will telling her, "My dad wasn't scared of much, but he stayed away from Skunk Lake. Old man Crea was dangerous, and unless he murdered someone, we left him alone."

"Harriet talked a little about Jimmy. Said she'd heard he was a nice boy who came from bad seed. Seems his mother was quite a bit younger than his dad. Harriet called Jimmy's dad 'the Swamp King' or some such thing. He knew that lake and those woods better than anyone. They lived in a trailer somewhere up there, and Harriet said the missus was forced to entertain 'Jacks.'"

"Jacks?"

"I think she meant johns. Harriet tut-tutted about it and said that Carl Grandgeorge was a known Jack."

"Hmmm. Not seeing the connection."

Georgia's eyes sparkled. "Harriet said that Jimmy might have been the product of the Skunk Lake business—as she put it. It seems that Jimmy resembled his mother but not his father. His father was short with red hair and green eyes, and Jimmy is medium height with dark hair and brown eyes."

Red raised her eyebrows. "Hmmm. Sounds like fodder for a *telenovela*."

"Just passing the information on. You know with all the home DNA testing, a lot of family secrets are being revealed."

Red smiled inwardly as she thought about the reality of DNA evidence in law enforcement. On television, they get results immediately. In the real world of investigations, it was known as "get in line and good luck."

Georgia stood to leave. "One more thing. Scotty has agreed to accompany me to Charlesville in case your little furball gets ornery."

Red hoped Blue could wait until tomorrow. Maybe she could get him to eat something when she got home.

Georgia read her worried expression and walked over, giving her a half hug. "We nurses are good at taking care."

40

FIRE

After the door closed behind Georgia, Red called Oscar, her neighbor, to check on Blue. She stood in front of the window, waiting for him to call back. A young couple with a baby stroller walked down the sidewalk. They reminded her of how she was unable to have a child with Will. Even after all these years, she still felt a pang that Will died without an heir. For the years they were together, Blue was their surrogate.

After a dangerous miscarriage, she'd had a hysterectomy. For a week after the surgery, she'd stayed in bed and refused to come out. One day, Will brought home a tiny puppy given to him by one of his constituents. She remembered the tender and amused look on his face as he'd reassured her, "Red, honey, at least we don't have to worry about a college fund." She'd picked up the little poodle and agreed. "I don't think he'd do well on the SATs."

While she was musing about Blue's health, the dealer from Georgia called back. In his soft Southern drawl, he told her he'd made arrangements to buy a Civil War coin collection from someone in Minnesota.

"Do you have a name?"

"Well, that's the problem. The guy said his name was Grandgeorge, but he hadn't found the provenance papers on the collection yet. Said he'd get back to me but never did."

Red's hand tightened on the phone. "Grandgeorge? Are you sure?"

"Ma'am, it's an old Southern family name around here. I definitely remember."

"But you didn't purchase the set?"

"No, ma'am. Not without the papers. He might have tried somewhere else."

The dealer had no more to offer. Red ended the call and uttered, "Connections?"

When Red's phone rang again, she answered immediately, expecting it to be Oscar calling back. It wasn't Oscar from next door, though. It was the 911 dispatcher. "Red, I just got a call about a fire at the Grandgeorge Place. They're gathering the volunteers and should be out there in ten minutes or so."

A rush kicked in immediately. "Is anyone in the house?"

"I don't have details. It sounded like a younger woman who called it in. She said, 'Help! It's on fire!' but she hung up before I could get any more information out of her."

"Tell the fire chief I'm on my way, and see if you can get back to the person who called." As she ran to her car, Red called the Grandgeorge house but got no answer. She also called the number she had for Derek, and it went immediately to voicemail. "Oh please, I hope no one is inside."

Red arrived before the fire truck, and as she sped down the gravel lane, she saw smoke above the tree line ahead of her. "Please let it not be the house!" She tried the Grandgeorge number once again. This time it went directly to an answering machine.

The pines and aspens along the driveway stood stock-still in the afternoon heat, as if they were awaiting something to happen. Red concentrated on the road, pushing the accelerator as far as she dared.

She hated dealing with fires. Last winter, a teenager had died in a fire, and she could still conjure up the smell of the charred wood, soggy from the water from the fire truck. It wasn't a campfire odor. It was the odor of death, and as she sped along, she pictured the neglected mansion encased in flames.

To her relief, when it came into view, the house was intact with no

The Pines Were Watching 213

evidence of fire. However, behind it, gray-black smoke clouded the blue sky above the forest.

She pulled up in front of the sagging porch and called out, "It's Sheriff Red. The fire trucks are on the way." Without checking the house, she hurried down the path to the summerhouse. It was in a clearing, but because of the dryness of the spring and most of summer, the woods were ripe for the grass and the trees to catch on fire, and the house could easily be in its path. The absence of wind today was a blessing.

Caddie stood on the edge of the clearing as if hypnotized by the flames pouring from the summerhouse.

Red yelled above the roar of the fire. "Caddie, step back!" Heat from the flames warmed her cheeks. She ran toward the girl.

At the sound of Red's voice, Caddie took a step toward the burning building, crying, "But my journals are in there!"

Red saw the hunching of the girl's shoulders and recognized that she was ready to bolt into the burning building. "Stop, Caddie!"

Instead, the girl lurched forward. Red did one of the fastest sprints in her life and reached the girl before she could run into the building. With a leap, she was able to tackle Caddie and wrestle her to the ground. Panting in the choking air, she grabbed Caddie by the arm and hoisted her up. "We need to get out of here!"

Half carrying and half dragging her, she moved Caddie back to the path and away from the intense heat. Caddie looked at her with wide eyes. "Why would he do this?"

Red tugged her back further. "Let's get you to the house and let the firemen take care of this."

Behind her, the first firemen arrived. "Can we get the truck back there?"

The path was mainly a footpath but wide enough that the truck with the water could inch through.

"How bad is it?"

Red kept her hands on Caddie. "It doesn't look good. I hope you can get it under control so the woods don't go up in flames."

"The summerhouse...it's all burned up. My...my journals were in there. Why would he do this?"

Suddenly the area was filled with activity as the firemen brought in the truck, shouting orders and running toward the summerhouse. Red concentrated on keeping hold of Caddie and moving her away from the activity. Caddie stumbled like her legs couldn't hold her anymore, and as Red worked to keep her from falling, she glanced over the girl's shoulder and was sure that she saw someone in a green jacket disappearing into the woods.

"Caddie! Stand! I want you to go back to the house!" She let go of the girl's arm, praying Caddie wouldn't turn back to the fire, and ran to the edge of the woods where she'd spotted the man. When she peered into the woods with the overgrown shrubs and bramble, she saw nothing. Around her, the air was filled with smoke and shouts and activity, but inside the forest, it was quiet, almost dead. She saw no evidence of a man in a green jacket.

I must be hallucinating.

She turned back and caught up with Caddie, who was walking toward the house. "Caddie, what happened?"

The girl kept walking, ignoring her question. Red realized she needed to get her someplace that felt comfortable and safe before she asked about the fire.

When they reached the house, Geraldine was pacing on the porch. As soon as she saw the two of them, she ran down the steps and swept Caddie into a hug. "Oh my God! Are you all right?"

Caddie burst into tears. Red would have to wait to hear her story.

41

WHAT CADDIE SAW

Red sat in the kitchen with Caddie and Geraldine. Outside, the firemen continued to work, but the activity had died down. Caddie had washed her face and put on a clean T-shirt and shorts. She still smelled of the fire. Geraldine sat close to her daughter, and the resemblance between the two was striking.

Taking a sip of the water Geraldine had given her, Red studied Caddie. The teenager with an attitude was gone, replaced by a scared young girl. Instead of the raccoon eyes of too much makeup, Caddie looked plain with a hint of the prettiness that her mother probably once had.

"Tell me what happened?"

"I wanted my journals."

Red waited, but the girl didn't speak again until Geraldine prompted her. "Tell her about the journals and what you saw."

Caddie's voice was so low, it was close to a whisper. "I...I didn't want to go back there—you know, because..."

Red nodded. "I don't blame you."

"But I used to go to the summerhouse sometimes when it was really hot and write in my journal. It was a special place..." A tear slipped down her cheek. "You know, kind of like mine because no one else used it."

Geraldine interrupted. "Carl built that place for Rebecca, but after Clyde took off, she forgot about it."

"Yes, but Derek kept it up, and I think..." Caddie stopped. "I probably shouldn't tell. Um...I think he had a woman there a couple of times."

Red leaned toward the girl. "Can you tell me about it?"

Caddie stared at her feet. "Sunday before last, I saw Mrs. Crea's car, and I saw the two of them—you know—like walking down the path to the summerhouse."

Angela had told her that's when she had her last summerhouse encounter with Derek.

"Are you sure it was Mrs. Crea?"

Still staring at her feet, Caddie spoke with hesitation. "Um...maybe. But I don't want to get Uncle Derek into trouble." She paused. "Okay, I guess I saw her car, and I saw Uncle Derek walking down the path. And she...uh... she wasn't in the house or with Gramma Rebecca or anything."

"And it was Mrs. Crea?" Red prompted, keeping her voice gentle. She didn't want to scare Caddie into not talking.

"Um...I saw someone with Derek. I don't know if it was her because the trees were in the way. But her white car was parked by Uncle Derek's truck. I know it was her car because it surprised me when she used to visit that it was so banged up."

"Did you tell anyone about this?"

Caddie looked at her mother. "I might have told Mom?"

Geraldine narrowed her eyes and was about to say something when they were interrupted by Joe Held, the volunteer fire captain. Red stepped out to talk with him. "What's the story?"

"Looks like the building is totaled, but we were able to prevent a grass fire or something worse."

"Any sign of why it caught fire?"

Joe grimaced. "Oh yes. Definitely set. We found a couple of red gas canisters tossed into the woods. I'm guessing our man, or woman, is the one who smells like a gas station."

"Uh-huh. Well then, get your gasoline-sniffing dogs out. I thought I saw someone wearing a green jacket disappear into the woods." She pointed in the direction of where she had sighted the jacket.

The Pines Were Watching 217

"I'll get the dogs on it right away. Want to take a look?"

They walked down the path that was becoming all too familiar to Red. More tire tracks and ruts in the grassy walkway. The fire truck pumper sat parked at the edge of the clearing. She remembered when Pearsal County got the new truck, and Joe proudly told the ribbon-cutting crowd that the engine held five hundred gallons of water. It had come in handy last winter with the cabin fire that still haunted Red.

All that remained of the summerhouse were charred timbers and debris. Her crime scene was destroyed, and if the summerhouse held any more evidence, it was lost. Was that why the fire was set? Did the building contain clues the forensic team hadn't found?

She shook her head. Caddie's journals and whatever they contained were now ashes.

When Red returned to the kitchen, Caddie's chair was empty. "Where did she go?"

"Said she couldn't stand how she smelled, and she was going to take a shower."

"Geraldine, what do you know about Derek using the summerhouse?"

A flush rose up her cheeks as she looked away from Red. "I don't know anything about it. Derek and I barely speak to each other. He's a hard man to figure, especially since he got back from the military. Keeps to himself. Sometimes I think he's like that teapot on the stove, simmering and ready to blow. And sometimes he's sweet like he used to be."

The pumper truck grunted and beeped as it backed out of the summerhouse path. Geraldine stared out the window with a sad expression. "Things were good here once—at least for a little while." She turned back to Red. "Derek is good to us. I know we don't have a lot of money, but he takes care of the bills, and he works hard. He's not a bad man."

But maybe he's a murderer.

Geraldine walked over to the sink and grabbed the dishcloth to wipe the table, even though the table was clean. She spoke softly. "I'm sorry if I was snippy the other day. It wasn't a good day." She gazed at Red. "Caddie told me how you kept her from trying to run into the fire. Thank you. She can be headstrong."

This was a good time to try to get more information from Geraldine.

The fire truck and volunteers were gone, and the house was quiet. "Do you mind if we sit for a little more until Caddie comes back?"

Geraldine sat heavily in the chair with a long sigh. "I can't talk for much longer. Rebecca will be up from her nap. I'm surprised she slept through all the commotion."

Red clasped her hands, resting them on the table. "I understand Arlis Henley was your cousin."

The sadness Red had seen in Geraldine when she talked about how things were good for a short while returned. "Arly and I were close cousins for a while. I don't know what happened. I got married and Caddie was born, and Arly just wanted to party. She went a different way than me."

"Do you know why anyone would want to hurt her?"

Geraldine put her elbows on the table and massaged her cheeks. She appeared to choose her words carefully. "She was sweet on Clyde the same way I was. When he married me, we kind of fell out...you know, like she was really pissed."

"But that was a long time ago. What about now?"

"We talked sometimes. She had that job at the Golden Deer, and I thought maybe she'd turned things around. But..."

Red waited.

"I talked with her before all this happened. She was excited and said she was coming into money, and she'd be able to buy a house and stop partying."

Red pictured the new television in the trailer and how she said she had important friends who would get Tommy back. "Did she say where the money was coming from?"

Geraldine shook her head.

Red had one more thought. "When you talked with Arlis, did you say anything to her about Caddie seeing Derek and Mrs. Crea walking to the summerhouse?"

A flush grew on Geraldine's cheeks. "We were just chatting, you know. I might have mentioned it."

Rebecca's high, twittery voice rose from the living room. "Girl, I think I'd like my supper now."

The Pines Were Watching 219

Geraldine pushed herself up. "I gotta go. But I wish I'd called Arly again. Maybe she'd be okay if I'd found out more."

Or maybe you'd also be down in St. Paul in the morgue.

The front screen door slammed, and Derek called out, "What the hell is going on?"

Geraldine seemed to do a metamorphosis from the caring cousin to a shrew as she called out, "We're in the kitchen, and your damned summer-house is gone."

Derek strode in, his face dark. "What are you talking about?" He wore a green jacket and smelled of gasoline.

42

THE CHAINSAW

Red pulled herself to her full height. "Derek, we need to talk, and I think it would be best if you came with me."

"Why the hell should I talk with you?" Derek's jaw tightened. "What's this about the summerhouse?"

Geraldine blurted out, "Someone burned it down."

Derek's face reddened as he stared at his sister-in-law. "What?"

"Caddie discovered it and almost got burnt up." Geraldine's face slackened, she gulped, and she burst into tears. "I can't take this anymore."

"Oh my God." He stood, arms loosely at his side, as Geraldine sobbed. As if in a trance, he stepped over to her and wrapped his arms around her.

Watching the two of them, Red remembered her remark to Georgia about being in a *telenovela*. This was not the scene she expected. She hadn't seen any evidence that Derek had a tender side until now.

As Derek comforted Geraldine, Rebecca called out in a high, irritated voice, "I need some help here."

Red walked down the hallway to the living room, where Rebecca sat in her usual chair wrapped in an afghan despite the warmth of the room. "Say, girl. I'd like my tea now. I saw Clyde in the window. He'd like some tea as well."

Red raised her voice. "Did you say you saw Clyde?"

The Pines Were Watching 221

The old woman frowned as she looked up at Red. "Who are you? Did Clyde say you could come in?"

Red tried again, "Did you talk with him?"

She pointed to the front window. "He was right there. I saw him."

Red suspected she'd just seen Derek and decided not to pursue it. "I'll see if we can get you some tea."

"And a biscuit, and don't put any of that margarine on it. You know I like butter."

Back in the kitchen, Geraldine sat at the table, wiping her eyes and hiccupping. "Sorry, it was too much."

Red told her Rebecca was waiting for her tea. "And she said she saw Clyde in the window."

Geraldine brushed the comment off. "She's always seeing Clyde somewhere. She's gotten it into poor Caddie's head that her father is out there."

Derek watched them with an expression that went from confusion to anger. "What do you need to know from me?"

To avoid further drama, Red simply replied, "Derek, the fire was set by someone pouring gasoline on the building. You smell like gasoline, so I have to ask."

She expected an explosion from him, but instead he bowed his head, shaking it. "I wouldn't destroy that building. My dad built it for Mother. It was the only decent thing about this whole place that he ever did for her."

"Why do you smell like gasoline?"

He rubbed his eyes. "What? Oh. Damned chainsaw. Couldn't get it started, and I spilled a little gas on my boot when I tried to fill the tank."

"Can you show me the chainsaw?"

He turned to the hallway and walked ahead of her. He stopped at the living room doorway but didn't greet Rebecca.

"I'd like my tea now." The old woman's voice rose.

"Gerry will get it for you."

Red followed him out the front door and onto the porch. His pickup was in the turnaround. Without a word to her, he opened the tailgate and took out the chainsaw. It smelled of gasoline.

Red nodded, noting that this wasn't much of an alibi for the arson. Unless they're electric or battery powered, chainsaws always smelled like gasoline. "Derek, can we talk? Too many things have happened that seem to be connected with the Grandgeorge name. I need you to come in."

His lips tightened into a thin line. "Unless you want to arrest me, I have to stay here and figure out what happened."

"Is there somewhere we can talk privately?"

He pointed to the side of the house. "There's a couple of lawn chairs over there." Without waiting for her response, he walked in that direction. From the back, he had a posture of defeat. God, she wished Waltz were here. He was the expert in these kinds of interviews.

The Adirondack chairs were weathered, and the white paint was peeling. They fit with the general shabbiness of the mansion. They sat on uneven patio stones. Weeds had grown up between the cracks in the stones, and many of them were completely covered by grass and moss. It reminded Red of the photos she'd seen of Chernobyl years after it was abandoned. Almost like this place also had a nuclear meltdown.

"Why don't you tell me your story, Derek. Where were you this afternoon?"

He sat, hunched. Underneath the two-day growth of beard, Red detected a deadly paleness.

"I was out scouting for trees to cut."

"Here?" She indicated the forest around the house.

"Further north."

"Skunk Lake?"

He frowned. "No. Why do you ask?"

"Arlis Henley was found on Fire Tower Road."

He sat up straight with his teeth gritted. "I had nothing to do with her."

Red backed off, remembering interview tips that Waltz had given her. "Don't push it," he'd said. "If you hit a roadblock, change direction."

"Okay. Let's start again. You are connected to Joanie Crea's death because she was found on your property, and you are connected to Arlis Henley because you were seen going to her trailer before her body was found."

He looked surprised when she talked about Arlis. "How did you know I'd gone to see her?"

The Pines Were Watching 223

Red said nothing. Bud Campbell had been right about seeing Derek's truck.

Derek ran his hands through his hair with an almost imperceptible groan. "I can't explain anything except I think my brother Clyde is involved."

"He's here?"

"I don't know. But others say he's been around."

Red leaned closer. "Tell me why you think he's involved." A cloud obscured the sun for a few moments. She couldn't read the expression on his face, but his voice was filled with tension.

He took a deep breath. "Clyde had...has my father's meanness and my mother's charm. I didn't inherit much of either." He bowed his head. "He could be secretive and vengeful."

"He's been gone for a lot of years. What makes you think he's back?"

"Arlis told Gerry she'd heard that some guy named Clyde was gambling at the Golden Deer."

"But you haven't seen him?"

He shook his head. "Mother claims he's here. And Caddie says she thinks she saw him."

"But you haven't."

"I sometimes feel like he's watching—but no." He made a move to stand. "Are we done here?"

Hardly.

"Derek, tell me why you were seen at Arlis Henley's last week."

His hands made fists and then relaxed. "Sometimes...I used to visit her trailer, have some beers." His voice dropped off.

"You partied with her?" She fought to keep an even tone.

"Not for a long time. I couldn't stand that she kept that little boy shut up in the other bedroom." He shifted in the chair. "I went there last week because of what Gerry said about Clyde being at the Golden Deer. I wanted to find out if it was true. I knocked, but no one answered, so I came home."

"Was her van there?"

He looked up as if trying to remember the scene. "It was after dark, but I think it was there."

"And you didn't see her?"

"I haven't seen her in a couple of months. Are we done now?"

Red wasn't sure whether to believe him. She thought about her brother, Lad, who could conceal a lie so easily. Her initial reaction told her to be cautious, although her gut said he was telling the truth. She wondered what Waltz would have thought.

A flock of Canadian geese squawked as they flew in a vee overhead. "Tell me about Joanie Crea. Did you have something going on with her?"

Derek looked startled. "What? The nurse that was found in my summerhouse?" He emphasized the word *my* as if she'd been an intruder. "She was Rebecca's nurse. I had nothing to do with her."

"But you were seen together."

He paused. "Late last May, she came here. I was outside getting ready to leave. She seemed really worried and asked me if I'd noticed whether anything was missing from the house."

"What did you tell her?"

"I asked her what she meant. She was kind of twitchy and just shook her head and said, 'I'm not sure.'"

Derek fixed his attention on something beyond Red. "Then she asked if anyone wearing a green jacket had been around the house. I was so surprised by the question. It caught me off guard. You see, Clyde used to wear this green letterman's jacket all the time." He rubbed the back of his neck. "I hated it because he wore it like he was the big man on campus. I guess I was kind of gruff when I asked her what she meant about a green jacket, because she turned around and left without saying anything else."

"And the other nurse? Angela?"

Derek sighed. "It didn't last long. We weren't a good match."

"But you took her to the summerhouse, didn't you?"

The color rose on his face. "That's really none of your business, is it?"

"When it comes to murder, everything is my business." Red's temper was rising. Waltz wouldn't approve, and neither would Will.

He pushed himself out of the chair. "I have to see what happened to my house." His tone was sharp and abrupt. "If you have more questions, I'd like to have a lawyer present."

Red hated when people asked for lawyers—not because it was a legiti-mate request but because so often they did it because that's what they saw

The Pines Were Watching 225

on television dramas. "Derek, I'm not accusing you of anything. I'm just after answers."

"Well, I don't have them."

She stood up, trying to keep the irritation out of her voice. "Just one more question. If your brother is truly back, but he's not here, where would he be?"

"Ask Bella Crea." He spit the name out.

"Who?"

"Jimmy's mother. She mixed it up with him back then."

The disgust in his voice sent a shiver down her spine. Was Jimmy's mother in danger, too?

43

BELLA CREA

It was dark when Red walked in the door of her house. Oscar had reported earlier that when he'd checked on Blue, the dog was sleeping on the recliner. He refused to go out and refused to eat anything.

Red listened for the familiar sound of Blue trotting out to greet her and was met with silence.

"Hey, pup. Where are you?"

She found him on Will's recliner with his eyes closed. His breathing was even, and when she patted him on the head, he opened his eyes and looked at her. She felt the nubbin of his tail wiggling as she stroked his back. "Still feeling blue?"

She carried him out to the patio and set him in the grass. He squatted to pee but appeared to have no energy. She brought him back in and offered food and water. He took a few laps of the water before gazing up at her as if to say, "Can I go back to sleeping now?"

Red's throat ached as she tucked him back into the recliner. "Listen, boy, Georgia is taking you to the vet tomorrow, and we'll get you all fixed up."

Too much going on to have a sick dog. She microwaved a frozen dinner and sat at the kitchen table with her head filled with worry. She sensed that the killer, whether it was Clyde Grandgeorge or Derek or a stranger, wasn't done. Her gut told her that somewhere in this story was someone with a sickness who was exacting revenge. Who would be next?

Her thoughts turned to Lad and his long-ago disappearance. Neither she nor her parents had been able to trace him, although before her mother died, she received a postcard sent from Denver. All it said was, *Hi!*

Was Clyde Grandgeorge the lost brother like Lad? If so, why didn't he simply show up at Grandgeorge Place and claim it? And what about Bella Crea? Who was she, and why had Derek said Clyde would be with her?

Her hands turned cold as she pictured the two dead women—both strangled and their bodies moved. Why? Was this the work of the lost brother?

Too many questions. Red stripped and showered, letting the warm water run down her back and relax her.

In the morning, Blue remained on the recliner until Red took him outside to pee. He didn't appear to be either any worse or any better. She confirmed with Georgia that she and Scotty would take him to the vet early in the afternoon. "We promise we won't feed him chocolate on the way—or grapes."

Outside, the sky was a hazy shade of blue with a few yellowish-tinged clouds. The air hung still and heavy, holding the early morning dew in a soft grip. Beyond the line of trees, which obscured the western horizon, a thick storm front simmered.

Before leaving for work, she phoned Waltz with a measured, "How are things? Did you get the evidence to the lab?"

Waltz answered in a pleasant tone. "I think I've got the family thing settled. It's a relief."

Red debated whether to ask him more about it. She sensed he wanted to talk. "Can you tell me about it?"

He cleared his throat. "The age-old story. My dad has been on the mental and physical decline for some time but stubborn, as the old cliché goes, as a mule. He broke his hip the day after we interviewed that Crea guy."

Red sympathized, since she'd dealt with her mother's dementia for a number of years after her father died.

"Sorry, it was complicated because he wasn't making much sense and we'd never done the paperwork to make me his power of attorney."

Red thought about her own situation. "I was fortunate that my dad, before he died, made sure things were in order for Mother. I think even though she hadn't been diagnosed yet, he knew her mind was failing."

They talked for a few minutes about caring for aging parents and the toll dementia took on everyone. "Wish they either had a cure or a quick out for it. I don't want my kids to have to go through this with me." Waltz sounded tired.

Red wondered who would be there for her if she took the same route as her mother. Right now, her only heir was a five-pound poodle. "One day at a time, I guess." She was immediately embarrassed that she'd just muttered a tired cliché and quickly changed the subject by filling him in on the fire and the interview with Derek.

Waltz was quiet for a moment when she was done. She sensed that he wasn't happy that she hadn't waited for him to do the interview.

"What do you think?" he finally asked.

"I think I need to find the missing brother."

At the office, she had Billie get an address for Bella Crea. Jason walked in while she was putting some notes in the computer. She reviewed with him her interview with Derek but left out that she might have seen someone with a green jacket. "Derek told me to talk with Jimmy's mother."

"Oh yeah. My grandma lives at Lakeside Senior Apartments. She likes to gossip about the residents and told me someone named Bella used to be a party girl but you'd never know it now. Do you want me to talk with her? I mean, maybe she would be more open to a man."

Red was tempted. "No, would you go back to the Grandgeorge Place and talk with Derek again? Maybe he'll tell you a different story."

"I don't like him."

"Be polite, then. And if he says he won't talk without a lawyer, let it go."

Red reached the door to the senior apartments just as Rance Westerling, the caretaker, trudged down the carpeted hallway with his keys jangling.

The Pines Were Watching

"Can I help you find someone?" he yelled at Red.

She smiled. Rance wore a jet-black hairpiece, which contrasted so completely with his pale white skin that he looked like a walking corpse. He was too vain to wear a hearing aid.

"Just going to drop by and see Mrs. Crea."

Rance nodded like he understood, smiled vaguely, and wandered off. "Have a good day, Sheriff."

The second-floor hallway was dimly lit, and Red noted how shabby the carpeting in the publicly subsidized building had become. She had looked at Lakeside back when her mother was still able to function at home. By the time an apartment opened up, Mom was beyond independent living.

She stopped in front of number 206 and listened for any rustling inside. Across the hallway, a television blared through the thin walls, muffling the sound of her knocking.

When no one answered, she tapped harder. "Mrs. Crea, it's Sheriff Hammergren."

She thought she detected a slight creaking of the floor inside, but no one came to the door. She tried the handle, and to her surprise, the door was not locked.

"I'd like to talk with you, Mrs. Crea," she called, opening the door.

She was answered by the soft ticking of a wall clock. The apartment smelled slightly of boiled cabbage. The heavy curtains were drawn against the midmorning sun. A small night light plugged into a socket in the kitchen cast the only light into the room.

"Mrs. Crea?"

"Leave me be," said a shrill voice. The old woman was seated in a rocking chair in front of the curtained window.

"I need some information." Red kept her voice low and soothing. She quietly closed the door and walked over to the woman.

The darkened apartment living area was over-furnished with a sofa, love seat, two easy chairs, and a rocking chair. It reminded her of an impoverished version of Rebecca Grandgeorge's living room.

The walls were bare except for the clock. Even in the poor light, Red could see that the clock was old and made of ornately carved wood.

Mrs. Crea must have noticed how Red looked at it because she snapped, "That's mine. They've taken everything else, but that's mine."

"It's a beautiful clock," she said gently. "It must be old."

"You don't fool me. I won't give it to you." Still, her voice softened a little.

"I need to talk with you about Clyde Grandgeorge."

The chair creaked on the thin carpet. Mrs. Crea was small, her facial features sunken and skeletal. Still, even in the dim light, Red could see a hint of beauty. The worn look on her face and the suspicion in her eyes veiled the fact that she wasn't nearly as old as she looked. She had none of the broadness or roundness of her son.

When Mrs. Crea didn't respond, Red tried again. "I'm told you knew Clyde Grandgeorge. We are trying to locate him."

"Bastard. All of them." Bella rocked harder, the chair squeaking with the motion.

Red tried a different approach. "Did Jimmy tell you about his wife, Joanie? We're trying to find who killed her."

"The clock is mine," Bella spit out. "You can't take it from me!"

Red squatted down in front of her and placed her hands squarely on the rocker to stop its motion. Bella opened her mouth, revealing a loose top denture. "Always after something, but I wouldn't give up the clock."

"Who, Mrs. Crea?" The woman's vehemence was unnerving.

"The mother's sins are visited upon the sons to the third and fourth generation." Her voice grew hard.

Red settled back on her heels to try to sort out the woman's words. "Did your husband try to take the clock?" She spoke like she was trying to calm a child.

"He didn't take my clock. I wouldn't let him."

"Did your son hurt you?" Red repeated the question with a little more force.

Mrs. Crea sat stock-still in the chair, her hands gripping at Red's wrists, like claws. "Jimmy is a sweet boy," she whispered.

"I'm sure he is."

The grip on Red's wrists loosened.

"Mrs. Crea, did Clyde Grandgeorge give you the clock?"

The Pines Were Watching

"What? That boy? He was a bag of hot wind. So high and mighty with his dad's fancy car. Not like his father at all."

"Carl Grandgeorge gave you the clock?"

The woman let her arms fall to her sides. "He gave me my only begotten son in whom I am well pleased." She clamped her mouth shut and closed her eyes. "Leave me be. The clock is mine."

"Bella? Do you know who killed your daughter-in-law?"

She turned her head away from Red, and a single tear slipped down her cheek. "Skunk Lake knows. It's an evil place."

Red could get her to say no more.

Once back in her car, Red rested her head on the steering wheel. "Dear God," she uttered. In the distance, she heard the muted rumble of thunder.

44

SKUNK LAKE

Red reviewed all the notes on the two cases. Will had once told her, "Remember Occam's razor. The simplest explanation is preferable to the more complex one."

Thanks. Nothing seemed simple right now. She had four possible suspects—Jimmy by virtue of being the ex-husband, Derek, an unknown man in a green jacket, and the mysterious brother Clyde. Jimmy had a decent alibi for the night of Joanie's murder; Derek did not. Was this what Occam's razor meant?

Red went over the interview with Jimmy. He was home, and Alma Wooster could testify to it. His light was on, and he said he'd heard her talking on the phone at 3:00 a.m. Something about it again niggled at her but was not enough to put him high in the suspect category. As far as she knew, Jimmy had no relationship with Arlis other than having Tommy in his youth group.

Then there was Derek. An ache rose up the side of her head as she thought about all the inconsistencies around Derek. No alibis, contact with both victims, and body found on his property. On top of that, he simply had a dangerous edge to him. She remembered how Geraldine compared him to a simmering teapot. Had something with Joanie or Arlis caused him to explode?

The Pines Were Watching 233

Then there was the mystery man in the green jacket. Seen at Indian Mounds Park. Spotted by Harriet Lundblad. And possibly glimpsed by Red at the fire.

Finally, Clyde Grandgeorge. Gambling at the Golden Deer and supposedly seen by Rebecca Grandgeorge and Caddie. Another man in a green jacket or the same man in the green jacket?

Red gazed out the courthouse window, trying to piece this all together. The day was hazy and humid, ripe for a big storm. She willed it to clear. Right now, she didn't need to have her staff dealing with storm damage. On top of everything else, she needed to redo the schedule for next week and figure in the vacation requests, leave requests, and the two openings on her staff.

Will had told her, "Ninety percent of my time as a sheriff is dealing with staffing and personnel. That gives me ten percent to actually catch the bad guys."

Red stretched her arms over her head. "Well," she spoke to the framed photo on her desk that was taken after she married Will and before he was decimated by the lung cancer, "I'm not doing too well with my ten percent."

Voices rose outside her office. "Sheriff?" Billie called out, knocking on the door. "You have a visitor."

"Come in."

To her surprise, Derek Grandgeorge walked through the doorway. His face was drawn with tension lines around his mouth. Red motioned for him to sit.

Before Billie closed the door, she asked him to bring in two cups of coffee. From her bottom drawer, she extracted a box of granola bars.

"Here," she said, handing Derek a bar. "You look like you could use something to eat."

Derek nodded, ripping the wrapping off the bar. He finished it in two bites.

She took out her notebook. "What can I do for you?"

He sat, hunched in the chair, resting his arms loosely on his lap. "I saw the ruins of the summerhouse, and it was too much. It brought back things that happened a long time ago with my brother, Clyde. If he's around, he's dangerous." He took a shuddering breath as he stared at his lap. "I need to tell you this."

Red considered halting the discussion and giving Waltz a call. If this was a confession, she needed his expertise. However, Waltz was dealing with a demented father, and Derek was talking. She nodded at him.

Derek's eyes were bloodshot and weary. "Clyde and I were always different. Like I said yesterday, he had my father's meanness and my mother's charm. I didn't inherit much of either." He looked up at the ceiling for a moment as if to gather his thoughts.

Billie walked in without knocking, carrying two Styrofoam cups of coffee. Red pointed to a spot on the desk. "Leave them here. Thanks."

Billie stood uncertainly in front of her desk.

"Thanks, Billie," she said with a flat emphasis.

Reluctantly he backed out the door.

Red watched until the door latched, then she said, "Go ahead."

Derek took the cup of coffee and held it in both hands. Outside, a motorcycle zoomed by, breaking the silence in the room.

"I want to tell you about the bear. Then maybe you'll understand my brother." He tipped the coffee to his lips, then pulled it away without taking any. "He used to beat up on me and tease me about being a chickenshit. Clyde was a bully just like my dad. But he was right about one thing—at twelve, I was still scared of the dark. One night, I decided to show him and walk down the path to the summerhouse. I wanted to prove to myself that I wasn't a chickenshit like Clyde kept saying."

Derek looked at the wall beyond Red with a faraway expression. "The moon must have been full and high that night, because it was light along the path. I was almost to the summerhouse when something came crashing behind me. I froze. My heart was beating so hard I thought it might explode. A bear stood no more than six feet from me. His mouth was open, and he was panting like an old horse."

He stopped and took a sip of the coffee. The expression on his face did not change.

"I don't know how long we stared at each other before it occurred to me that he was scared, too. I started to think about it from his perspective. The old bear was out just trying to get a bite to eat when this white, gangly creature blocks his way. I decided I must look pretty absurd to him. I started to laugh. The bear was backing away when Clyde came whooping down the path with a rifle. Before I could stop him, he took aim and shot the bear in the back. The bear squealed and crashed into the woods." He shivered. "We found his carcass a couple of days later. I think it was a slow death."

Red's shoulders tensed. Was this a true story, or was Derek gaslighting her to make a point?

"Clyde had a cruel streak in him. I don't think he felt a thing when we found the bear. All he said was that he wished he could take the head for a trophy. I didn't show him, but I cried for the bear. I covered it as best as I could, but the scavengers picked it apart. The next spring when I went out, all that was left were bones. To me, that part of the woods still smells of dead animal."

Derek set the coffee cup down and stared across the desk directly at Red.

"Eighteen years ago, the night Clyde left, I came home to find Geraldine on the porch. She was pregnant, and he had kicked her. Blood was caked around her nose, and one of her eyes was swollen shut."

He clasped and unclasped his fists. "Gerry used to be a sweet thing. Not too bright but good-hearted."

Laughter from the outer office punctuated the stillness in the room. Red leaned toward Derek. "Was something going on between you and Geraldine?"

Misery etched his face. "It never went beyond a kiss. I felt so sorry for her. The same way I felt about the bear. She hadn't done anything wrong except get pregnant."

"But Clyde found out?"

"That's why he beat her up. He didn't even want her, but she was his." Derek stared down at his feet, his shoulders sagging. "When he came home that night, I took after him with a baseball bat. I chased him down the path to the summerhouse. He was drunk, and I was crazy."

His body seemed to draw inward. "I hit him and he fell. I kept hitting him until he didn't move anymore. Then I left him."

He rubbed his neck, peering at Red with anguish in his eyes. "I can still see him in that damn green jacket, blood running down the side of his head."

Red waited a few moments, then asked softly, "What happened next?"

Derek shrugged. "A couple of hours later, after I'd cooled down, I went back. It was like I was searching for the bear all over again. God, I was scared." He paused.

"And?" Red prompted.

"He was gone." Derek spoke in a whisper. "He was gone. When I got back to the house, his Mustang was gone, too. I haven't seen him since."

Red leaned back in her chair, the notebook empty on her lap. She rubbed her cheeks before speaking. "Derek, why do you think it was Clyde who killed those women? You haven't seen him in eighteen years."

Dully, he replied, "Because the last thing he said to me was, 'I'll see that you pay for this.'" He opened his mouth to say more, then drained his coffee instead. "That damn green jacket. Joanie Crea in my summerhouse. What else can I believe? He comes back to haunt me."

A tightness pulled at the muscles in Red's back as she watched Derek. She wanted very much to believe him, but she wondered if the anguish masked a total craziness. She thought about Lad and how his face never revealed his true thoughts.

The phone rang. Red ignored it.

Derek stretched his legs in front of him. "I keep trying to put it together. Why the nurse? Did it have to do with her visits to Mother or Caddie? Maybe he was angry because of the abortion—the baby would have been his grandchild—or that Joanie was married to Jimmy Crea. Jimmy once picked a fight with him after he got together with Gerry. He gave Clyde a black eye. For Clyde, that was unforgivable."

"You mean you think Clyde was exacting revenge on Jimmy? Tell me more."

Derek closed his eyes. "It was part of the whole craziness back then. Jimmy dated Geraldine before she married Clyde. Gerry doesn't like to talk about it, but I know Clyde married her because she was pregnant. I've never been sure, though, about Caddie."

The Pines Were Watching   237

"What do you mean?"

"Like maybe Clyde wasn't the father?"

In the middle of this tense meeting, the word raced through Red's head. *Telenovela.* She pressed her lips together to stop the insane smile that wanted to creep out.

"Derek, yesterday you told me to talk to Bella Crea. What was that all about?"

Derek rubbed his temples. "My dad and Clyde used to visit her at Skunk Lake. She...ah...was the swamp version of a hooker, I guess. Dad took me there once when I was thirteen. It wasn't a good thing."

The light coming in from the windows dimmed as darker clouds obscured the sun. Red's jaw ached, telling her the low-pressure system was moving in. Storm clouds were gathering, and it fit her mood.

"Early this morning, I drove up there. You know, to where they used to go. I needed to find Clyde and ask him why—why all the craziness."

Red sat up straighter. "And what did you find?"

"I remembered a road. The place has changed a lot, and it took me a while to find it. But I found the road. It's just a rutted, overgrown track, but someone had driven on it enough to pack it down." He blinked with a dazed expression. "The old trailer that the Creas lived in was there. I thought it would be run-down and overgrown with weeds, but someone had kept the lawn up. I knew it wasn't Bella because she was in the senior apartments." His voice drifted off.

"And?"

"The door was unlocked, and I knew Clyde had been staying there."

"Did you find him?"

"No, but I smelled him. He used to use an expensive cologne. Not like one you'd buy at the drugstore. God knows why. It had a piney scent to it."

"What did you do?"

He shrugged. "I looked around, and he wasn't there. But I'm going to find him, and when I do..."

Red raised her hand. "Why don't you leave it to us to find your brother. Maybe you could go home and get some rest. You look terrible."

Derek stared at her for a few moments before nodding. "Sure."

"One more thing." Red showed him the photo of the scrap of paper she'd found by Fire Tower Road.

"Does this mean anything to you?"

He squinted at the photo as he read aloud the faint words, "Green jacket." He shrugged. "I don't recognize the handwriting."

Outside the window, clouds obscured the sun.

45

THE CREA LAND

Red walked Derek to the door. "If you see your brother, please call immediately."

He left without replying, and as she watched him, she wondered if she should have detained him. Her gut, the one that Will said was so accurate, told her yes and no.

"Damn it! Would you make up your mind," she muttered.

Billie looked up. "Did you say something?"

As soon as she sat down, she called Waltz and filled him in on her interview with Derek. He sounded sympathetic. "Sorry I couldn't be there. Sometimes body language tells you more than the words."

"I would have to say that I think he was basically telling the truth. I should have gotten more out of him, though."

Waltz laughed. "You are so Minnesota humble. I've watched you in action. You can squeeze blood from a stone."

"Thanks for the cliché. But I'm lost here. I have a bad feeling that whoever killed those women isn't done."

"Why?"

Should she tell him about her dreams and her spotting of the green jacket? She shook her head. Intuition and gut feelings didn't stand up in court. "I don't know, but I worry about Geraldine. If Clyde has truly come back and is filled with revenge, I'd think he'd want to take it out on her. After all, isn't it the husband who usually kills the wife?"

Waltz's voice turned serious. "All too often that's the case. Speaking of husbands killing wives, we need to talk with Jimmy again. Guilty people often change their stories after they've had a chance to think about it."

Red pictured Jimmy with his jovial expression and his slight paunch. "When are you available? We can bring him in."

"I have paperwork to take care of to get Dad into a care facility. I'll drive up tomorrow, and we can bring in both Jimmy and Derek."

"Maybe by then I'll have found the mysterious Clyde." She planned to drive north to Skunk Lake and check out the trailer.

A half hour later, the county engineer brought several maps of the northern part of Pearsal County to her office. He unrolled the first one. "This is about five years old. I don't see any roads into the swamp—at least none we've had to maintain. Maybe Jimmy should come in and show you where they used to live."

Red preferred that Jimmy not know that she was searching for the old Crea property. "I'll think about it. Thanks."

Instead of Jimmy, Red called Cal. Cal, one of her dispatchers, had retired in the spring. He had an uncanny memory of places and people. With Cal around, the county did not need to use Google. Plus, he was usually more accurate.

"Hey, Cal, it's Red. How's the fishing?"

Cal coughed before answering. "Terrible. Hammer Lake isn't giving them up this year. And yes, I know you are short-handed, but I shall remain retired."

Red laughed. "Sure you don't want a few shifts? I can arrange it."

He made a growling sound. Red smiled because whenever Cal was irritated, that was the noise he made. "I'll stop kidding you. I know you are retired. However, if you ever get the yen to come back, I'll kick your replacement out."

"Uh-huh. What can I do you for?"

She quickly explained that she was looking for the road to the old Crea place. "It's not on the newer maps. At least I can't see it."

"Ah yes, back in the day, we called that Crea place our red-light district.

The Pines Were Watching 241

I'm told people found their way even if the road wasn't more than a dirt track." He paused. "Not that I ever went there."

"I'm sure you didn't."

"Poor Bella. Married Harley Crea when she was sixteen and he was forty. I doubt her 'party' lifestyle was one she chose herself. Came from dirt-poor people, I'm told."

Red thought about the woman she'd visited this morning. She'd looked worn out, aged beyond her years and afraid. What a sad life. "Cal, do you know how to get to the old Crea place? I know it's near Skunk Lake, but I don't see any roads or accesses up there."

He was silent for a moment. Red pictured him calculating through all the information in his brain. "It's tricky, but there is an old access road. It's not on the maps anymore. It got flooded out shortly before Harley disappeared. He was the Swamp King, and everyone assumed he probably got drunk and sank into the bog somewhere. If I recall, Bella never asked us to find him. She and Jimmy moved into town, and we didn't look too hard for him. Last I knew, the property was still in Harley's name, but taxes were up to date."

"She never had him declared dead?"

"Not that I recall. I wondered when Jimmy came back with his accountant degree if he would do something. You could check with the assessor, but I doubt the land's been transferred." He coughed and cleared his throat. "Maybe Jimmy and Bella think old Harley is still alive."

Just like the Grandgeorges think Clyde is alive. Interesting.

Red was able to get directions from Cal to the road that was no longer on the map. It was time for a site visit.

She called Jason. "Want to go for a ride?"

"Sure, as long as wherever we go has beer."

"I hear we might find some old hooch."

"Hooch?"

Red had to remind herself that Jason was a millennial. He didn't grow up with stories from grandparents about backyard stills. More likely he heard stories about basements filled with grow lights and marijuana plants.

She gave him directions and said they'd meet off the county road near where Cal thought the access road might be. "You know, where Nelson's collapsed barn is?"

"Sure, see you in an hour."

She needed to hand Blue over to Georgia and Scotty. As irrational as it was, she didn't want him going off with them without an explanation. Will used to laugh at her when she'd sit on the patio and talk to the dog about her day.

"What are you going to do if he argues with you?"

"I'll arrest him and send him to the shelter." Since Pearsal County didn't have an animal shelter, it was hardly a threat.

Besides, the only fight Blue ever put up was when she had to give him his heartworm medicine or a bath.

When Red arrived at home, Georgia and Scotty were already waiting. Scotty had Blue wrapped in a towel and was talking softly to him. "He's not very perky. And I can hear his stomach rumble. Good that we can get him into the vet."

Looking at Blue, so small and vulnerable in Scotty's arms, she had to fight back an ache in her throat. She stroked his head. "Listen, old pup. These nurses will take good care of you."

The air was still and heavy as Scotty and Georgia drove away. She hoped the weather would hold for them. A low rumble of thunder replied.

As she watched the car disappear down the road, her phone rang. "Sheriff, it's Billie. Jimmy Crea is here, and he's really mad. I think you'd better come."

"Sorry. Tell him I can see him later this afternoon. Jason and I are meeting at Skunk Lake. Please don't say anything about where we are to him."

"Ah sure."

As soon as she ended the call, she regretted mentioning Skunk Lake to Billie. She pictured him accidentally passing it on to Jimmy.

Through the pines in front of her house, she saw the sky light up behind a band of dark clouds. She needed to get up north quickly and find the access road.

. . .

The front bringing in the storm appeared to be moving slowly as Red drove north on Highway 25. Several cars and trucks were parked in Eddie's lot—the mid-afternoon drinking crowd. For a moment, she wondered if any of them had spotted a man in a green jacket. They tended to gossip with each other—retirees from the cities and old fishermen from the area. Maybe if they didn't have luck finding the Crea trailer, she'd stop and ask around.

She'd heard that Mac fired Wayne, and the conversation at the jail didn't go well. As much as she disliked Mac, at least he stuck to his guns on this. She was still working with the county attorney on the charges. Another paperwork headache to attend to. Finding who killed the women was first in her mind.

Large raindrops splatted on the windshield as she turned off the highway and onto County Road 18, the road that passed by Indian Mounds Park and Fire Tower Road. Weak lightning flashed, followed by a low thunder. If she was lucky, they'd find the trailer before the brunt of the storm hit. The park was empty of cars. She thought about the shoe she'd discovered and wondered what Joanie had been doing at the park. Angela had told her Joanie was meeting someone up north. Was this the meeting place? If so, who was she meeting, and where was her car? Had she gone there to meet with Clyde Grandgeorge or the mystery man in the green jacket? Again, if so, why?

Red almost missed the turnoff by Nelson's collapsed barn. The building, with its roof caved in and its frame tilted to the side, hadn't changed much in the years that Red had worked for the sheriff's department. In fact, when she was a teenager, it had once been a place to party until the roof collapsed on a couple of her classmates and they had to explain how they got hurt to their parents. Over the years, the partying had moved on to Fire Tower Road. She imagined that the inside of the building was still littered with empty beer cans and liquor bottles. It was a wonder that no one had set the old barn on fire.

As she turned onto the gravel, the rain came down harder. Jason was parked near the old barn and sat eating a sandwich. By the time she pulled up next to him, the lightning flashed a bright white and the thunder vibrated the ground. Rain quickly came down in sheets. Red sat in the car, cursing the weather as the wind picked up, swaying the pines behind the old barn.

Jason made a dash to her car and slipped into the passenger seat.

"Well, boss. I'm thinking this isn't a good time to find an abandoned road."

She felt like she was so close to something. So close to maybe finding the mysterious Clyde, yet Jason was right. Even if they sat out the storm, the road in these lowlands would be impassable.

As if to seal the deal, her radio crackled to life. "Sheriff, trees down and power off in town."

"We'd better get back. Stay close to me in case the road is flooded." She watched through the downpour as Jason sprinted to his car. As she backed out onto the county road, she again cursed the goddess of weather.

46

BLUE

Driving back to town with the rain pouring down and the wind rattling the windows of the car felt similar to driving through a blizzard. At times, Red could barely see the road ahead of her. If she hadn't been the sheriff, she would have pulled over to wait it out.

Several reports came through with calls about downed trees and utility poles. One of the downed trees was across from Norma Elling's house. It reminded her that an angry Jimmy Crea had wanted to talk with her. It was hard to see the mild, almost milk-toast Jimmy barging into her office and unsettling Billie. She must have touched a sore spot when she visited his mother. Only child, protective—could mean something or nothing. After all, Jimmy had just lost Joanie, and his nerves might be raw.

The rain began to lighten as she neared town. Her neck and shoulders ached with the tension of trying to stay on the road. She ran through a list of to-dos in her head to deal with the storm. First was to make sure no one had gotten hurt.

She pulled into the parking lot of the courthouse to a few sprinkles and a sky that was growing lighter as the clouds swept east. The rain had washed away the heavy air and left behind the sweet smell of wet shrubbery and newly mown grass. Ed stood in the doorway of the building, wearing a raincoat.

"Wet enough for you?" He pulled off his baseball cap and shook it out.

"How's the old building?" She pointed to the door. "Any damage?"

"Nope, not even a wet basement. But hooey, did it come down for a while. Least we didn't get any hail. Those farmers down south were plenty worried, I'm sure."

With climate change, some parts of Minnesota had suffered drought followed by torrential rains with nowhere for the water to go. The southern part of the state had experienced unprecedented flooding. Some of it could be attributed to the corporate farming practices that drained the wetlands for more acreage. Still, the rural wags refused to believe it had anything to do with a man-made problem. Pearsal County and the surrounding area had been spared for the time being. Other than a warmer and dryer-than-normal summer, the forest appeared to flourish.

Crews were already out restoring electricity. When she reached her office, a ray of sunshine pushed through the clouds. Perhaps if she and Jason had waited it out, they might have found the trailer Derek spoke of.

She asked Billie into her office. She caught him right before shift change. Billie was not known to hang around a second longer than necessary. "Sorry, Billie. Can you stay for a few minutes and tell me about Jimmy?"

"Oh, he was mad when he walked through the door. My grandma used to say something about spitting tacks. I think I got what she meant when I looked at him. Red in the face and everything."

"Did he say what he wanted to talk to me about?"

Billie wrinkled his brow. "I think he said something about Randy telling him you talked to his mother, and you had no business going there."

"Randy?" She thought for a moment. "Oh, he must have meant Rance, the caretaker."

Billie's face brightened. "Yeah, that's what I think. Anyway, when I told him you were up at Skunk Lake, he left."

Red opened her mouth to remind him that she had specifically instructed him not to tell Jimmy where she was. She pressed her lips together, remembering Will's advice about choosing your battles. Billie was trying, but he was scattered, and since he'd passed his probationary period, moving him out of his position would be a major headache.

The Pines Were Watching 247

"Okay, you can go." After he hurried out the door, Red pulled up her notes on her visit to Bella and added that Jimmy wanted to talk with her. She considered giving him a call, but when she glanced at the clock, she saw that it was now after five and she hadn't heard from Georgia or Scotty.

She tried Georgia's number, and it went directly to voicemail. "It's Red. Just checking to find out your ETA. Hope the vet visit went well."

When Georgia hadn't called back in ten minutes, she tried Scotty. She got a no-service message. She experienced a sudden empathy for her parents when Lad would disappear. She remembered how irritated she'd be with them. "Come on, you know he'll show up." And then one day, he didn't.

Reports came in about spotty damage throughout the county. Mostly downed trees. The hospital emergency room only had one casualty. It was the usual chainsaw injury. The guy had cut all the way through the tree and into his thigh.

All was calm in Pearsal County except Georgia and Scotty were not back. At six, she called the veterinarian's office in Charlesville.

The vet, a woman with an Eastern European accent, told her they had missed the appointment and hadn't called to cancel. "I must charge for that."

Red hardly heard her words as she ended the call. Where were they? She made several more phone calls, including to the state patrol to be on the lookout for Georgia's car. When her phone finally rang, she nearly dropped it in her worry and haste.

"Red, it's Lou. I thought we had a poker game tonight, but no one is here."

Red struggled to keep her voice even. "They didn't make it to the vet appointment, and they're not answering the phone. I've got the highway patrol on alert. Maybe they had car trouble."

After another twenty minutes of pacing and getting nothing done, Red grabbed her laptop and headed home. Lou was already in the driveway, holding a pan of lasagna. "I made it for tonight. We might as well have it."

They sat at the kitchen table while the lasagna heated. Lou sat up straight with her hands folded in front of her. She was not one for a lot of words, but when she was amused, she had a dazzling smile. The worry in the room was palpable.

"You know, Red, I've been thinking about Tommy Henley. What if he knows something about who killed his mother but he's afraid to say? Could it be the guy in the green jacket?"

"I doubt he will speak with me. He's too scared. I'm sure over the years his mother has warned him not to talk to 'the law.'"

"I did a training course on talking with children last year. Do you want me to try? I don't think he's scared of me."

Red quickly sorted through all the roadblocks to using Lou. She wasn't a peace officer or a contracted psychologist. But she did have a lot of experience talking with teenagers at the family planning clinic, and she was a certified family nurse practitioner. Could she draw Tommy out?

"Let me think about it."

"Aha! The bureaucrat in you is speaking."

"You sound like Scotty."

The timer on the oven dinged as the kitchen filled with the smell of lasagna. Despite her worry, Red realized how hungry she was. Before eating, she checked her phone and also called in to dispatch to find out if they had any news of her missing friends. Red's head pounded.

"I need to take something for this headache before I can enjoy your delicious supper. I didn't know you were a chef along with your other skills."

"The secret is to not follow any of Scotty's recipes."

While Red was in the bathroom, she heard voices. Quickly taking the Tylenol, she hurried to the kitchen to find Lou holding the door open for Georgia and Scotty.

Scotty walked in, her hair damp and flattened, as if she'd been wearing a stocking cap. She started talking as soon as she spotted Red and Lou.

"You wouldn't believe what happened to us. We've been escorted the last ten miles by the highway patrol." Her eyes suddenly lit up. "Really cute officer named Grady."

"Is everything okay?" She looked through the doorway for Georgia.

"Well, we didn't make it to the vet."

The Pines Were Watching 249

A car door closed. Red stepped to the back door just as Georgia walked in carrying a very limp little dog.

Red looked at Blue and then at Georgia.

Georgia smiled sympathetically. "He's fine. Just tired from all the activity. Poor smelly little thing." She handed him over to Red, who worked to not show the relief that flowed through her body. Blue licked Red's hand and wiggled as she held him.

In the next ten minutes, Red heard a jumbled story of the two women lost in the downpour, car in the ditch. They'd walked down a driveway to a little farmhouse where an old woman took them in. The woman, who was at least ninety, according to Scotty, claimed to be able to heal small animals.

"She was shriveled—you know, like one of those apple dolls. Downright scrawny," Scotty said. "But she had magic hands. She held Blue, rocked him, and he was cured!"

Red looked at Georgia in disbelief. "Has she been drinking? An old lady in a farmhouse healed my dog?"

Georgia looked back at her with calm eyes. "Scotty forgot to mention that she also gave him a magical potion."

"What?"

Blue, now comfortably resting on Red's lap, lifted his head. His eyes were as clear as she'd seen them in a year. Gently, he licked her hand.

"Okay," Scotty said. "So, it was a little Pepto-Bismol or Maalox or something. But she did put a spell on it."

The room erupted in laughter. After things quieted to a few hiccups, Scotty asked, "Anything happen around here?"

Despite the relief of having her dog and her friends back, Red felt edgy. It was that odd sensation like someone was watching them. Before they left, she admonished them, "Listen, we haven't found the person who killed those women. I want you to be on high alert, and for heaven's sake, lock your doors."

Scotty furrowed her brow. "You are serious."

She didn't share that she thought the next victim could be Geraldine Grandgeorge, wife of the missing Clyde and cousin of the dead Arlis.

After they left, she offered dry dog food to Blue. He chewed a few nuggets without much enthusiasm. She'd have to take him herself to the

Charlesville vet if he didn't seem better in the morning. Imagine, she thought, explaining to her constituents that she was skipping out on the investigation because her dog had an upset stomach.

She stroked his fur. "Little pup, you really need to get well because I have a crime to solve."

That night, she fell into a fitful sleep filled with dreams of trying to get away from a dark presence. She tried to cry out, but no sound came from her until she was startled awake by a high yip from Blue. He seldom barked, and when he did, it was usually to scare away a chipmunk.

"You okay?" He lay next to her in bed, his ears pricked. "Did you hear something, or were you having a nightmare, too?"

It was 4:32 a.m. as she sat up and strained to hear what had awakened Blue. The house was silent other than the ticking of the clock on the bedroom wall.

As if to answer, Blue jumped off the bed and trotted into the living room. He stood by the patio door and yipped again. Red walked out wearing only Will's large-size T-shirt.

"What is it?"

She snapped on the patio light and peered out. Beyond the light was only the darkness of the forest between the house and the lake. "I don't see anything."

Blue remained on alert.

"Maybe this upset stomach has addled your brain. There's nothing outside."

Pushing open the patio door, she stepped out, and Blue followed. Blue went to his favorite tree and lifted his leg. He probably simply needed to go out.

Still, she sensed that something wasn't right. A rustling sound near the corner of the house caught her attention. She crept in the direction of the sound, aware that she was barefoot and unarmed. Quickly she peeked around the corner but saw nothing.

"Just a continuation of my dream, I guess." When she returned to the patio, Blue waited by the door. "There's nothing for you to bark at." She picked him up to go back inside when it struck her. It was a fragrance that

The Pines Were Watching 251

didn't fit with the outdoors. Something piney and artificial. Just like what she'd noticed in Joanie's house.

Quickly she brought Blue in, pulled on a pair of jogging pants, and slipped into her shoes. She thought about getting her gun that was locked up but opted for the large flashlight she kept by the back door.

Back outside, she walked around the perimeter of the house, using the flashlight to illuminate the woods close by. Nothing moved, but the fragrance stayed in the still air.

47

A LITTLE DEATH AND A LITTLE COLOGNE

Blue woke Red up by licking her cheek just after dawn. The rumbling in his stomach had stopped, and he gazed at her with bright eyes.

"A little old lady fixed you, huh? If I'd known all you needed was some Pepto-Bismol, we could have avoided yesterday's drama."

The air was fresh and cool, cleansed by the storm yesterday. While Blue trotted to his tree, Red took a walk around the outside of the house. She saw nothing out of place, and the fragrance she had detected in the middle of the night was replaced by the smell of the dewy grass in her yard. Maybe she'd imagined it.

Still, she had a feeling.

Her first chore of the morning was a phone call to Jimmy. Hopefully he had cooled down. When she called, it went immediately to voicemail. To her chagrin, she realized it was only seven in the morning—not a good time for anyone to get a call from the local sheriff. She left a brief message asking him to call her.

Sipping instant coffee, she sat at the kitchen table with her laptop going over all her notes. None of the pieces of information were coming together to paint a picture. Two women strangled but bodies left in different parts of the county. Details that didn't add up—a slip of paper near where Arlis had been found. The key to Joanie's house in Arlis's

The Pines Were Watching 253

mouth. Joanie's shoe found near Indian Mounds Park. Various sightings of a man in a green jacket.

She sat back and thought about the key. It linked the murders, but if the killer had shoved it in, why? She and Waltz had discussed it briefly after it had been found. They both agreed it might be a sign of rage or revenge. But again, why? They also agreed to keep this information between them and Waltz's team. As Waltz said, "Sometimes the killer slips up with a detail only we know."

She closed the lid of the laptop, patted Blue on the head, and told him, "I'm going on a possible wild goose chase to Skunk Lake. I'll ask Oscar to look in on you. Okay?"

Blue walked away, jumped on Will's recliner, and settled in. He'd eaten his breakfast and appeared to be back to normal.

She arranged for Jason to once again meet her on the access road and hoped it wouldn't be too muddy to get through, if indeed a trailer existed like Derek had described.

As the day brightened, the gloom that encased Red eased away. She thought again about Occam's razor. A simple solution. *No*, she shook her head, *it's never simple when you take a life.*

Red turned in at the falling-down barn, noting tracks in the gravel road. Jason hadn't arrived yet, which meant someone else had been on this abandoned road. She parked and called in for a report from last night. Storm damage was minimal, and it appeared that the county slept well except for a 911 call from Alma Wooster. She thought someone was in her house.

"Did one of the deputies go out?"

"Yes, didn't find any evidence of it. However, Alma was worried because she woke up around three to find Jimmy's light on. When she called him, it went right to voicemail."

She told the dispatcher she'd be up at Skunk Lake for a couple of hours and might be out of cell range. Jason arrived as she was ending the call.

They took the county SUV. Jason drove slowly because the further down the road they went, the softer the road base. "It looks like it turns into a mud track up ahead."

"Derek claimed he found his way to the Crea trailer. I'm wondering if he was spinning a tale."

Jason turned to her. "I don't understand why you haven't arrested him. He probably burned that summerhouse down because he thought it had evidence. The guy's a spook."

Deeper into the woods, the pines gave way to ash and poplar trees. The forest floor was thick with evergreen shrubs, tamarack, and sedges. For a few moments as they inched their way down the road, she studied the beauty of these woods and the greenery that would soon be turning autumn brown. How endangered was Skunk Lake due to man and mother nature? Would all the ash trees be gone once the ash borer beetle got this far north?

She was jarred from these thoughts as Jason braked just before standing water obscured the road. "Looks like we're in for a hike, eh?"

Red was glad she'd worn her hiking boots and had slicked down with mosquito repellent before driving to the broken barn. "Are you doped up?"

Jason nodded. "Hate this stuff. It makes my nose run."

His comment reminded her that Jimmy had said cologne and perfume made him wheeze.

They were able to bypass the standing water by slogging around it. On the other side, the tire tracks they had followed continued. Derek probably was telling the truth about being up here.

They walked about a half mile until they came to a small clearing. The air was filled with the sounds of birds and frogs and crickets. Ahead was an old trailer that must have been a model from the early 1950s.

"Do you think Jimmy grew up here?"

Red folded her arms, studying the property. It was surrounded by boreal forest and swampland so thick it was hard to think that anyone could get in or out other than by the road. Twenty feet from the trailer was a pole building, its sides rusted, and its metal roof covered with moss and debris from the shedding forest.

The whole place should have looked abandoned, except a small grassy yard in front of the trailer had been tamped down by foot traffic and a worn path led from the trailer to the outbuilding.

Jason stepped to the trailer, but Red grabbed his arm. "Wait. Let's listen."

They stood in silence while the sounds of the swamp and forest filled

The Pines Were Watching   255

the air. Other than the birds and a couple of squirrels climbing an aspen, the grounds were quiet.

"Okay, let's check out the trailer and see if Clyde Grandgeorge is actually staying here like Derek claims."

Red knocked on the door and called out, "Hello! It's Sheriff Red Hammergren. Can you let us in?"

Silence.

She called again, "Can you open up?"

She nodded at Jason as she opened the screen door and turned the handle on the door, still knocking. She expected it to be locked. People didn't leave their Northwoods trailers unlocked because of vandalism. The knob twisted, and the door opened inward. Red took out her flashlight, still calling out.

"It's the sheriff. Can you come to the door?"

Red had been in many trailers that resided on isolated property in Pearsal County. Because the county had few zoning restrictions, people could drop their trailers without worrying about protecting the environment with things like septic systems and drain fields. Over the last decade, many of the places had become meth labs, adding to both crime and chemical pollution.

She half expected to see a lab setup. The living area of the trailer consisted of a love seat and another upholstered chair. While the trailer smelled of mold, it didn't have the dirty, neglected look of a place edging its way back to nature. Over the musty odor was the scent of something earthy and piney. The same scent she'd smelled by her house.

The kitchen had an old LP gas stove and a refrigerator that wasn't turned on. Instead, a Styrofoam ice chest sat on the counter. When she opened it, nothing was inside except a melted bag of ice.

Jason stood in the doorway of the first bedroom. It was hardly big enough to hold more than a cot-sized bed and a small dresser. The mattress on the cot was bare, and stuffing leaked out where the mice had eaten through.

The back bedroom was big enough to hold a double bed. Again, the mattress was bare, but a sleeping bag had been spread over the top.

"Someone has been living here."

Derek might have been correct.

They searched through the trailer but found nothing to indicate who had been using it. "I guess I will have a chat with Jimmy to see if he knows."

Outside, the sun had risen to midmorning brightness. Red pointed to the outbuilding. "Let's check it out."

As they walked the worn path to the building, Red experienced a feeling of suffocation in her chest, like this spot, this clearing, was closing in on her.

Jason chatted as he surveyed the land, "Boy, this is nice, isn't it. Would be a great place to come during deer hunting season. I'll bet I could snag a buck."

In the warmth of the sunlight, the deer flies had discovered the two of them. Red was glad she'd worn a baseball cap because they loved to land in hair and take bites out of the scalp. She batted them away as they circled around her head.

Will had once told her, "Never visit the woods on a still day in summer without having your head covered and your socks rolled up over your pants. If the deer flies don't eat you, the wood ticks will."

"Thanks," she'd groused. "Remember, I grew up as a town girl. Lykkins Lake wouldn't allow the bugs inside the city limits."

Now, with the mosquitoes and flies, she looked down and wondered how many ticks had invaded her body.

The pole building had a large sliding door, wide enough that a car or truck could get through. The door was firmly padlocked.

She stared at it. "Why would someone leave the trailer unlocked and the outbuilding locked?"

"Maybe because there was something valuable inside? Like a snowmobile or an ATV?"

They walked around the side of the building to a small window. It had been painted over.

"What are the secrets in here?" she asked aloud.

"I have a bolt cutter back in the cruiser. Do you want me to get it?"

Of course she wanted him to get it, but legally, without a warrant, she couldn't say yes. Yet, her gut, that damned gut of hers said she needed to find out what was in the building.

The Pines Were Watching 257

Studying the window, she said, "You know, when I was a kid, I once shimmied my way through a basement window when I...uh...came home a little late and the house was locked. Maybe we heard something like a call for help in the building?"

Now she had stepped over the edge of a legal search, and her stomach clenched as she made her decision. "Let's see if we can open the window just to peek in."

Jason stared at her. "Uh, boss, you're sure?"

"We're not doing an illegal search. We're checking for a meth lab."

He shrugged, and between the two of them, they tried to lift the window. It was painted shut. "Should we break it?" Jason looked around for something to smash the window.

Red shook her head. "Let's rattle it, and maybe loosen the paint."

They rattled the window and then tried pushing it up. It budged a little. Sweat beaded on her forehead as she and Jason worked the window. Would this be worth the back and shoulder pain she'd experience later?

After three attempts, the window slid up a couple of inches. Enough that they could peek inside.

Jason grunted, pushing harder on the window. With one last heave, the window opened.

"What's that smell?"

A little death. A little cologne.

The beam of the flashlight rested on two cars. A white Ford Escort and an old Ford Mustang.

It was time to get Waltz and his team back to Pearsal County.

48

THE TRUNK

"We've located Joanie Crea's car," Red spoke into the phone. Reception was spotty but good enough to hear Waltz say he and his team would be there as quickly as possible.

While they waited for the BCA forensic team, Jason cut the lock on the door. Inside the building, the air was hot and stale and mixed with the odor of cologne and something else.

Jason sniffed. "That's more than a dead smell."

Red did a cursory inspection of the building but stayed away from the two cars. Best to have the scientists check it out. She noted that the Mustang, with long-expired license plates, looked to be in good condition. The tires were inflated, and from a distance, she could not detect any of the usual Minnesota car rust from salted highways.

A quick check of the license plate confirmed the white Ford Escort belonged to Joanie. She had not been kind to it. It was dirty, like it had been driven on gravel roads. It had rust around the wheel wells and a couple of old dents.

She instructed Jason to go back to the old barn and direct the forensic crew. She asked the dispatcher to locate Jimmy Crea. She wanted him in the interview room with Waltz. The same with Derek Grandgeorge. She

The Pines Were Watching 259

also put out an alert to look for a man in his early forties with blond hair wearing a green letterman's jacket.

In the minutes of quiet on this land hemmed in by thick forest and swamp, Red sifted through all she knew. The pieces were lining up but still jumbled.

She and Waltz had talked earlier about the two cases. He'd been puzzled. "Usually a murder is about money, control, or jealousy. I don't see it here with either of these cases."

Maybe she needed to start by following the money. Joanie had withdrawn a $50,000 inheritance. The state of her house and her car would indicate she hadn't spent it on herself. However, she was concerned about things of value being taken from her patients.

Red's thoughts turned to Jimmy. She hadn't looked into his finances, but she knew he lived cheaply in a room at Norma Elling's. He was the treasurer for his church, and Rose had reported money missing but then said it had been an accounting error.

Connection? Maybe?

Derek Grandgeorge lived in a crumbling mansion. Again, she hadn't investigated his finances. Could he make enough money to maintain the place and support Geraldine, Caddie, and Rebecca? If he had a relationship with Joanie, which he denied, was he after her $50,000?

Then there was Arlis and her statement that she was coming into money.

On top of that, the mysterious man in the green jacket who claimed to be named Clyde had lost money at the casino. Who was he?

"Damn," she said aloud. "None of this is adding up."

Her radio squawked, and the dispatcher said they hadn't been able to locate Jimmy. Norma thought he'd gone out for the day, and he wasn't at his office or answering his phone. Grandgeorge was cutting logs on his property, according to Geraldine, and wasn't answering his phone.

She stood at the opening of the outbuilding, staring at the two cars and lost in thought when Waltz tapped her on the shoulder. "Hey, so we meet again."

He smelled of coffee and a hint of men's aftershave. Definitely not either the mystery odor or the strong scent of drugstore cologne that Harv Smith seemed to bathe in. "You know, Waltz, it would be nice to get together some time when we're not dealing with death."

For a moment, an amused smile crossed his face. "Such a thought."

She told him she and Jason had done a cursory check to make sure there were no bodies in the seats of the cars. Otherwise, they hadn't touched anything.

Waltz nodded his approval and set his team to work photographing the car and examining the area around the cars. The building itself held very little other than a few yard tools, a couple of red canisters of gasoline, and an extra canister of LP gas.

"This car is a beauty." He pointed to the Mustang. "Geez, I haven't seen one in such pristine condition since I went to the vintage car show in North St. Paul last year."

He walked around it, taking notes before trying the door. It was locked. The two of them bent over the window and peered in. It appeared the leather seats were in almost new condition.

Waltz sniffed. "Smell that?"

"Cologne and death?"

"You are astute."

"Astute? Nice word. Not normally used to describe a rural sheriff." A little tension slipped from her shoulders as they bantered.

They moved to the Escort. It was unlocked, and when they opened the door, they found the floor had been swept clean. Again, the pine cologne smell. The more she smelled it, the more it made her slightly nauseous.

"Wait." Waltz held up his hand and knelt by the floor of the passenger side. With gloved hands, he inched out a delicate gold bracelet jammed under the floor mat.

Red stared at it, picturing the bracelet on Arlis's thick wrist. "That belonged to Arlis."

Connections.

Opening the trunk of the Escort, they found a tarp similar to the one Red had seen last week in the back of Derek's truck. When they pulled out the tarp, they found a shoe, one that matched the one Red had discovered at the wayside rest. She examined it, and a little piece of the puzzle fell into place.

Waltz peered at it with a grim expression. "Jimmy killed his wife?"

"Or someone set Jimmy up."

"Hmmm."

Jason joined them as they watched the team inspect the Escort, collect samples, and take more photographs.

Waltz supervised with a low-key touch. "Careful there. Don't miss the latch. Let's get another photo of the tarp."

Matt arrived and brought a thermos with coffee. "Thought you could use this."

Securing a possible crime scene was painstaking work and for Red, who wanted to be doing something, boring. She tried the dispatcher a couple of times, and they reported they hadn't located either Jimmy or Derek.

While she waited, she called Lou at the clinic. "Hi. Remember how you offered to talk with Tommy Henley?"

"I thought you got all tied up in bureaucratic red tape about having me interview him."

"I'm not in a bureaucratic mood right now." Red filled her in on what she was looking for and called Debbi, the foster mother, to let her know Lou would be stopping by. "How's Tommy doing?"

"Not well. Doesn't want to eat. Just plays video games."

"Is he talking?"

"A little. He said something to one of my kids about how he should have saved his mother. If he hadn't wanted that video game so badly."

"Poor kid." She told Debbi about Lou's visit. "Lou knows that if he doesn't want to talk, she won't push him." When she ended the call, the back of her head throbbed with a headache—the kind that said this was not going to be a good day.

Waltz's team moved to the Mustang. As they inspected it, Waltz pointed to the trunk. "I don't like locked trunks at a crime scene." He stood by as one of his team used a slim jim to open the locked front door.

Once inside, he reached down and popped the trunk.

A chill ran down Red's back as she peered at what was inside. "Oh my God."

Death and cologne.

The decomposed body looked like it had been tossed in the trunk either in great haste or great anger. The skull had tufts of blond hair and an indentation on the right temple. The skeletal legs were pulled up into a fetal position.

Her thoughts turned immediately to Derek Grandgeorge. Had he killed his brother in his rage all those years ago? If so, why hide the body at the Creas'? And why hadn't Jimmy reported it? For a moment, her knees locked as she tensed up.

She stood back and watched the forensic team carefully document the state of the body and take more photos. Her instinct would have been to move it immediately to see if it yielded any clues for identification.

The phone interrupted her. She was tempted to let it go to voicemail since the caller was unknown. At this moment of drama, the last thing she needed was Harv Smith calling to report a barking dog. Reluctantly she answered. "This is Sheriff Hammergren."

The voice on the staticky line was high-pitched and hysterical. "He called Mom to say he was coming for her. When I told Uncle Derek, he said he was going to kill him at last. Hurry! Something bad is going to happen!"

"Caddie, where are you?"

"I'm in the house, but Mom went to the summerhouse."

"Who called?"

Caddie let out a sob. "He said he was my dad, and it was time to claim what was his."

"How long ago did he call?"

"I..." Her voice rose. "I don't know. Maybe fifteen minutes? Please do something!"

"Listen." Red fought to keep a calm tone. "Stay where you are and lock the doors. Okay?"

"But what about Mom?"

"We're on our way."

The line went dead.

49

THE BROTHERS

Damn it! Damn it! Damn it!

"Waltz," she called out. "I have an emergency." She didn't add that she might need his team once again at the Grandgeorge Place.

Jason stood watching Waltz's team, as if in a trance. Pearsal County didn't often yield decaying bodies in trunks of old cars. She grabbed him by his arm. "Come on! We need to get to the Grandgeorge Place now!"

The bright, cloudless day seemed to respond to the drama on the ground when darker clouds obscured the sun. As they ran to the cruiser, Red looked up and muttered, "Don't you dare storm on us."

The leaves on the trees, awakened from a summer stillness, began to rustle, and the wind whispered through the pines. It was not a poetic sound, more the sound of suppressed anger. Red pictured the Swamp King emerging from the mire after all these years. When they reached the cruiser by the crumbling barn, it was hemmed in by one of the BCA cars.

They wasted precious minutes getting by the BCA car and almost ended up stuck in the boggy earth. While Jason manipulated the vehicle, Red called Caddie back. After numerous rings, it went to voicemail. She tried the number she had for Derek, and the call failed.

Just as they finally pulled onto County Road 18 and headed west around the bog and the lake, Red's phone rang. Lou's name popped up.

Red skipped any of the social niceties. "What did you find out?"

Lou spoke for about five minutes before ending the call. Tommy had confirmed what Red now suspected and had described the man in the green jacket.

She gripped the phone, angry with herself for not picking up the clues earlier. "It was all there in bits and pieces." She pressed her lips together into a tight grimace. "Why didn't I put it together?"

My only begotten son in whom I am well pleased.

Closing her eyes, she made a mental list of all the pieces and felt the tightening of her stomach. Another murder was about to happen if they didn't get to the Grandgeorge Place in time. Will's voice, calm and measured, broke through the noise in her head. *Trust your instincts and stay calm.*

"Easy for you to say. You're dead."

"What?" Jason glanced at her and quickly back at the road. "Did you say something?"

Raindrops began splattering onto the windshield. Driving west, the storm intensified. Jason pushed harder on the accelerator, and the cruiser skidded on the slick pavement.

Red tried Caddie again, and again it went to voicemail. She also tried Derek and Geraldine with no results. As they passed the cemetery before the driveway to the mansion, lightning reflected off the granite gravestones. Red imagined seeing a man in a green jacket disappearing into the woods. She blinked hard, and the vision disappeared.

"Great," she mumbled. "Seeing things now." No time for visions or humor or anything else. They were in a race to save another person from being killed.

The cruiser slid on the wet gravel as the windshield wipers slapped away the rain and mud. Jason gripped the steering wheel with white knuckles.

With a calmness she didn't feel, she touched Jason's shoulder. "You're doing good. Almost there."

Her heart thumped inside her ears, and she wished the cruiser to go faster.

The radio came alive.

The Pines Were Watching

"Sheriff?"

"Go ahead," Red yelled over the din of the road.

"We're sending Matt and another deputy. They're about fifteen minutes out."

Fifteen minutes might be too late.

The sky lit up in a sickly green-white hue from a flash of lightning as they pulled up to the big house. Derek's pickup and a dark SUV were parked in the turnaround. Blood pounded behind Red's eyes.

She ran up the steps and ripped open the screen door. "Caddie, it's Sheriff Red. Can you open the door?"

She signaled Jason to follow her.

The deadbolt slipped open, and Caddie stared at her with wide eyes. In the living room, a trembly voice called, "Clyde? I know you're here. I saw you. Come see your mother."

"Where are they?" Red took a step toward the living room but stopped when Caddie held up her hand.

The girl's voice shook. "The summerhouse. Derek said..."

Red interrupted, "How long ago?"

Caddie's lips quivered. "A little while. Not long."

"What did Derek say?"

"He said he'd find his brother and get this all over with. That's all." Caddie's eyes filled with tears. "Mom went after him. I tried to stop her."

A clap of thunder hit with such intensity that the floor vibrated. Windows in the house rattled, and suddenly the place went dark.

Red pointed to the living room. "Stay with your grandmother and away from windows." She turned to Jason. "We need to get to the ruins of the summerhouse."

Dashing through the downpour to the cruiser, she swung open the door and grabbed her flashlight. Above her, a streak of lightning shot across the sky, followed within seconds by the crash of thunder. She ran around the side of the house to the summerhouse path, cursing her gun, which rubbed against her thigh, the rain, which dripped down her face, and the stupidity of men. Jason huffed alongside her.

Wind blasted through the pines lining the path to the burned-out building. In her peripheral vision, all Red could see were the shadows of the trees, obscured by the rain, and the ominous white flashes of lightning. The ground gave beneath her feet. She felt like she was running on a wet sponge.

Spots formed in front of her eyes, and her stomach tightened with a sickening grip as she ran.

"Hurry!" They didn't have much time. Her shirt was drenched and sticking to her, and her lungs cried out. It seemed like it was taking too long to get to the summerhouse. "Where is it?"

Suddenly, in front of her, just beyond the beam of the flashlight, she saw movement.

"Stop!" she yelled. "It's Sheriff Red."

The figure disappeared around a slight bend in the pathway.

The rain and the wind roared in her ears. Her foot caught a root, and she slid to the side. Jason grabbed her arm before she fell.

Righting herself, she kept running. Moments later, she reached the clearing and the blackened skeleton of the summerhouse. The charred beams appeared darker and more foreboding in the downpour. She signaled to Jason, and they stopped about ten feet from the gaping hole that was once the door. Straining, she listened for the sound of humans above the roar of the storm. For a second, it was deadly silent, then thunder crashed once again. And a voice rose from the other side of the building.

"It will end here."

Then a shrill scream. "Stop! Oh, please stop!"

50

IN WHOM I AM WELL PLEASED

They sprinted around the blackened building. Jason slipped on the wet ash and debris, backpedaling to stay upright. She ran ahead of him, concentrating on the sound of the voices. A bolt of lightning illuminated the cleared area behind the summerhouse. Framed by the flash of brilliance, two men struggled at the edge near a line of old-growth pines. Geraldine stood behind them, her hands over her mouth.

Brother against brother.

The dark one held a baseball bat. The other, with blond hair, wore a tattered green letterman's jacket.

Thunder rumbled and the ground shook. Red yelled to Jason, "Get Geraldine out of here!"

Geraldine stood stock-still, rooted to the drama in front of her. Jason grabbed her arm and tugged her away. She fought against him. Red prayed he had the strength to move her away before she became the next victim.

For a moment, the two men turned to watch as Jason half dragged Geraldine around the side of the summerhouse.

"Stop!" Red pointed the flashlight beam at the two men.

Derek held the bat in both hands, ready to swing.

"Don't do it!" A clap of thunder buried the sound of her voice.

"Goddamn you!" he roared.

Again, Red yelled, "Stop!"

Derek hesitated for a second, glancing at Red, then back at the man in the green jacket. His hesitation gave the man just enough time to react. In a split second, he lunged, aiming a vicious kick at Derek's knee. Red heard the thud of the impact. Derek groaned and fell, the bat flying from his hand.

Wind blasted a sheet of rain at Red as if the earth wanted to hold her back.

The man in the green jacket grabbed the bat and, without hesitation, charged Derek, the blond wig flying off his head.

He moved so quickly; she didn't have time to pull her gun out. Instead, she gripped the flashlight and pointed the beam directly at the man in the green jacket.

Blinded for a moment, Jimmy Crea slowed.

"It's all over, Jimmy. You don't have to pretend anymore."

"You!" he roared, lifting the baseball bat. "You should have left my mother alone!"

Ice shot through her veins as he swung the bat and hit her solidly in the left arm. The blow sent a bolt of white-hot pain up her arm and into her neck. She stumbled but remained upright. He was back at her with the quickness and power of unrestrained rage. Instinctively, she jerked back the flashlight in her right hand and aimed at his head with all her strength. The blow was too low and glanced off his shoulder.

He launched himself at her, his eyes on her holstered gun. She backed away, losing her balance. He was upon her in an instant as the two fell to the wet ground, the rain pounding down on them. She was on her back, her left arm numb. She grappled for the flashlight as he threw his weight on her.

Red began to see dark spots in front of her eyes as the weight of his body pushed the oxygen out of her lungs.

Jimmy spit out, "You ruined it! This place is mine! Carl promised my mother he would take care of both of us."

With the fingers of her right hand, she was able to inch the flashlight over until she could get a grip on it.

The Pines Were Watching 269

"Jimmy, you murdered three people and beat up a little boy. This place is not yours and never was!" She gasped out the words, fighting for oxygen.

He let up slightly, just long enough for her to gather all the energy she had left and swing the flashlight. This time it hit his temple with a sickening thud. His eyes widened, and he collapsed.

She rolled away and into a stand. "It's over."

Jason ran back, his gun drawn. "Are you all right?" He stared at the blood trickling down the side of Jimmy's face. "What did you do?"

"I bashed him with the flashlight. Should have shot him instead." Catching her breath, she added, "Meet the man in the green jacket."

51

THE PIECES

Red refused the attention of the doctor in the emergency room. Her arm would be sore and bruised, but nothing was ripped or broken. Let them tend to Jimmy's head and Derek's knee. She needed some quiet time with Waltz to put the puzzle together.

They sat in her office as the evening faded and streetlights of Lykkins Lake snapped on. Red pointed to the one she could see from her window. "That's what tripped me up."

Waltz sat back in the chair in front of the desk and folded his arms. "Tell me more." His expression was both bemused and serious.

In her exhaustion, she thought she spied Will standing behind him. She blinked hard and continued. "Alma Wooster was Jimmy's alibi for the night Joanie was murdered. She'd seen his light go on, and Jimmy told us he'd heard her on the telephone. If you recall, it appeared to be a solid story."

"Except?"

"When we searched his room this afternoon, we found a light timer. Similar to the one Joanie had in her house. It was programmed to come on at three a.m. and go off fifteen minutes later. Jimmy's second phone, the one we found hidden in his closet, had a record of a call to Alma at three a.m.

The Pines Were Watching

Of course, Jimmy knew what Alma said because he was the one who called her."

"Clever."

"Except he was busy at that time hauling his ex-wife's body to the Grandgeorge summerhouse."

Red reached up with her left arm to scratch the back of her head. An ache shot through her, and she groaned. "Damn that man. Whacking me with a baseball bat."

"I heard you walloped him with a flashlight. Pretty dramatic."

"Don't remind me, and please don't tell my constituents that I couldn't get my gun out in time. They still think I'm a competent shooter because Will was. You know, the Hammergren legacy."

They both laughed, but it was a tired sound.

"You have more to say about all the clues, don't you?" Waltz shifted in his chair.

For a moment, he sounded like Will, who could read her so well.

"I wish I'd known about Jimmy's other phone. Maybe after Joanie was found, I should have searched his room. Might have prevented another death."

Waltz's expression registered sympathy. "You had no basis for searching his room. Remember? He had a solid alibi."

Red stretched her back by sitting up straighter. "But if I had, I would have found that he called her on Sunday before she went to Indian Mounds Park. And I would have found the call he made to the tipline accusing Grandgeorge. It had me puzzled because I was sure it was a male voice trying to sound like a woman."

Waltz leaned forward. "What else are you beating yourself up on?"

"Blood in the urine."

"Excuse me?"

"Jimmy was treated for hematuria—according to my anonymous source two days after he murdered Joanie."

Waltz scratched his head. "STD of some sort?"

"Nope. It's a condition that happens to wrestlers and weight lifters. It was probably from hiking from the road to the summerhouse while carrying Joanie. Except I didn't put it together, even though we knew the body had been moved."

Outside, a truck rumbled down the street. Red was both bone-tired and still filled with nervous energy. "One other thing that I didn't catch."

"There's more?"

"I smelled cologne in Joanie's house and other places. A woodsy-piney kind of smell. I didn't attribute it to Jimmy because he said he was allergic to all perfume."

"And?"

"The day he came into the office with Harv Smith, Harv smelled like he'd bathed in a bottle of Brut, yet not a wheeze or a sneeze from Jimmy. I should have caught it."

"Convicted by cologne, eh? That's a little too much for me." Waltz yawned, stretching his arms. "I think that's my signal to turn in. I hear the B and B has a great breakfast, and I need to be fresh for interviews tomorrow. They're keeping Jimmy overnight at the hospital for observation."

Red groaned. "Which means I have to pay overtime to have a deputy guard him."

"Ah yes, budgets and personnel. Glad I have a boss to take care of all that."

As he walked out the door, he left a slight scent that reminded her of Will's aftershave. *Men and their scents*, she sighed.

Tomorrow would be the beginning of a painstaking process to make a tight case.

The next day, they brought Jimmy to the interview room. He sat down with a dazed expression and an aw-shucks shrug. "Listen, I don't remember anything from yesterday. I took some of those pills the doctor gave me to help me sleep. Must have had a bad reaction. I don't know how I got to the Grandgeorge Place."

Waltz ignored Jimmy's comments but spoke in a friendly tone. "Jimmy, tell me about yourself and the Grandgeorge family."

Jimmy raised his eyebrows. "There's not much to say. I was hardly

The Pines Were Watching   273

connected with them at all except when Clyde stole my girlfriend." He smiled to himself. "I got over it, though."

"Were you angry at the time?"

"Of course. I was a dumb teenager. I admit that I kind of stalked them back then—you know, watched from the woods. It was crazy, but I got over it."

"And Carl Grandgeorge? What do you know about him?"

Jimmy wrinkled his brow, looking confused. "Carl? Not much."

"Your mother said he gave her a clock."

And her only begotten son. Red watched as Jimmy's face turned from confusion and bemusement to a growing anger.

His cheeks reddened. The aw-shucks expression disappeared, and he spoke in a low, controlled voice. "You leave my mother out of this."

Red wanted to push him with everything she knew—Carl being his father, Clyde stealing his girlfriend, and whatever Arlis had over him. She stayed quiet, hoping her face and body language weren't giving anything away.

Waltz continued with a friendly tone. "Why were you at the Grandgeorge Place yesterday?"

Jimmy chose his words carefully. "It's real hazy. The pills, you know. I guess I must have gone there because I was worried about Geraldine. We used to be good friends, and when Joanie was found there, I was sure Derek was responsible. He's crazy, you see. Burned down his own summerhouse. Pretty weird. And look what he did to Arlis. I knew they were linked."

Waltz rested his arms on the table with his hands clasped together. "What do you mean by linked?"

"The murders. That Henley woman and my wife."

Red joined the questioning. "Jimmy, how do you know they're linked?"

He spoke with a thoughtful expression. "Everyone does. Ask Harv Smith. Maybe he was the one who told me. They were both strangled, right? And then there was my wife's key they found on her." He shrugged. "They must have been linked."

Red tried to keep the excitement out of her voice. "What about this key?"

Perhaps it was the look on Red's face or the way Waltz shifted in his chair, but it was like a light went on behind Jimmy's eyes. He stiffened. "Listen, my head is really hurting from where you hit me." He glared at Red. "I could sue, you know. I didn't do anything wrong, and I'm not saying any more without a lawyer."

Jimmy's expression reminded Red of the fat little boy racing out of her parents' bedroom all those years ago. Red stood and with pleasure said, "Jimmy Crea, I'm arresting you…"

A week later, Red sat at the table in the back of Georgia's Antiques as Scotty cut the deck. The bruise on her arm had faded to an ugly yellow, and she was able to lift her arm over her head without wincing. The poker club members peered at her until Georgia finally said, "Okay, Sheriff. Spill."

"It's an ongoing investigation. I can't tell you the details."

Scotty laughed. "You don't have to. Everyone in town is talking about it. We, your junior sleuths, have put the story together. All you have to do is nod if you agree."

"I'll stick to my poker face, thank you."

Scotty was the first to speak as she dealt the cards. "I can tell you that Harv Smith is struggling. He and Jimmy were good friends—or so he thought. But I overheard him saying that the church's books were all off and several of Jimmy's customers were looking into his work. Seems Jimmy had a long-term serious gambling problem. The speculation is that Joanie stopped bailing him out and that's when he started stealing from her patients."

Georgia agreed. "That's what Joanie was onto. Murdering her might have been a crime of passion, but it was also to cover up the mess he was in. Lynne from the nursing office told me she used her inheritance to pay people back."

Red sorted her cards without comment. They'd uncovered Joanie's journal in one of the packed boxes in her house. At least two pages had been torn out. Red suspected the one she'd found by Fire Tower Road had been in her car and fell out when Jimmy dumped Arlis's body. The diary carefully documented what she had discovered.

"Furthermore," Georgia continued, "before Joanie was murdered, she

The Pines Were Watching 275

talked to her boss, Clarise, about the suspected theft. As a public servant, Clarise should have reported all of this to you. Instead, she sat on the information—probably because she didn't want anything bad to reflect on her. What a twit!"

Scotty looked perplexed. "What we don't understand is the whole charade with the green jacket. And why he would go after Arlis Henley."

Lou answered. "Here's the talk at the clinic. I was told someone knew someone who knew all about Arlis."

Red raised her eyebrows. "Maybe they can make a statement. Hearsay always goes well in court."

Lou smiled. "Well, the hearsay is that he took on the identity of Clyde in order to direct attention to the Grandgeorges, but Arlis recognized him at the Golden Deer. She was blackmailing him. And he beat up poor little Tommy to make sure he didn't say anything."

Lou had been able to get Tommy to talk, and he identified Jimmy as the person who'd hit him. He also told Lou that the reason he went to Rose Timm's to find his mother was because Arlis had said something about getting money from that old bat Rose. Red wasn't sure they'd be able to use that information in court but was confident they had enough to make sure Jimmy stayed in prison.

A forensic analyst was going through Jimmy's financials, and they were a mess. The analyst had uncovered losses in both online gambling sites and several casinos.

Georgia said thoughtfully, "Maybe in the end, he really wanted to be Clyde. The wife, the jacket, and the expensive cologne."

"Creepy." Scotty sipped her beer.

Red put her cards facedown. "Are we going to play poker or what?"

"No, we're going to put the case together for you."

Red leaned back and listened to her poker club as they outlined the case. They didn't have all the details, but they had the gist of it. It was up to her team and Waltz's team to sift through the evidence and make a compelling case for court. After that, it was up to a judge and jury.

"Earth to sheriff." Scotty leaned forward. "Did we get it right?"

"It's an ongoing investigation. I'll let you know when we have Jimmy convicted and put away for good."

At home, she sat on the patio with the stars scattered across the clear sky. Blue rested comfortably on her lap. "You know, pup, I truly don't understand human behavior. Why Jimmy waited all these years to act out his Clyde fantasy and why he went to so much trouble. It makes no sense. The Grandgeorge Place isn't worth it. Derek's a reclusive wreck, and Geraldine is no prize."

Blue lifted his head and licked her arm. A car pulled into the driveway, and Waltz walked around the side of the house to the patio. "I see you have a date with your dog."

"He's a good listener, and he doesn't try to pry information out of me like my poker club pals."

He settled into a lawn chair with a slight wheeze. "Not in great shape these days."

"Care for a beer?"

"No." He clasped his hands on his lap. "Just wanted a quick talk away from the madding crowd."

"Ah, literary allusions."

He shrugged. "I was a lit major until I realized quoting Shakespeare wouldn't get me employed."

"Me? I taught junior high science and math. Certainly had no trouble finding employment. I hated the education system bureaucracy, though."

"So you became sheriff and spend your days with spreadsheets?"

They sat in silence as the crickets sang.

"I interviewed Geraldine today. Did you know that Caddie is Jimmy's daughter?"

Red shifted and set Blue down. "I suspected. I think Jimmy also knew. He decided that if he set Derek up for the deaths of the two women, he could have the Grandgeorge Place and Geraldine. How about that for a motive? We've got money, jealousy, and revenge."

They talked about all the little clues and pieces to create a full picture. "It really started with little Tommy Henley. Jimmy in his wig and jacket beat him to keep him quiet. Tommy was no dummy. He recognized Jimmy right away. And Arlis didn't say anything because Jimmy was her meal ticket."

The Pines Were Watching

"Poor kid." Waltz pushed a hand through his salt-and-pepper hair. "My first job after college was with child protection. I lasted two years. The stories were too wrenching. I'd rather deal with dead bodies than broken kids."

The moon peeked over the tops of the pines. Red stared at it. "I still don't understand the key. Clearly it was what finally tipped the scales on Jimmy. But why did he shove that key in her mouth?"

"My guess? I think she found it on him after Joanie was killed and dangled it in front of him. She was trying for more money."

"Can we use it?"

He raised his eyebrows. "We can use the fact that no one outside of my team knew about it."

"That was a huge slip."

"Jimmy let his rage take over, I'd say."

Red agreed. "Same thing with setting the summerhouse on fire. Geraldine told Arlis that Caddie had spotted Joanie and Derek going to the summerhouse. That's probably why he put her body there and why he set the place on fire. Except Caddie was wrong. Angela was Derek's lover, not Joanie."

Waltz took a deep breath. "I'm guessing we won't get Jimmy to admit to any of it."

Blue broke up the session by trotting to the patio door and yipping. "Bedtime, I guess."

Waltz stood. "I'll see you in the morning. We have another session with Jimmy and his slick lawyer."

She watched him walk away, a not-so-handsome widower with a sparkle to his eyes. She felt Will's hand on her shoulder and heard a voice inside her head. "He's not a bad guy."

"No, Will. Not yet. But maybe someday…"

Blue wiggled when she picked him up and opened the door. "It's you and me…for now. Time to get a good night's sleep so I can get back to sheriffing."

Outside her house, the pines stood quiet.

What the Fields Saw
Book #3 in the Sheriff Red Mysteries

Decades of secrets surface when a high school reunion spirals into a deadly reckoning.

When Sheriff Red Hammergren welcomes billionaire Vance Judson back to Lykkins Lake for his high school reunion, his return stirs up more than nostalgia—it unearths old grudges, long-buried betrayals, and a reckoning sixty years in the making. At the same time, a young podcaster, drawn to whispers of an unsolved hit-and-run from the same era, begins asking questions—questions that cut too close to the truth and put a target on her back.

What begins as unease soon turns to fear when reunion attendees start turning up dead and the podcaster vanishes without a trace. Red races to untangle a mystery that refuses to stay in the past, knowing the next victim could already be marked. With help from her friends, she pieces together a history stained with privilege, silence, and revenge. Each bit of evidence brings her closer to the truth—but also closer to a killer who has already waited a lifetime to finish what was started.

In a town where loyalty is a dangerous currency, Red must determine who is paying for old sins—and who is collecting the debt.

Get your copy today at
severnriverbooks.com

ACKNOWLEDGMENTS

A big thanks to Brian Smith, Sheriff of Kanabec County in Minnesota. He provided insight and details on the day to day running of a rural law enforcement agency. His dedication to his community was clear and inspirational. Thank you to my writer's group Jan Kerman, Carol Williams and Randy Kastner who first met Sheriff Red a number of years ago. Thanks to Julia Hastings and the staff at Severin River Publishing for all your support and expertise. A special thanks to Jerome for all the years he's supported my writing dreams.

ABOUT THE AUTHOR

Linda Norlander is the author of *And the Lake Will Take Them* the first in the Sheriff Red Mystery series. She is also author of A Cabin by the Lake mysteries and the Liza and Mrs. Wilkens mysteries. Norlander has published award winning short stories, op-ed pieces and short humor featured in regional and national publications. Before taking up the pen to write novels, she worked in end-of-life care. Norlander resides in Tacoma, Washington with her spouse.

Sign up for the reader list at
severnriverbooks.com